take me home

ALSO BY SOPHIE PARKIN

all grown up

take me home

SOPHIE PARKIN

review

First published in 1999
by REVIEW

An imprint of Headline Book Publishing

First published in paperback in 1999

10 9 8 7 6 5 4 3 2 1

ISBN 0 7472 5741 8

Typeset by
Letterpart Limited, Reigate, Surrey
Printed and bound in Great Britain by
Clays Ltd, St Ives plc.

Headline Book Publishing
A division of the Hodder Headline Group
338 Euston Road
London NW1 3BH
www.reviewbooks.co.uk
www.hodderheadline.com

To all my great female friends (you know who you are!) and especially my sister Sarah

And for Sylvia Scaffardi

CHAPTER ONE

Sarah Jane doesn't know about rules.

Remember – look, don't touch! Strict rules govern strip-a-gram excitement. Banana sex, peel back and watch.

None of them had known what to expect, but the reality was gorgeous. They stood admiring the young Marlon Brando with slicked hair, narrow, sharp eyes and bee-stung lips. He was a beauty in a place of beasts, even Honor was thinking that, and you could see Sarah Jane's reaction. Her eyes grew large and hungry as soon as she realised this was her present. She could hardly keep her hands from jumping to his sides, touching him, helping undo the Velcro on his easy-strip shirt to display his well-oiled, hairless muscled chest that gleamed like a professionally polished sideboard.

The music was loud, pumping dance music. The boy moved, gyrating, smouldering, 3D calendar sex on display. He was working his audience, the only audience that mattered, Sarah Jane. She was growing excited, dancing with him, moving closer, hustling him into the darker corner of the room, away from the centre stage of the dance floor. Closer to a cowering Honor, sitting up at the mirrored bar.

The whole thing was too much: Honor walked in and felt it, stumbling down into the darkness of the club. Flashing white and red lights momentarily lit the space. Confusing the steps she clung to the steel rail for support, missed one and banged her knee on the glass banister rods. One way to make an entrance to the Underworld, but not one she would have chosen.

Honor couldn't quite believe she was watching Sarah Jane and a strip-a-gram. What on earth am I doing here? she thought. The darkness, the thumping music, the alcohol, the cigarette smoke-screen lit up by pulsing coloured dance lights, heightened her unease.

Like Hades – 'abode of the damned' – it was hot and cram-packed. The gold-ringed, smart-not-casual designer-label men and their women looked like extras from a late seventies film. Girls leaned their heads coquettishly to the side, eyes wide and glazed, fringed heavy with mascara. Some held straws attached to baby-coloured cocktails stuck in their glossy pursed lips like teats. Uniform highlighted hair, blowdried and layered. Skirts barely covering bottoms, feet shod with sharp high heels or heavy lumpen clods. Easy prey girls, to a nectar concocted of drugs and slick, scented men, searching for a means of escape. Easy prey, girls, just pray.

'Deliver me from evil, for thine is the kingdom . . .'

'God I was off my head last night.'

'Off your face.'

'I could have pissed myself.'

'Yeah. Great night.'

Clubland, anywhere.

Prayers don't help you escape hell, you've got to want to leave – alone. Honor wanted to leave. 'I'm going,' she said.

'Oh don't. Don't go. It's just getting fun. It's just getting started. Don't be such a killjoy.'

Honor was unused to this secret world, where gangland uniforms seldom change. She looked around the club, away from the centre stage, watching for other people's reactions.

Maybe, she thought, having children makes your morals prudishly tighten as your stomach muscles slacken, but Catherine had children and was whooping along with the rest of them. What was wrong with her, Honor?

Meanwhile Sarah Jane was stroking her long red-painted fingers up her legs, pulling aside the splits in her skirt to reveal her expensively stockinged thighs. Her hips moved backwards and forward with the rhythm, compulsively bending her knees, shimmying her bare shoulders, shaking her head of sleek, blonded hair. Her breasts wobbled alluringly in her uplift strapless bra and seemed in danger of spilling out of the Monroe-style drawstring top. You could see they were real.

Honor was embarrassed. She swigged back her glass to enable herself to watch, but still felt uneasy. She wasn't able to enjoy the provocative fun of the situation; it was only comic-book sex, like Quentin Tarantino violence. 'Lighten up, laugh!' she heard herself saying but couldn't respond.

Then it changed, suddenly the performance stopped and Sarah Jane's face switched channels: she'd had a lot to drink and enough drugs. Maybe she wasn't all there. You could read her eyes, she was somewhere else, though her body was present and performing. Nobody stopped her, they were all too amazed, caught up in the flow.

This was to be the hen night to end all hen nights. Twenty of Sarah Jane's closest friends would be meeting on Friday at seven thirty at Sid's Place for drinks, then on by eight forty-five to the Med, the restaurant. By twelve they would be leaving for the first nightclub. That was the plan in theory. Catherine and Gem had organised it all for Sarah Jane and they had told Honor, the fourth of their close-friend quartet, not to worry about arrangements, just to turn up and wave goodbye to Sarah Jane's last weeks of freedom.

As Catherine said to Gem on the phone – 'Poor Honor, she has enough trouble getting a baby-sitter organised for Jack, we can't ask her to do anything else.'

'It'll be a miracle if she turns up on time. I still don't know why she insisted on going through with it all, I couldn't be a one-parent family. She works so hard, poor thing,' agreed Gem, reaching for her nail accoutrements.

'I don't know. At least she has a male in the house who doesn't demand sex from her: all he needs is feeding, and she's good at that,' replied Catherine, taking her coffee, a pen and a pad before settling herself into a velvet armchair in the corner of her office. She wrote at the top of the page – things to do.

'I know, it must be nice staying at home at night watching a video together all squadged up. A bit like having a big talking dog.' Gem pushed at a cuticle.

'If that's all you want, you can have my husband David, I'll send him over to you this evening as soon as he gets in. You know he's always fancied you. I'm sure if you fed him the right brand of dogfood he'd be loyal.' Catherine was busy doodling on her pad – pictures of dogs that looked like her husband, with pricetags around their necks.

Gem laughed before replying. 'Hmmm, it's a tempting offer, Catherine. If he was a dog what breed would he be?'

'A cross breed.'

'I'll stick with a hamster, they're less argumentative.'

'Hey! What about my sister's hen night?' Catherine burst in, sharply.

'I think we should go to Sid's place for drinks, since everybody knows her there,' said Gem.

'He'll probably give us a couple of bottles of free champagne to help us celebrate. You can't say Sarah Jane hasn't been a good customer over the years.' Catherine gently jibed at her absent sister. 'If he'd ever sold the place she would have come as a fixture and fitting.'

'He'll probably charge us double for the future years of lost revenue, with her happily married and blissful in LA.'

'Isn't that a contradiction in terms?'

'What? Being happily married?' Gem replied, knowing they were back on Catherine's favourite hobbyhorse. 'Just one question, if you hate marriage and David so much, why were you the only one of us four to get married?'

'Because I'm older and stupider than all of you? Because I'm addicted to shopping and if I can't have an account card at Harvey Nichols, I'll "scweem and scweem until I'm sick", as Violet Elizabeth said to Just William.'

'You're so highbrow Catherine! Why don't you leave him, instead of moaning?'

'David? If you look at it positively, he's cheaper than a new set of batteries for a vibrator. At least I can close my eyes and pretend it's Mel Gibson beneath the plethora of pouch pockets from business dinners. Quite frankly I can't see what the alternative would be, other than a different brand of misery. Look at Honor. What did honour ever do for Honor? Is it ever worth being an Honourable Honor? Don't tell me she finds it easy?'

Gem ignored the question and started to apply the first coat of beige polish upon her newly buffed, squared and Sally Hanson-coated nails. The repair kit was essential, her nails were following the path of her hair, her teeth, her eyes and inevitably her kidneys. Though she wasn't conscious of her physical decline, this is what happens when you habitually vomit everything you eat.

'Honor likes it being just her and Jack. The problem with you,

Catherine, is you've forgotten, you don't appreciate the nice things about being married.'

'I jolly well do Gem. I've just bought myself the most perfect Issey Miyake dress for my foolish sister's hen night. Do you properly appreciate being single and fancy free? Now then, where were we, where's the dinner to be held? Who'll have us?'

'If it's the right size I'll appreciate anything honey! Well, we really don't want to eat that much do we?'

'What about the Ivy?'

'Don't be ridiculous Catherine! You can't remember being a student can you? Let's go to the Med, then whoever wants one course can have it and if you want three and can afford it, it's up to you. It's also only a stagger from Sid's.'

'All right, I bow to your plebeian knowledge Gem. I thought we were all a bit old for student life but you always could spot a bargain, no wonder you've always got money. Sid's Place, does anyone go there any more? I mean anyone over fifteen. And then the Med. I suppose the food is good?'

'It's not meant to be your hen night Catherine. It's what Sarah Jane is going to enjoy and everyone knows her in those places, and I hate to remind you . . .'

'I know, I know, I'm the oldest girl in the place and she'll have a whale of a time saying to everyone, "Hello darlings, no it's not my mother it's my sister, she just used the wrong moisturiser." I'm past the clubbing sell-by date.'

'Actually I was going to remind you that we don't all live off men, but I thought it was rather a low remark. You have to make allowances for human frailty. Which reminds me, the club should be decided then arranged otherwise we'll be waiting outside in some depressing queue and then we'll all feel like students. Your sister mentioned somewhere called Underworld.'

'Oh my God, don't talk to me about that place in the same breath as human frailty, they breed it down there in dark dank tanks.'

Catherine was trying to drag the conversation out. If it finished early she might have to do some work before the auction and lunch. As it was she couldn't bear to look at the stack of papers leering at her from the top of her steel and glass desk, beckoning with calls that really needed to be made.

'Sounds perfect! I take it it's tacky and if it's tacky they usually have good dancing music. It'll be just like the old days, Lionel Richie and Luther Vandross for the smoochie numbers.'

'Worse, tackier and more expensive, second-class stars in a third-class decor with first-class prices. I think a lot of "actoors" go there, once they've got their first paycheck from *The Bill*. And worse than that, Gem, I think it's full of women being paid for by men!'

'If that's what Sarah Jane wants, that's what Sarah Jane gets,' added Gem, determined to finish. She looked at her watch, she wanted to get to the gym before the lunchtime rush when all the best machines were grabbed.

'That's what she's marrying for. Let's get her a surprise like a strip-a-gram. Perhaps she'll forget the wedding and abscond with him.'

'You really are a horrible sister, Catherine. I'm glad I'm an only child if this is what sibling rivalry's like. You should be happy for Sarah Jane.' She blew at her nails to make sure they were dry and tentatively touched the edge of one. Unimpressed, she flapped her fingers around her head for the rest of the conversation, holding the phone in the crook of her neck and frowning at Catherine's unwillingness to share in her sister's frothy dream of the aisle. It was Gem's dream too, she didn't like it trampled – not that she would admit it.

'Oh you know I would be, if it wasn't going to make her so damn miserable.' Catherine gave in and began to cajole her. 'Okay, okay, let's pretend and make her happy. I can feel your steely gaze down the telephone wire, what do you say to a *Full Monty*-gram? She would love it and it's her last chance to gaze at a naked man without Josh about. What sort would she like?'

'She'd want somebody dressed like a telephone engineer or a builder.' Gem would too, the fantasy whisking her away from the almost clinical order of her existence. A lifestyle which some might call fanatical, was essential for Gem.

'I just thought that since she's marrying a bit of rough, she might like the illusion of something a little more sophisticated for her hen night.' Catherine looked at her watch and was delighted to see that it was time for her to lipstick her mouth again. She reached for her *Moschino* briefcase and pulled out the necessaries for lip service.

'Like a flight attendant? Catherine, you book the builder strip-a-gram and I'll book the restaurant and bar. If you do the club, warn them about the stripper.'

'I'll call you if there's any trouble and we end up with a Bruce Forsyth.'

'Whoever you get, could you make sure they don't look as though they've been left at the bottom of the laundry basket for the last twenty years?' Gem tapped her index nail gently on her desk and, happy that it was dry, began to put everything neatly back in its little case before depositing it in a drawer. She was ready to go. Catherine finished blotting her lips and began on the gloss.

'Don't worry, I'll specify.'

'Hey, I've got to dash.'

'Me too. Bye love.' Both were away before their phones were down.

Sarah Jane was exhausted. She had been working hard, shopping for the right clothes to wear. Now she had an unlimited supply of credit cards with somebody else's billing address, she was free to do just that. She had to have something to fill her days with since she had given up serious acting and auditioning. No more herding into deodorant and tampon auditions with a ready smile and a bum-length skirt, absorbing gut-pulling rejections beneath a friendly veneer. No more daily calls to her agent, waiting for the big part in films that never got made or never called her back, waiting for the first chance at a crack in a profession chocablock full of pretty blondes with good legs and neat smiles, just like her.

Shopping was what Sarah Jane really liked. Even when she had no money she'd happily spend a shameless afternoon in Sloane Street, Bond Street or South Molton Street trying on clothes that she could never afford. She refused to acknowledge the sneers of snotty sales girls. The clothes she had she bought second-hand from markets, or she paid impoverished student dress-designer friends to run up outrageous numbers, copies from old Hollywood movies for her auditions and night-club appearances, a little something that Raquel or Zsa Zsa would have worn. She'd pay them with promises (she was rich with those) of her future fame and their employment if only they ran up this one little favour as their investment in notoriety.

No one minded in the end with Sarah Jane, she was sweet and funny, loud and outrageous and could always be trusted to provide entertainment at a party. She was the one who'd stand in the middle of a table and sing a song, do anything for a laugh; a pretty child of a girl.

Soaking luxuriously in her bath oil until her pedicured toes began to wrinkle, it didn't take long for Sarah Jane to reach her boredom threshold. She began to write obscenities on to the steamed-mirrored wall with crude illustrations that made her laugh. She could get really good detail in now her stubby nails had been transformed with new cyclamen-pink nail extensions. She doubted if they'd have made Josh laugh.

Josh Todd, voted best-looking filmstar 1997, was prudish, strangely conservative about sex, and saw her as an innocent, an English rose. Sarah Jane wondered if she'd ever dare fart in front of him, let alone discuss her sexually chequered past.

Josh Todd, her fiancé, her intended, the man she was to marry in two weeks, her beloved? Yes, her beloved. She liked to try all the terms out, practise them though she still didn't dare try 'husband'. 'This is my hus . . .' That was about as far as she could get. She imagined it would become easier as the days slipped by, hoped that it would, until the day she said 'I do', the time she would sign her name, Mrs Todd.

These were fears she couldn't share, certainly not with her mother who would admonish her as ridiculous (whilst complaining about the price of the wedding). Her mother was so delighted with the idea of Josh as a son-in-law, she had said to him when they were first introduced, 'I can't believe you want to marry Sarah Jane. We really are so pleased.'

'Why? Does she have some nasty disease I don't know about?' Josh had replied almost seriously. Luckily Sarah Jane had dealt with her thrush the day before they'd met.

If not her mother or even her sister, who'd been through it all before, who was she supposed to ask about the sick sadness rising from her innards that jolted her awake at night? Her sister Catherine's advice would only encourage her to develop fear until it encompassed everything. Sarah Jane wished she could make both her step-father and Catherine like Josh a little, but her step-father was downright racist. Any anti-American jibe he could muster was thrown in the ring. Catherine covered up with smart lines like, 'Just the idea of weddings makes me nervous!' As though they hid her sneers at Josh's lack of sophistication, which no amount of her charismatic charm could conceal. Sarah Jane watched her family dissect everything, from the way he ate to the views he expressed. He was a blundering alien in the ridiculously genteel atmosphere of her mother's country house. But Josh loved their Englishness and she couldn't bring herself to tell him they were all laughing at him.

Sarah Jane decided she had to forget about her family, she wasn't even going to be living in the same country as them any more. Fuck them, she thought, but remained unconvinced by her own rebellion, praying the upset wouldn't keep churning around her body, wishing she could please everyone. Sarah Jane didn't want much, just everybody's love and approval. Who could she discuss her fears with? She couldn't even think about them herself.

'Fuck it. I am beautiful. I am loved. I am getting married. And what's more, I'm getting married to the movie star Josh Todd in two weeks. YEAHH you jealous bastards, eat that!' She shouted into the mirror, jumped out of the bath and ran twice around the flat naked, before turning over her Shirley Bassey tape, pushing the volume up to sing 'Hey Big Spender', naked to the window and anybody who was watching. The gang of workmen on the scaffold opposite thought it was Christmas, but Sarah Jane didn't care. Bored with Bassey out-singing her, she replaced her with the *Pal Joey* soundtrack in a flick of a switch. Something light with Rita Hayworth's thin voice duetting with Sinatra.

'That's more like it, Frankie baby! Now how about a little joint-ette and a glass of Chablis for Sarah Jane. You've been so good today and haven't touched a drop all the time it's been sitting in the fridge. After all, it is your hen night, you're allowed to enjoy yourself,' she said out loud, wrapping a towel around her wet clean hair and a thick white bathrobe about her long lean body. She looked like the blonde version of the 'look no make-up I've just jumped out of the shower', surprise photo of Liz Taylor wrapped in towels, perfect, beautiful. Her eyebrows gently arched upwards making her violet eyes look wider, her tanned clear skin looked tighter for the towel's twist, her lips too naked in their baby pouting pale softness.

Lounging comfortably on her sofa, inhaling luxuriously on her joint and sipping from her glass, the world seemed blissful. Looking ahead, all Sarah Jane could see was the Californian sunshine, a leisurely poolside existence surrounded by the rich and famous. A waiter proffering 'Another glass of Halcyon Daze, modom.'

A late spring sun slid through the living-room windows and lit the yellow-ochre walls to a rich gold. Erratic paintings from junk shops hung lopsidedly on the walls, flea-market furniture cluttered the carpet. In the kitchen, washing up had been waiting to be done for days, gathering patiently on top of every available surface. Towels and dirty washing were meant to live in the bathroom but rarely made their destination, scattering the floors instead on their unattended journey.

The bathroom was full of make-up, which miraculously managed to stay put, apart from the odd long-lost lipstick hiding in a jacket pocket. It was the mirror that kept it there, lit about with small bulbs that always made Sarah Jane think if she looked any good in that she looked a million dollars in the outside world. Amongst the powder for cheeks and chins, the pencils for lips and eyes, sat fat mugs of un-drunk tea and coffee stagnating into plant life.

Sarah Jane was a slut and she didn't care, there was simply no shame to her. She carelessly flicked the channels of her TV and gave up in favour of a glossy fashion magazine. Now, she was a contented slut. When she finished her joint and the glass of wine she would drift into her bedroom and start trying on all of her new expensive clothes.

When she had signed the credit card for them, even though she knew the bill was heading straight for Josh, she had had to close her eyes. Such a ridiculous amount of money to be spending on clothes, it could've paid her rent for a couple of months! But Josh had told her to do it, he didn't want her turning out tacky on the honeymoon in the South of France, she had to be able to measure up to the French babes in Cannes. He had even told her the labels he wanted her to wear. Their honeymoon would conveniently coincide with the festival and his new film.

'Oh, but it will be grand, no more auditions, they'll be begging me to take roles when they see me in some of the outfits I've bought.' Sarah Jane was dreaming smugly, imagining how the

Hello! interview would read until the joint burnt its way down to her fingers and made her jump. Cross, she stubbed it out in a convenient mug and stamped into her clothes-strewn room, only to discover there was no space to try anything on, so she hauled the whole lot back into the living room.

CHAPTER TWO

Catherine had been right. Honor had only just managed to get herself a baby-sitter and didn't know what on earth she was going to wear. She rushed back from work on the bus, as fast as the bus goes stuck in Oxford Street traffic. She'd already forgotten about the dress she'd bought on Saturday. That's how her head was; too busy to remember a thing but her main responsibility, Jack.

Each morning the boy screeched into her room transmogrified into a Formula One racing car, an aerial bomber, Batman, or a hamster. ('You can be the baby hamster and I'm the mummy who has to protect you because the hunter's coming. Don't cry now, I've got you a worm to eat,' Jack would say pushing a warm plump finger into Honor's sleep-sodden face, duvet pulled over their heads like earth mounds.) With Jack she didn't need an alarm clock, she knew with his first noise that it was half past seven.

Each morning she got up, made him breakfast and his lunch-box, found his clothes, watched him brush his teeth, comb his hair, wash his face, pack his games kit. At the same time she showered, dressed, and thought about a cup of tea before racing out the door to get to school as the bell clanged through the playground. Then she jumped on a bus to work, hustled for a seat so she could sit and gaze blank-minded for fifteen minutes and be *compos mentis* enough to devise a menu. She would cook for the day, not stopping to eat lunch, picking at everything, hurry back to school, pick up Jack, get back home, collapse: Honor's life.

Tonight was different. This Friday she had arranged for Jack to go home from school with a friend and stay overnight until after lunch. She could even fit in a hangover if she wanted, an inevitability these days if she drank more than two glasses of wine and she wasn't menstruating. What had happened to her body after Jack was born? It was a complete mystery to her, along with the rest of the world.

Food was the only thing Honor did know about, its taste, texture, colour, nutrition and the balance of matching flavours seemed to be in-built in her genetic make-up. If she had bothered to take the time to examine the rest of her myriad talents with as much confidence, she would have realised how strong and able she was – kind, loving and bright – but that had not been Honor's way, until now. Now she was trying to change. Grab her self-deprecating victim-mentality and throw it out the window. But it was hard, sometimes it clung to her like wet dough when she'd run out of flour.

Honor's ability as a mother she took for granted, anyone could do that, she thought. Anyone would do the best and try to do the right thing for their child, she argued with others at work, it was natural wasn't it? She couldn't understand child abuse, it upset her, she couldn't begin to believe a parent could behave badly to a defenceless innocent. But if she thought back, there was a time when Jack was small and Honor was alone and isolated. In the days after Jeremy had left she had understood it well enough then, the small step from holding a baby, to strangling it.

Jack was only a little baby with a face twisted by his constant demands. Honor was only young, she had no idea of the never-ending rituals that needed to be performed. As soon as one was finished, the next began, feeding and changing, winding and comforting. Remembering so much baby knowledge was like doing an A-level practical twenty-four hours a day with no revision. It hadn't come naturally to Honor. Remembering to wipe Jack's bottom the right way – down: to always hold his head; to lie him on his stomach, face to one side; learning to do everything one-handed whilst holding the baby. Filling and plugging the kettle in, going to the loo or chopping vegetables for dinner turned into ten-minute wrestling ordeals. Honor had felt like some old run-down auxiliary engine to Jack's perfect three-month dynamo. Sometimes it felt like Jack was stealing his energy from Honor's failing resources, sucking her life-blood like a leech, prospering as she withered. She wept for her lack, prayed to say 'No' to his demands. The flat was chaos, but Honor had been worse. One day when Jack had pitched his cry at that unignor-able level, the screech individually manufactured to touch the mother's chord, Honor had hauled herself over again to his cot. It was late, she wanted to sleep, needed to so badly. He was fed and clean, what more could he want? She began to scream at him, once her impatient coos didn't work, and then couldn't stop.

'What do you want now!' she shouted back, a desperate response to his baby bleats, and had found herself picking him up and shaking his bewildered small rag-doll body, before throwing him violently back down in his cot, unable to touch him.

'I can't do anything else for you. I can't!' she sobbed until his cries had her begging. 'Just please let me have some sleep, please, please, please.' When he kept on crying all she could do was scream louder. 'Shut up, shut up, shut up.' She slammed the door on him and collapsed weeping on the sofa, bawling louder than him, a pillow pulled over her head to distance his piercing cries from her ears, until in their separate cots they howled themselves wet-faced to sleep.

The next morning she'd been full of remorse. Terrible cancerous remorse which grew to giant proportions fed with plenty of top-grade, succulent guilt. So bad that when her granny had called her, her regular confidante, she'd allowed her to tell her mother. She knew her granny couldn't do anything: she was in a home for 'ageing gentlefolk' outside Bournemouth.

'Oh Granny, why can't you leave that horrid place and come live with me? I'd look after you,' Honor said regularly and always her granny replied, 'But sweetie thing you have the baby, I couldn't manage the stairs, I don't like London and I would miss watching the sea from my window. You have your life to make in front of you, and it will be brilliant. God's just giving you this so you'll have a comparison.'

Honor laughed, her granny always had a reason for everything. When her mother called she'd confessed, she had to, she was frightened. Scared of what she might be capable of. Honor knew she could have killed her baby, Jack. Finally she even told her mum about Jeremy leaving the month before, something her pride had forbidden her to do. She found it hard enough admitting to herself that she and Jeremy were over, that having a man's baby guaranteed nothing. That she was so worthless, fat and ugly that he couldn't bear to be near her, not even as she held his own flesh and blood.

Honor repeated to her mother, as she had to her granny, the last conversation she had had with Jeremy.

Jeremy had said the baby was making too many demands upon

him and he wasn't able at this time to fulfil his role as a father. He'd said that since it hadn't been his decision to get pregnant (as though it had been anybody's but God's) and it had been Honor's choice to keep the baby, then keep it she must. He didn't want to stay any longer in the flat, not with those sleepless nights, he had enough of those at work being a junior houseman. He had his career to think about. He'd said the problem with Honor was that she didn't even begin to realise what important life and death decisions he had to make being a doctor; living this way meant he risked endangering his patients.

Anyway, he didn't want to get attached to the baby; it wouldn't be fair, he added as though being kind. She could keep the flat, a precious housing-association one, mysteriously in a mansion block of private housing. He'd be staying at a friend's, taking a few things until he could collect the rest, either the following weekend or the next. He'd said he would ring, let her know what was happening, but it all depended on his shifts.

In the usual Jeremy way, he hadn't. Honor had come to expect that of him, all the way through their year-and-a-half affair. Reliable, as Honor's mother always said, wasn't Jeremy's second name.

'Maybe he used up his quota at work,' Honor mumbled generously, because she loved him.

Jeremy was an only child born to ageing wealthy parents. Tall and dark, he was almost as dark-haired as Honor but his eyes were as blue as hers were green. His skin retained his holiday tan all year round, giving away his Mediterranean origins, until his harsh public-school voice shattered any romanticism that came with such looks.

'You see I've got to be honest I can't kid myself or you any longer. I don't love you, Honor. I don't think I ever did. Look at you, at this place. How can any man want to come back to this!'

He looked around the living room in bewilderment, eyebrows raised as though seeing it properly for the first time. Bags of nappies were strewn across the floor, clothes small and large littered the chairs and sofa, the table remained laid with used breakfast and an array of soggy old breast pads. The kitchen area was worse and made the rest of the room stink of day-old nappies that hadn't been put out to the bins.

Jeremy turned back to Honor, standing there at four o'clock in the afternoon still in an old towelling dressing gown. At least she'd had a bath that day, but her hair lay wet and straggled with its damp curls limp about her tired, bloated face. 'I couldn't stay with you, you're a boring mess, you must realise that?'

Honor's face had raced, with this talk, through the full gamut of emotions. Though her brain was still unable to grasp the implications, her head was nodding dumbly like a car-window Corgi. Jeremy had wanted to make it clear, he was trying his best. He said she seemed hardly to be there most of the time, her brain seemed to have been addled by this baby thing, but he didn't like to be too cruel so he added to soften the axe blade, 'I did once find you attractive. I remember you being quite pretty in candlelight. It's a pity, it would have been nice if it could have worked, but the timing's all out. We took a chance, you can't expect to win every time.'

As he'd gathered bits into a bag, he had spoken as casually as if he had just missed the afternoon matinée. His mind was on other things, the smooth, cool blonded beauty of Melissa, the friend whose flat he'd be moving to, also doing her exams. But Honor didn't know that, all she could think was, He must be right, it's all my fault.

Thank God the baby had had better timing than his father, crying out with some desperate plea so that Honor could go rushing out of the room to him, hold on to some bit of human warmth to comfort herself. Bury her messy head against his tiny perfect one. Their faces scrunched identically in their individual pain, Jack's with the misery of a dirty nappy. He bleated his cries for help but all Honor could do was to weep silently, her tears running down his blue and white striped, combed-cotton back. She remained silent until she heard the door slam and the lift descend. When she wailed all she could say was, 'Poor little Jack,' over and over again. 'Poor little Jack.'

It took a lot of courage for Honor to tell her mother, she couldn't bear to hear the 'told you so' on the other end of the phone.

Martha, Honor's mother, had never liked Jeremy but she was kind and practical in her reaction. She even made Honor laugh, joking about Jeremy's upper-class pretentions, designer clothes and vintage wines. Honor relaxed and told her mother how in the fit of rage that had followed the upset she had taken a pair of scissors and secretly mutilated every garment, pair of shoes, book and tape that remained uncollected. Just subtle snips here and there that he wouldn't notice at first and wouldn't render them useless, nothing too visible, just little reminders.

'For the first time since Jack was born I felt I'd done a really constructive day's work, I thought I'd turned the corner with managing it all. Why didn't you ever tell me, Mum, that having a baby was like putting an exploding grenade into your life?'

'Because if that was true for everyone, nobody would procreate. It's just your circumstances, darling. I remember your dad was marvellous, cooked the dinner every night and realised he had to send his shirts to the laundry if he expected them ironed. I never ironed another shirt after that.' This was just what Honor didn't need to hear, Hail to the Father. The absent, philandering father. Her mother continued in Mrs Minerva fashion.

'Now what do you want me to do? Just ask and I'll tell you if it's possible. We'll work something out. Do you want to come home for a bit and I'll help you look after Jack for a week or two?'

'Thanks Mum, but I'd still have to come back and sort all this out.'

'But you'd have a rest. I'll come and collect you, and afterwards we can sort out something regular. You could leave Jack down here for the occasional weekend, once he's off feeding. Now what are you going to do about money? Your father wonders if fifty a week would help?'

Honor had gone on the dole for the first couple of years, had her rent paid by the council and, with the odd private dinner party to cook for, had got by. All made easier thanks to the black economy and her friends, Gem, Catherine and Sarah Jane doing her culinary PR and arriving for baby-sitting duties with bulging carrier bags from Sainsbury's. She'd swallowed her pride, but after a few DSS interviews she was an old hand at that. Honor's brother Simon stayed with her in his university holidays and helped out. When he wasn't girl-picking in Bologna he enjoyed the male au pair playground perks.

Now Honor had a job as a weekday chef in a small, busy restaurant with a more reliable pay packet and, with weekend dinner party supplements, got by. Jeremy had disappeared but for mysterious twice-yearly postcards from exotic destinations. One day if she could be bothered, for Jack's sake, she'd trace him, send him the bill for his son's upbringing, or send Jack to public school with all invoices to be sent to Jeremy's posh private consultancy, she joked. The truth was she didn't want Jeremy to have any part of Jack, she wouldn't even give his name to the Child Support Agency. Jack was Honor's and Jeremy had been the walking sperm bank. At least she'd made sure he was a handsome, clever donor, even if he was an emotional retard with a total inability to give or receive love. Honor wondered if she'd ever marry. What man would take on somebody else's child?

For the last six years her friends had been trying to match-make her with 'suitable men': good fathers for Jack, reliable money machines for Honor. Sometimes she looked at these offerings and didn't know what they were supposed to be suitable for, poor creatures, but they weren't for her. The day after the dinners, she'd ring up Catherine and ask what on earth was she supposed to find attractive in a boring, balding, overweight lawyer whose wife had just left him to nobody's surprise for the scuba-instructor on holiday. Catherine always tried to find her financially stable men. Gem, who knew Honor liked foreign films and poetry, always matched her with impoverished artists. Sarah Jane was always trying to pass on her leftover gorgeous but feckless actors so that they wouldn't feel so hurt when she left them for another.

Sarah Jane had always been the leader in the serial monogamy race, until now; everything was changing. Sarah Jane was getting married.

Tonight at Sarah Jane's hen party, Honor could dress for herself, not for some mystery man's trial approval that always made her want to put on a baggy, shapeless, awful, high-necked thing, in rebellion. For the first time in ages she'd gone and bought herself something new, not second-hand or charity. She had bought a slinky, knitted emerald dress that she would wear with her new uplift bra. She wasn't sure she'd have the nerve to wear the bra, the cleavage from her full breasts left her self-conscious. Tonight she wanted to feel proud and un-threatened, the brilliant green dress matched her eyes and made her feel desirable, it made her feel good.

Before she could feel any of those things, there was clear-up time.

Arriving home she was greeted by the usual breakfast mess on the living-room table, a light still on in Jack's yellow room, and a mixed carpet of cereal and toys. First, she ran a bath, pouring in lots of bubbles, and then found a toy box into which to throw everything. She stopped at an immaculate trail of dominoes set up on their heads like a maze, leant down and playfully flicked one spotted bar at the start; they crumbled headlong down like a train without brakes, one after the other. Shit! she thought, realising she would have to re-set Jack's efforts if she didn't want to upset him. No time now! and she scooped them in handfuls into the box before dumping it in his room, a quick whizz with the Hoover until the floor was spotless and the rest of the mess had been hidden away behind cupboard doors.

In her tiny blue bedroom she kicked off her loafers and pulled off her clothes, throwing them into the laundry basket at the end of her Victorian bed. It was supposed to double as a mini sofa once its seat was down, but was used more as Jack's acrobatic climbing frame in his commando set-ups.

Naked, she turned and caught the shock of her body in the mirror, not recognising the stranger, the strangeness of her own flesh. The relaxed crumpled belly, cellulite-dimpled thighs, sagging breasts. At thirty-two, did these really belong to her? She replied with a quick suck-in of her stomach and went to stand in front of the other mirror that always made her look taller and thinner. She pulled her shoulders back and straightened herself tall to properly confront the mirror. 'Gem would kill to have breasts like mine or at least have a cleavage,' she reassured herself, not utterly convinced. She turned three-quarters to wonder at the faint silhouette of a hip bone before she realised it was a bruised shadow, from her pillow fight with Jack.

'I'm loveable and curvaceous. Honor, you are beautiful.' She parroted back at herself from her positivity tape that she'd been falling asleep to at bedtime. Each night she listened to the repetitive lines, hoping miracles would slip into her unconscious so that she would awake to a new positive body image the next morning. The next best thing to a new body, she supposed. She couldn't afford surgery or even a health-club membership, but she could afford a tape. She kissed her mirror image and smiled dimples into her cheeks, half-pleased, half-embarrassed. It must be half-working. She used to throw up at the sight of childbearing stretchmarks, too much like offal. She wouldn't even cook offal, not since she'd seen what had come out of her at Jack's birth.

The self-help tape told her over and over again, she had to accept it all, love all of her, nice bits, nasty bits, all the bits with all her heart. She was trying, she knew what the smooth American voice said was right, so she conscientiously hugged her belly by crossing her lower arms over it, holding on to her squadgy hips, fingers dipping into her flesh. The area between her legs was still off-limits. She prayed that men would be braver than her in those little-explored territories.

Turning about to switch an old Johnny Guitar Watson tape on, Honor jogged, singing to her turquoise bathroom walls stuck with shells. 'I'm stronger than a locomotive and that folk-saying is true . . .'

Bunching her hair into an elastic band, she touched her toes five times, just to prove she still could and gasped at the forest growth upon her legs. Somewhere there was an unused Bic razor. Searching her bathroom cupboard and finding one behind the Mickey Mouse bubble bath, she pulled it out showering dinosaur plasters over her head and the floor. That was the problem with her method of tidying, hiding it all behind cupboard doors waiting for the mess to arrange and fix itself, it never did. Everything she put away was always trying to prove Newton right, it seemed she couldn't open a cupboard without its contents reaching for the floor. She stopped and took the trouble to put the catapulting plasters back in their box and place them on the proper shelf next to the Calpol and TCP. Constant reminders of Jack. She listened for his voice through the music, or a rata-ta-tat of machine-gun fire but heard nothing and smiled with mischievous irresponsible pleasure at the luxury of being alone.

Fully armed with razor, pumice stone and loofah, she slid into her hot bath, her dirty toenails rising above the suds as her head gently subsided, and she gazed at the myriad postcard destinations that filled the fake fishing net that was strung across the ceiling.

'Ahh blissssss,' she whispered to the bubbles, water swimming over the edge and dripping to the floor. The wet warmth seeped through her skin, only her head and the islands of her knees left dry: eyes closed, body still – serenity.

This is how it was to be single, thought Honor.

Single people didn't have jumping Jacks with their arms full of plastic dinosaurs plummeting into their bath, pretending a leg was a submarine. Imagine!

Honor let her mind swim to a pale blue, distant past, she could just about remember it. The quiet that led to anxiety, fears that grew desperate, the need for blocking loneliness. Now she dreamt to recall all that freedom, the bliss of sloping into an afternoon eighteen-rated movie, shopping for one, staying out and sleeping in, jumping on a train to Paris spur of the moment. No responsibilities.

It was only a game. She could play it because Jack would always be back showering noise and joy with tearful needs. Not that you never get lonely and depressed, just you and a small child, fighting for some adult sanity through the baby squish. Every day was filled with survival, making ends meet, keeping stomachs fed, minds occupied, bodies safe and conjuring up fun; as for the soul, it was squeezed with love. With Jack she would never be alone, not for the next ten years at least. It was safe to dream.

CHAPTER THREE

Catherine Herbert, Sarah Jane's only and elder sister, is quite unlike her, even to look at. Sarah Jane's blonde wild-eyed prettiness, outrageous behaviour twin-peaked with innocence, contrasts to her sibling's glossy magazine beautiful looks and capability. When Catherine moves her head, her dark groomed jaw-length hair obeys like a TV ad, her fringe sits upon her eyebrows with ruler-cut obedience and doesn't move until it's told to. Where once her body glowed for months under sunbeds like a silky brown berry, now she is as pale as the moon, fearful of skin cancer. She keeps her elegant milky body perfect to a size ten, and, if she slips, she enters the other side of her wardrobe, larger sized clothes bereft of labels. Only she will know the difference, she thinks. She drinks only mineral water, coffee and alcohol, usually a good white wine, vodka, or champagne – less fattening, she doesn't care that the bubbles eat away at her tooth enamel, why should she when all her teeth are capped? She exercises her tummy strenuously until she aches and the strong muscles show no signs of having held a baby, let alone two. With her still-perfect breasts (she wouldn't breastfeed for fear of marking and sagging) Catherine can confidently look in the mirror and exclaim, 'Perfection!' to herself, but only when dressed; the ugly scars of child-bearing will always be there when naked. At a certain point in every seduction, the lights go out, in privacy and respect for her past bodily functions.

Catherine slips on the expensive silk of her new dress and it glides over her slim limbs and hairless armpits, glides over her satin-held breasts, stomach and bottom. She maintains that what you wear under your clothes is as important as what you wear over them, it doesn't matter whether you fuck your husband or not, there might always be somebody else at the party. Often she holds this in mind and wears no underwear at all. She knows David her husband always notices. He grows aggrieved through an evening as she crosses and uncrosses her legs, flashing a darkness to some handsome stranger in a room. Not for him, he thinks.

On those nights, when they go home together, after the tense empty car journey, David will unlock the door to their house and, in the silence that says everybody is asleep, will close the door and turn on his wife. He will ram Catherine against the hall wall, he will tear at her new dress, ladder her stockings and push himself hard into her in his excitement. Sometimes he will wait, pull her up the stairs by her groomed hair, appreciating its softness with his large thick hands that have paid for it. Like a well honed bully-boy victim, he will throw her on to the carpet, grip her by the shoulders, pinning her down with his long heaviness, biting at her breasts and neck, marking her paleness until he relieves himself inside her with short hard grunts.

Catherine and David never 'make love', they 'fuck' – fuck off.

Catherine doesn't say a thing, make a sound or change her distant smile that taunts him on with her unavailability. So she comes with the surreal excitement of violent tension, then she feels bad.

David cries when he comes, wetting her perfumed skin with a mixture of snot, saliva and tears. She turns from him in disgust, his sobs have lost their effect. For another week or month he has used up his 'rights' to a disgruntled, emptying kind of sex. He snorts away the last of his snuffling and returns to his cold metal tone, when she says, 'I'm going to have to get a new dress now, you've ruined this one.'

Over the years she has said this in a range of tones from jocular to sultry, now she says it blankly but always inside she feels sick. A sickening sadness.

'Buy a new dress. You would do anyway, I pay for it all in the end. You must be the most expensive whore in London,' he says getting up, adjusting his clothes and walking towards the adjoining bathroom.

'I suspected you might be well versed in that department. I only hope you wear a Durex with them,' she shouts after him. He turns on the taps to drown out her voice and blows his nose.

Before bed and silk pyjamas, she will have a cigarette, to calm her nerves (and because David hates her smoking, though he indulges in fat cigars), a bidet or bath to soothe her punished soreness and a camomile tea to help her troubled sleep. She will climb into their bed next to her snoring drunken husband, maybe she will have a brandy too, to help her stop thinking and enter black dreamless sleep; the only sort she cares to remember.

Why does she do it when she knows the predictable outcome? Catherine can't even claim it's for excitement any more, so she puts it down to boredom. It is easier to see it as an adjunct to boredom, the games of dishonesty, no longer fun or playful. A little something to alleviate the dullness of a pointless marriage? Perhaps.

She must have loved him once, Catherine often reasons with herself, she must have, but now it is so far back she can't be sure she ever did. They have grown apart, if ever they were together. He is too coarse, she thinks, vulgar, setting his ambition above everything. The successful do not have to work that hard. She is afraid she has chosen a failure. He bores her. With him, she bores herself.

'Remember Catherine, he's a good provider and that's worth a lot!' her mother tells her, any time she shows herself to be more than just dissatisfied with the situation. 'Do you think with your job you could afford that house? Discovering young unknown artists might be exciting but it won't cover the dresses. Let him be and you can both get on with whatever you want to do within the security of the marriage. It won't hurt you to turn your back and be a little discreet. It's how good marriages survive. Just grit your teeth and smile.'

'I dare say you're right,' she finishes the discussion and locks back her pain. Catherine and Sarah Jane's mother, Henrietta Gossop, was a fine-looking haughty creature; she would have made an excellent president's first lady.

No gritting teeth tonight, nothing can happen. David is out for a business dinner, he has rung and told her. This means he will be back in the early hours of the morning satisfied by some woman, a secretary who thinks herself a PA. A girl whose light head has been turned by the charisma of his musk power, impressed by the cut of his suits, his fine cotton shirts, silk ties and enamelled cufflinks, all chosen by Catherine, his wife. A bottle of cheap champagne (but it is champagne) and dinner, will secure a sympathetic ear, some impressed youthful enthusiasm and twenty-three-year-old sex. He will say he's separated, this gives them hope and is not entirely untrue, for he is separated from the world, friendships, his children,

Catherine. The more separate he becomes the more he clings to his work, his office, his lawyer's title.

Hard bitch Catherine who offers him iced vitriol when he asks for sympathy, just a little compassion. He has forgotten that she once kissed him softly and whispered sweetness to his ear, how she offered her tummy to him to stroke, full and warm with their baby and love. He has forgotten how he threw up at Ben's birth, disgusted to see Catherine's sex turned to gore, desire to pain. The years he wilted at her touch, he has forgotten.

Now Catherine rebukes him, on the phone, in the house with her pushing, teasing cruelty. She always was too clever for him.

'Business dinner. Oh really darling, working again on a Friday night, how awful for you?' she mockingly commiserates about his 'special' client dinners, that make him bearable for the weekend.

'I have to pay for the dresses somehow, bitch,' he whispers. Bored with the screen of words both can translate. A cloaked repartee of vituperative volleys.

'Yes, you do don't you. I wonder who will be home first? I'm out to Sarah Jane's hen night. Don't worry about the children darling, Helena's in tonight,' she adds as an afterthought, as though he worries about such things. Why should he, they are for her to worry about, he earns the money after all. What does she do, apart from spend it?

'Hngh,' he snorts. 'Enjoy yourself.'

'Oh don't worry, I'll make sure of that!'

'By the way when are you going to get a proper job, earn some real money and join the real world, Catherine?' He throws her name out of his mouth and puts the phone down, not waiting for her goodbye, believing he has the last word.

The phone call with David made Catherine wish she was going somewhere with a reason for not wearing underclothes. It might be a girls-only dinner but we're not going to single sex places, she realised and a thrill whizzed through her veins. The Issey Miyake dress that she'd bought was too elegantly sculptured, perfect for a Royal Academy opening but never dirty-dancing. So she pulled out a sleeveless silk jersey in a dark smoked blue-grey that unbuttoned down one side; a dress she'd always had success in.

Catherine was in such a good mood with her evening all planned, she decided to stop her work early, pick her children up from school, take them out to an Ed's Easy Diner. They could have milkshakes and cheeseburgers and it would make it easier to ask Helena, their au pair, to take them out to a movie in the afternoon and relieve her of parental duties so she could sleep in tomorrow. Get some quiet in the house, a change from their incessant bickering and fights over computer games, music and videos. She intended staying out late.

'What are you doing here?' was her son's thirteen-year-old negative enthusiasm to Catherine picking him up from school. He usually took the bus home by himself. It was bad enough being seen with Helena but at least she was young and wore boots with her short skirt. Helena was all right, he quite fancied her.

'Ben darling, I thought we could all go out for tea. Have you seen Augusta, oh there she is. Augusta, over here darling. Ben come back, don't go off in the other direction. We're going, now, Ben, come on.'

'Okay, okay, Mum. Cool it. You don't have to nag.'

Once all seated in the car, both in the back to stop them arguing about who would go in the front, Ben asked, 'Next time you pick us up, can you wear a pair of jeans and a floppy jumper? All the boys stare at your bosoms in that dress. It's embarrassing.'

'I don't think so, it's a compliment to me at my age.' Catherine laughed.

'It's too short for your age.'

'I like your dress Mummy, I think it's lovely. Can you buy me one?' said greedy Augusta.

'It's embarrassing to *me* Mum, and if you think you're so old you shouldn't wear it. Don't you know you're not a teenager any more! And Gus, stop being so creepy, "I think it's lovely",' Ben mimicked his sister, 'you make me want to puke. Anyway, where are we going?'

'Where would you like to go? It's up to you two if you can come to a decision between yourselves without arguing.'

'Ed's,' they both shouted. Catherine smiled indulgently at their predictability.

'Okay, okay, Ed's it is.'

Catherine parked the car on the yellow line outside and sat up on the barstool by the window to keep an eye on it, wedged between her children. Augusta liked being out with her mother who always called her by her proper name: Gussy sounded too babyish, she felt like an Augusta. Sitting up at the bar of the 1950s American-style diner, she was unsure of who she wanted to impress the most, the good-looking young waiter who looked like the lead singer of Blur, or her mother, so she smiled her all-round sickly smile for both of them and sneered intermittently at her brother. She had favours she wanted to procure. Ben had no doubts, he'd show who was cool around here.

'Mum! Did you get my Snoop Doggy Dog CD I told you to. Did you?'

'Ben what are you having? The cheeseburger and french fries, like Gussy?'

'Mummy, I'm Augusta, not Gussy.' Crestfallen, betrayed by her own mother. Her mouth slid to a cynical grimace, her head turned firmly away unable to look the wearer of the 'Hi, I'm Gary' badge in the face. He'd think she was a baby, though she was almost eleven.

'No fear, I want the chilli burger and chips.'

'I thought you said it was too hot last time?' Catherine unthinkingly queried.

'I did not! Did you get my Snoop Doggy Dog?' he repeated loudly for the waiter's benefit, who smiled back in acknowledgement of his taste. Ben's charmless scowl tried to hide the smile.

Just like their father, she thought, more interested in impressing strangers than family. Ben's scowl is just like David's too; amazing considering they never see him, it must be in the genes. She couldn't wait to be out of the house tonight, away from her charmless son and sycophantic Lolita-esque daughter. How did they turn out so horrible when they had been such sweet small things?

'I hope Auntie Sarah Jane doesn't have babies,' Catherine thought out loud.

Augusta pondered on this one. Ben ignored it.

'I think she'd have beautiful babies. Uncle Josh is so . . .' said Augusta.

'You haven't even met him, how d'ya know he'd even let you call him "Uncle". Why does he want to marry your sister, Mum?

Sarah Jane's all right but there's bound to be better in LA.' Ben filled his mouth with chips before continuing. 'All he has to do is look at you and see what she'll look like when she's old.'

Catherine shook her head in disbelief. They champed at their burgers and Catherine at her bit, before smiling a seductive thank you to waiter Gary, as he lit her cigarette. Ben caught the exchange in the mirror, his mother and the waiter, he looked away in disgust. How could somebody so old still be interested in sex? He'd make her get the CD this weekend. Definite! And then he'd play it really loud on Sunday morning!

'You should smoke Death cigarettes. You're going to die of cancer soon anyway.' Ben threw the bored curse in the air averting his eyes. 'Then me and Gus could sue the cigarette company and be rich!'

'Thank you for the suggestion but I'm quite happy with this brand,' she grimaced back, reminding herself of her mother.

Ben smoked Death cigarettes. He didn't tell his mother but he was working his habit up to eight a day. Death suited his and his friends' defiant image and gave them a hobby other than sticking their tongues into squeamish girls' mouths when they wanted to put other things in them. Cigarettes were a willing substitute. Ben was growing up faster than his mother or father cared to notice. Augusta wasn't that far behind, she still hid behind a childish façade to glean extra gold pickings from her distracted parents. David and Catherine remained innocently oblivious to their children's behaviour, but then their lack of interest in the family home extended to the family too. They were four unconnected beings who had been flung into a unit for no discernible purpose but to survive. Their house was an experiment for the dispossessed.

CHAPTER FOUR

'You'd better go now,' Gem turned and said to the boy lying on her arm, still wrapped in her white Egyptian sheets.

She had been kinder than usual, had given him a coffee, but now she wanted him to leave. She needed to have a shower, scald herself with water, scrub herself clean from the encounter, change.

Opening her windows both ends to let the wind sweep through and carry the reminding odours back outside with it, to erase the act, she needed to be alone, to be able to forget about last night's encounter.

Gem had prayed he'd got up in the middle of the night and left, disappeared, leaving no number, nothing. In the end she wished she hadn't brought him home at all, but sometimes she did foolish things in an effort to forget.

'At least I haven't eaten all the Reece's Peanut Butter Cups that are lurking in the bottom of the fridge. Then I'd be feeling truly bad,' she spoke silently in her head. 'At least I haven't done that, yet, but there's still the rest of the day to get through.'

Lots of conversations went on in Gem's head, made up dialogues or playbacks cast with different conclusions.

She would have preferred to go back to his place then she could have left as soon as the sex was finished, but you could never be sure how clean their sheets were, what godforsaken holes they might live in. A lot of boys still lived at parents' homes, not an option Gem wished to explore.

'Thanks a lot. I thought you were pretty fabulous too. Sure you don't want a fuck for the coffee?' he smirked resentfully at Gem and her virgin-white home. She ignored his tone.

'No, that's all right. Coffee's compliments of the house. I've got to get on with some work now. Sorry to be so abrupt, it's just the way it is.'

'Yeah sure. No trouble.' Steve, or whatever he was called, got up.

He was dressed quickly. Jeans, shirt, loafers, no underwear to search for and impede his speed. Gem was up, pulling the blinds, looking out of the window. She didn't want to look at him now, his elegant young muscled body, his face almost too pretty, although she'd hungered to look and admire him last night. She was disgusted that he wasn't wearing underwear, but in the darkness she had been aroused.

'Don't mind if I use your bathroom for a slash, do you?'

'Of course not,' but she didn't want to hear about it, hear it.

Gem roped her bleach-clean bathrobe around her, picking up clothes from the night before, putting them back in her wardrobe, folding and hanging everything neatly. Emptying the ashtray full of used condoms into the main kitchen bin. Ugh, she thought, not remembering the howling pleasure that had filled them last night. A tuneless hum started in her head, she tried to hold on to it, waiting for some order. Pinning her bottle-blonde hair up, waiting, listening for the cistern's flush. She walked through to the sitting room/office, glad to be in its stark neat paleness, away from the intimacy of her bedroom.

Over at her desk, she sat pretending to make a list of what she had to do, when all she could think was, why was he taking so damn long? Then there was the click on the door as she busily rearranged her paints in their box in the order of the spectrum. Gem didn't look up, he walked to the front door.

'Bye then. See you around.'

'Sure, see you at the club sometime. Thanks.'

'Yeah, thanks. Bye.'

Exchanging phone numbers was out of the question. He was gone, and any bodily warmth with him.

Gem felt lost in the silence, she jumped from the pale carpet on to the sofa and lay there face forwards, sunk in the pillows, hugging them and trying to empty her mind. She tried blocking it out, corking up the feelings of disgust that coursed through her, from ear to toe, leaving her imprinted like a piece of Brighton rock.

She wasn't having any of it. She went to the fridge and pulled out the pack of chocolate that she knew waited for her and tore it open, stuffing it into her mouth until its sweetness made her feel sick enough to spit it all out. She tried to make sure none of it had gone down her throat. She swilled out her mouth with water to get rid of the rest of the chocolate and nuts, spitting them into the sink under the running tap. She went straight to the bathroom and brushed her teeth until her gums hurt and not one grain of sugar was left. She gurgled with a mouthwash until, mouth and throat disinfected, she was clean enough to step into the shower and start purging her body.

Gem was an illustrator. She was once a painter, but a painter has to eat. She worked hard all day, ate nothing, sent one piece of work off to the magazine and started another one, for a feature about pre-menstrual tension. She listened to continuous classical music, drinking only camomile tea to clean out her system, but she still didn't feel virtuous. Something lingered that she needed to get rid of, to purge with physical exercise. She wasn't thinking about last night, she refused to, but the feeling hovered like an irritating horsefly about her head, unable to find an open window out.

It was four o'clock, they were meeting at eight, that was enough time to get to the pool, have a swim and get back, dress and be in town for eight. She put away her pens and pencils, sharpening the ones she'd used, screwing lids back on to tubes, putting tops back on to bottles. Everything neatly in its place, ordered like the rest of her flat.

It was just her mind that spun in turmoil, like a defective Magi-mix with a missing lid. Each time she let the control button slip something messy and inappropriate jumped out, splattering her.

Gemma Daley was like her mother Anna in many ways; precise, tidy, they looked the same too. Gemma saw she wasn't going to age well, her and her mother's kind of prettiness didn't. The eyes might stay clear and blue, but they didn't look good in the surrounding peach wrinkles. Their hair, though a wonderful rich honey blonde, was too thin, the lips not fat enough. They would cave with age towards their open mouths. The high cheekbones would only give a gauntness once youth's cushioning plumpness fell away.

The years can be cruel to some flowers, early blossoms.

At thirty-three, Gemma maintained she'd never introduce a man she was serious about to her mother, it wasn't a good advert for the marriage prospects. The only thing you heard people say about Anna Daley was, 'She must have been pretty when she was young.'

It was too depressing. That's why Gemma kept her body so fit, almost as punishment for it being her casing. When she swam, she dived hard and crawled non-stop for forty lanes, goggles down and the muscles set hard in her jaw. Beware loafing, casual swimmers who gently breaststroked their way around the pool.

After her swim, she scrutinised the changing room mirror to see if anything had altered, if her arms had slimmed down, her thighs subsided. Even Gem could now see, without her period, the flatness of her stomach, the definition of her hips.

It's no good, she thought. I'm definitely going to have to wear something to cover the size of my bum, but I can show my stomach if I eat nothing tonight. She'd put her hair up to make herself look taller, wear the Mexican chain-belt that Sarah Jane had brought her back from LA.

Returning from her swim, the answerphone flashed its red-button urgency. She pressed the talk-back button to hear the messages, put down her rucksack and flipped off her trainers.

'Hi, hi it's Nick here from the other night. I hope you don't mind I asked Susie for your number since you forgot to give it to me the other morning. How about meeting up for a drink or something? Call me, my number's 352-7744.'

Boring, she thought. I didn't give him my number on purpose. He got a fuck, what more do these boys want?

'Hello Gemma darling, it's Mummy here. You haven't forgotten Granny's birthday, have you? I've bought a present and card, you can sign it when you get here for the lunch. Don't work too hard now. Daddy sends his love, unfortunately I don't think he's going to be able to make it back from Brussels in time, he said he's got too much on. Works too hard, like father like daughter. Don't work so hard, have some fun whilst you're young, go out with some boys, it would do you good. Anyway give me a call.'

Ahh sweet, she thought of her mother, just wished she didn't fuss so. Wished she had some idea of a world beyond Richmond, and sending her father's suits to the cleaners for his ever-protracted business trips.

Poor Mummy, not a clue. Sometimes Gemma wondered how her parents came to have sex, what her mother would do if ever she knew how many men she went through in a month. It was not something Gemma ever wanted to consider, so why she thought her mother should . . . Still she hadn't forgotten her granny's birthday and had already bought her a present of handmade French truffles that sat untouched in her fridge, but screamed as audibly as a siren to her.

'Gem, I've been thinking about you, you and my tongue again . . . Ant calling.' Ha ha ha. Gross git.

Gemma had learnt her lesson about giving her number out with Ant and his regular, salacious calls. She used to think it was fun, used to do the same to his answerphone, until he kept on with them after his wedding to Amanda. Even at the reception he'd tried to pin her to the flimsy marquee walls with his own 'pole' as he referred to it, whilst Amanda changed into her honeymoon outfit upstairs. Gemma had slapped it down with her handbag and said, 'Anthony, my morals might have dredged the gutter to sleep with you once, but I'm not down to sewer-level yet.'

That's how she told the story. In reality she'd mumbled a quick, 'What about Amanda?' before running off across the muddied lawn in case she was identified as the whore of Whitby Bay and stoned to death by the in-laws on the nearby beach. In the end it wouldn't have mattered, Ant had already left Amanda and his two-year-old daughter for somebody else. He'd discovered Amanda was having an affair with their French nanny. Modern life.

It annoyed her that her mother's call should be sandwiched, sullied, in between these two distasteful messages. She wiped the lot and got back to work on her hair. First the back-combing and bouffanting before inserting the hairpiece. The false lashes went on next, followed by polyfiller foundation, baby-pink lipstick, blusher and eyeliner. Four-inch stacks went on her feet, making her confident enough to expose the midriff between her short, plunging top and hipster skirt.

She took a last look at herself in the mirror, up, down and both sides, pressed her lips together hard as though making the colour indelible, and said, 'At least the tits are real.'

They were in the merry stage of drunkenness as the twenty of them wound their way from the bar, full of champagne, to the restaurant. Sarah Jane had been sufficiently fussed over, and given perhaps one too many glasses for this time of the evening, if she was going to survive without passing out (a well-worn party trick). Water was going to have to be filtered through her at some point. Catherine saw that as her sisterly duty, and refused to order any wine at the restaurant until three large bottles of mineral water were finished.

'Heil Hitler, mein Führer,' said Janine, standing up, clicking her heels, sticking one arm out and putting one finger beneath her nose to moustache her lips. 'Sarah Jane, was your sister always this liberal at home?'

'Always. You look rather good like that with your hair all short and greased down. If you had leather lederhosen on I could quite fancy you.'

'Stop teasing me. You know I'd wear them naked for you!'

'Quiet! Has everybody ordered?'

'Has everybody stopped ordering everybody else around?'

'Where's the wine?'

'Yes, have you ordered the wine? I'm not drinking any of this water, W. C. Fields told me fish fuck in it.'

'Some crab has crapped in it.'

'So have you! It's true it's probably been through us seven times by now.'

'Charming!'

'Talking of which I thought we'd have a game. It's called Lucky Dip. How many of us have shared the same men (at the very least a heavy snog) and then we can award them marks out of ten, so that any of us who haven't had the pleasure so far don't have to waste time and condoms with the dross. Anyone got a likely name?' Catherine said, opening the game to the hungry crowd who shouted out their responses. All politeness had disappeared. The wine was open, the bottles emptying . . .

'One at a time girls.' Catherine had declared herself master of ceremonies. 'I think my sister should have first go.'

Sarah Jane stood up, wine firmly in hand, and addressed the table. She looked radiant and happy, flushed with the attention. How brides look on their wedding day. It wasn't just her fellow hens who were admiring her, half the restaurant had joined them. The bare shoulders helped.

'It's my party and I propose the ever-popular . . . Mr Ant Benict, who's got into more holes than a winning golfball.'

Eight hands went up around the table and another six could

have gone up if the whole restaurant had been included in the game. His brother-in-law sat at the next table listening with an appalled interest as the scores were counted. Distracted from his business dinner as he tried to discover how Anthony rated on the girls' Richter scale, he spent the rest of the meal worrying about the possibility of AIDS, wondering if promiscuity ran in the family and contemplating how much his wife was like her brother.

'The winner of tonight's competition seems to be Charlie Longley, endowed in more ways than one, his sensitivity and oral skills seem to put him at the top of the league. He may be hard to seduce, shy as old Charlie is but he's obviously worth the effort. Let's hear it for Charlie.'

The table busily clinked glasses and in unison replied, 'To Charlie.'

'And commiserations for Ant, though nobody feels sorry enough for him to start donating towards his obviously much-needed surgical enlarging scheme.'

'Raise your glasses please. To Ant, small in name because of his nature?'

'Very witty, Sara.'

The meal continued with food picked at and played with until the waiters could stand it no longer and the plates were cleared. A few girls ordered puddings. More wine was drunk. The other tables left. Sammy smeared blood-orange mousse across her naked breasts and got Janine (an executive film producer) and Misha (sometime children's presenter) to lick it off. At that point the manager gave them the bill, service charge included, and invited the hen night to pay up and leave, though his eyes seemed to say otherwise. Sarah Jane left the room like a Great Dane on heat, mounting each doric column in the room and simulating sex.

Outside, cabs were chaotically boarded, for those who couldn't be bothered to sober up in the night air. Honor walked, she felt she needed the sense of the ordinary around her before she descended into the disorienting youth culture of a nightclub. She couldn't remember the last time she had been dancing, apart from at a wedding. When they were at college they'd be in clubs two or three nights a week, no wonder they never had any money.

Gem had gone on ahead with Catherine to make sure they'd all get in to the exclusive Underworld 'celebrity bar' as a sign declared on the right of the cash till. An aggressive gum-chewing dolly at reception demanded eight pounds from everyone before they joined the darkness. A few of the girls sloped off home after the meal; a pregnant Diane couldn't justify a nightclub to her unborn child. Connie was still feeding her six-month-old son and justly said, if she didn't get home her breasts would burst like a pair of silicones at high altitude. Janine offered to subdue them. 'I've always wanted to taste breast milk, being a bottle-fed baby.'

'Rubbish, you just like sucking tits,' said a coarse voice in the dark.

Honor didn't want the pink champagne that somebody was putting into her hand, but she drank it all down anyway, like a good girl. Dragged on to the dance floor, she was glad to become invisible amongst the mass of jiggling bodies. Not for long, somebody had singled her out, was smiling an outrageously neon-white smile for Honor's benefit. She looked around her, still dancing, hoping it was meant for Beth next to her, but he bobbed his head close to her and in a thick Middle-Eastern accent offered her an array of drugs Sarah Jane would have died for and Honor would have died taking.

Sarah Jane had already discovered her supplies, pushed her way into the celebrity bar and found a former light middle-weight and an ageing ballad-singing pop star to provide her with a rolled up fifty-pound note and several neat lines of white dust to inhale, with a promise that he was allowed to lick the remaining snowy residue from her nose. Sarah Jane didn't object, she could hardly feel the wet warm tickle on her anaesthetised nostrils but just as he was about to move on to her mouth, Gem came to spoil it and pulled her away.

'Come on, Sarah Jane, your present's arriving.'

She pulled her downstairs in time for the entrance.

'A pressy for me! Oh goody, I love pressies and I should have lots of them. Gem, what is it? This is so exciting, I'm having such a brilliant time. Isn't it brilliant here? Oh Gem, isn't it great . . . Have the rest of this bottle,' she said and watched her present come down the stairs towards her.

Honor couldn't watch the performance any more, but watching the bargirl's expression was probably worse. She looked back, the crowd was geeing Sarah Jane on. She was down on her knees in front of Stripping Builder Jim, her hands were holding him and the contents of his jock strap seemed to be shrinking as her greedy mouth sought to envelop it, her hands trying to excite it back. The poor man looked terrified, it hadn't been part of his job description.

'I can't take this Gem. I've got to get home.'

'Neither can he by the look of it. Stay Honor, go on it's only quarter to two. I'll share a cab home with you at three.'

'I've heard that one before from Gem,' thought Honor and went to find Catherine to say goodnight.

'Honor, over here. You haven't met Mustapha and Gerald have you? They're diamond people, that's right isn't it boys? How about a glass for my friend Honey, of course we're both in the beauty business in case you couldn't tell.' Catherine winked, smiled and contained her laughter.

'You must be a model, no?' Mustapha, the smiley one, beseeched of Honor.

'No. But my friend here's an actress. She's playing a big part at the moment.' She bent to Catherine's ear to whisper. 'Sorry I'm a bit of a party pooper I'm afraid. I've got severe homing instincts. Catherine, can I pop round for a cup of tea tomorrow afternoon?'

'Of course Honey, give me a ring. Are you going to be all right?'

'I'd be honoured to give you a lift,' Mustapha offered graciously.

'No, I wouldn't hear of it, splitting up the party. I'll catch a cab on the street. Nice to meet you all, bye.'

As she turned up the stairway towards the door, she could already see Catherine had moved on to somebody else, Sarah Jane was snogging Misha with most of her clothes missing and was that Gem in the corner writhing with the strip-a-gram? It couldn't be. Not celibate Gem, she never did it with anyone. Either I've had more to drink than I'd imagined, or she has, thought Honor, stumbling up the stairs out into the darkness. The night-time madness of Shaftesbury Avenue full up to Cambridge Circus with packed coffee bars and cruising men made finding a cab hard. On Tottenham Court Road she hailed and heaved herself inside the familiar safety of warm leather and slippery seats. Honor relaxed and told the cabbie her address, home alone again.

CHAPTER FIVE

Honor raised her head to look into the lift and their eyes met and wouldn't disengage. She struggled with the heavy gate and instead of being embarrassed, couldn't look away. With an easy pull he'd released the door and given Honor such a warm smile that stepping through into the cage with him made her shy. This stranger was making her body behave oddly, either that or she was experiencing teenage regression or menopausal precociousness: hot flushes, goose pimples and feeling awkward about sharing a lift. How ridiculous! No matter how hard she tried to look at the floor, door, walls, her own fingers fidgeting in her hands, her eyes were drawn back to his face like a magnet. She tried to concentrate on her molars, biting at the inside of her cheek.

As he began to speak she felt her insides fold and collapse like a pancake.

'Hello there, my name is Harry Roberts. I'm your new neighbour. I've just bought the flat, I think it's above yours, no?' he asked charmingly.

His amused look disarmed her, as though he knew the immediate effect he was having on her. She wanted to hold on to the wall, feel something dead and solid, a bit of security against her blancmange body in meltdown. How could she answer? What was she supposed to say to this gorgeous man with his delicious Scottish accent and tousled floppy hair that fell divinely over one eye, whose broad shoulders pulled his white T-shirt across a muscular chest and whose jeans fitted him like an advert. Where were the words?

Honor began to open her mouth inadequately, and then closed it quickly when she realised nothing was coming out. Her name, she'd say her name and, and welcome. Welcome? She never said welcome.

'Oh good. I mean I'm glad that, sorry, welcome! I hope you'll be happy here.'

'I'm sure I will.' He was looking at her and thinking she was an idiot she was certain, even though her eyes had returned to studying the frayed carpeting beneath their feet. 'What's your name?'

'Oh I'm sorry. I'm Honor. Honor Summers, like Donna except different. I live in number nine, you must be in number twelve if you're above me.' Why had she said that? Why was she acting with all the sophistication of a Teletubby, when she could have said anything?

'No, I'm number eleven. There are only two apartments upstairs, ten and eleven.'

'Of course. Well, here we are.' Honor said, stating the obvious with the heavy clunk of the lift's descent.

She wanted to run as fast as she could and get on to the first bus going in the opposite direction, or stop time by saying something wittily impressive that would jump over all this embarrassing preamble and thrust them to intimacy.

'It's been nice meeting you,' was all she could come up with before she tripped out of the gates. Honor was not looking where she was going, her eyes had gone back to Harry's open-faced smile and the silent messages that passed between them. Imagined or real promises of predatory passion, caveman stuff. Once she was out and running, more limping, down the road to pick up Jack she realised the true awfulness of the situation. No make-up. In her hungover state she hadn't put a thing around her rabbit eyes, her skin less a blot on the landscape, more a blotched icescape with the bloodied remains of pulped seal pups, where her nails had dug in, in urgent excavations of blackheads the night before.

I must have looked awful, truly, that's why he was staring at me. Why don't I listen to Granny – 'If you keep picking, it'll never get better'? Aaagh. Please God of all earth swallow me up. A convenient cable hole had done just that and she'd been forced to laugh through her wrenched ankle.

'I didn't exactly fall flat on my face,' Honor said later, having described the awful sequence of events to Catherine, 'just enough to get a hole in my tights and limp out of the building as though I was a walking disaster. I couldn't even turn around and go back up to my flat to change. Not with him standing there looking so concerned as though I'd broken my leg, asking if I was all right. I can't tell you how embarrassing it was, Catherine, or how gorgeous he is . . .'

'I've never had a Scot,' Catherine interrupted. 'But I know what you mean, there's something sexy about that soft Gaelic accent. I'm thinking *Whisky Galore* rather than *Trainspotting*.'

Honor was sitting in Catherine's sunflower-yellow kitchen, looking out of the open French windows on to her idea of the perfect home garden. A camomile lawn, mossed stone walls tangled with camellias, sweet peas and trailing old-fashioned roses. In front, foxgloves, clematis, lilies, and a sprinkling of the first wild-coloured Icelandic poppies sprung between the fuchsia bushes. Next door's lilac waved new purple scents across the wall. Tubs of herbs sat around the open door. In the centre of the lawn sat a majestic old apple tree which by autumn would be groaning with the weight of fruit on its bent and stumpy body.

Honor's bare legs stretched out into the sun of the day. Tights off, her sore pink knee and bruised ankle basked in the warmth, her toes wriggling to be submerged in the cool lawn. She cradled the children's biscuit tin and a large yellow cup of tea in her hands. Her body harboured the hangover and not enough sleep after Sarah Jane's hen night. She could have slept in but her time clock woke her now as noisily as Jack's seven thirty alarm call, and she couldn't get back to sleep.

Instead, she lay in bed fantasising warm, sexy, romantic escapist dreams, with perfect celluloid faces, until forced by her bladder to get out of bed and confront her bathroom's cold lino reality.

Everything about Catherine's house and life seemed perfect to Honor (especially in her current state). She had a job she didn't need to make money from, as a partner in a small well-respected art gallery discovering new, exciting talent. Most of her work she could do from home. The daily grind of her children was taken from her by an au pair, and a wealthy husband who adored her enough to give her everything she wanted, including time and space. As if that wasn't enough she lived in this beautiful pale house in the cherry blossom-lined clean streets of Chelsea, where dog owners actually used pooper scoopers and doggy toilets. Even the winoes wore cravats and tweed jackets. Catherine had it made, Honor thought, like many others.

Why do some get and others not? thought Honor. How does

God manage to prioritise or discriminate? She had that faraway dreamy look as she considered the injustices of the world and hummed 'God Bless the Child' to herself.

'I've seen you look better but I've never seen you so smitten. Honestly Honor, anyone would think by your expression that he must look like a four-course meal by the Roux brothers. When I think of all the tempting offers I've put in front of you and not once have you bitten the bait! Sooo, when can we meet the highland fling?' asked Catherine, still not sitting down. She was always fixing and moving, preparing and sorting, elegantly unsettled like a beautiful butterfly, her hair catching the light, her clothes draped upon her like a catwalk doll.

'Catherine! He's just a neighbour! He's only just moved in and my chances of bumping into him again this year are about a thousand to one. I've only ever seen the person who lives in number ten twice in the three years she's lived there. It's complete fantasy stuff. Nice fantasy though,' she sighed.

'Can't you contrive a reason to go and knock on his door? Get the relationship going. Girl Lives Fantasy, shock horror! Okay how about, "Can I borrow some sugar," or a Tampax? Get it intimate. Or, "I'm just making some haggis could you help me with the stuffing?" You don't have to pretend you're Janet in *Dr Finlay's Casebook*, that's optional. Look, the worst you can do is humiliate yourself utterly Honor, and what's a little humiliation in the face of true love?'

Ahh the face of true love. All the shop-soiled expectations, straight from a storybook, hang your hat on a dream peg and watch it fall off the wall.

'Thanks a bunch. I thought I'd done that already, oh woman of wordy wisdom. Can I borrow a Tampax indeed!' All she could feel was sagging hopelessness. Honor stuffed another chocolate biscuit into her mouth, a reflex action like a child reaching for a dummy, and left it to melt on her tongue; now she'd got going she'd probably finish the tin.

'On the other hand I could ask to borrow a condom and ask him how to use one. Say I've forgotten it's been so long . . . What d'ya reckon?'

'Mum, don't eat all the biscuits, we want some,' said Jack, silently appearing to Honor's fright. He pulled the tin away from his mother's reluctant release. 'We haven't had anything! Greedy grown-ups grabbin' it all, you'll be fat Mum.'

'I'm fat already, but thanks for the warning.'

He was showing off especially, thought Honor, to impress Catherine in the only way he knew how, being boss to his mother. How sweet!

'Don't be so rude Jack, apologise to your mum.' Catherine defended her friend.

'Sorry, now can I have the biscuits and Gussy wants a drink of Coke and I do too. Please Catherine? What are you talking about Mum? You're always talking.'

'Things, different stuff. Jack, I thought you didn't like Coke, have some juice,' said Honor, suddenly the sugar-conscious mother, to no avail.

'I do! When I'm with Gussy. Juice is for babies.'

'Here you are Jack. Are you sure you can manage it all? Next time get that lazy old Augusta to do her own fetching and carrying, you can tell her that from me,' Catherine said conspiratorially to Jack, bending over to load him up. 'What's Ben up to?'

'I think he's on his computer but he might be in the square. Gussy's showing me her new videos her dad bought her, *Hercules* and *Tomorrow Never Dies*, all from America. Mum why don't we ever go to America?'

Honor and Catherine exchanged glances, and Honor gave one of the usual replies, 'We do other things, go other places. Maybe we will some day.' She tried not to give the automatic answer too often, 'We don't have the money.' The real reason.

'You always say that.'

It was already clear to Jack at school that other children had more than him with their Gameboys, computers, Nike trainers, whole houses to live in with gardens full of brothers, sisters, fathers, freezers, dishwashers and take-away McDonald's. Foreign holidays were just one more thing.

Honor found it hard, near impossible sometimes, trying to get the balance right, to show Jack how much more they had than others with nothing. One day maybe she and Jack would live in a house like Catherine's with a garden. Or maybe they wouldn't because she wasn't willing to pay the price of being with a suited man who worked in the city and brought home clients for her to cook cordon bleu dinners for, when she couldn't bear to talk to either clients or husband.

Honor knew Catherine hated that side, attending functions and appearing interested for the sake of your husband's career. She didn't want that life, to be nice Mrs Wifey, not for the price of a foreign holiday and a house in Chelsea. She wasn't that cheap. She'd rather be on her own without the drink problem, caffeine addiction, store cards, extra washing and gym membership. But if she loved him? Maybe that would be a different matter.

'Here's some popcorn for you two, and if you want some ice-cream later, Gussy knows where to get it from.' Catherine added the box to the balance of tins and Jack held it up to his chin to hold it in place, appeased by all the goodies he'd managed to snaffle.

'Are you sure you won't have a glass of wine, Honor?'

'No honestly I'm fine with tea, thanks.'

Catherine re-filled her blue glass with the cold white wine from the fridge and sat down beside Honor at the kitchen table.

'Are we going to mention last night, is it allowed?' ventured Honor, uncertain.

'Amongst participating hens, but I think it's a good idea not to mention one part of the evening to the groom. Well, I'm not going to, anyway!'

'So what happened after I left? Where did Sarah Jane and Gem end up? I thought I saw Gem with the strip-a-gram. I must have been drunk. Gem wouldn't.'

'Wouldn't she?' Catherine paused to pull on her cigarette and raise her eyebrows. 'I think there's a few things about Gem that are kept hidden, even from her nearest and dearest. I saw her leave with the strip-a-gram in a taxi.'

'No! But she's always saying she's celibate and not interested in men. I was starting to think she might be gay, or at least bi, like Misha. Whenever she gets drunk she slopes off with a girl. Gem never gets drunk, she likes the control.'

'Well she wasn't last night, she was definitely practising a little bump and grind with Marlon. Lucky her. He was great, I can't believe they're all like that. I'll be ordering all my take-aways from there.'

'And your sister!'

'I know, I know. All I can say is, thank God that kind of humiliating exhibitionism doesn't run in the family.'

'I was shocked to tell you the truth.'

'So was I. I couldn't believe he remained flaccid. He must have been terrified with Sarah Jane's gorgon's mouth coming towards his precious parts. It reminded me of that science fiction book I read at college that started with the man in blissful ecstasy as the space sirens took it in turns to give him fellatio. Quietly one turned away to put something in her mouth and came back on him smiling, just at that point he saw the glint of her new steel teeth descend upon him and fainted. I hope Gem got a better performance out of him.'

'Catherine, I didn't mean that. Poor man.'

'What? Which one?'

'Oh, all of them I suppose. With you around.'

'Honor don't disappoint me and say "poor David", otherwise I'll throw you out of the house.'

'Oh I wouldn't say that. David always seems happy enough, not that I've seen him for ages. How is he?'

'The usual. Busy, busy, work, work. We get along.'

Honor could sense Catherine's sensitivity on a subject that usually maliciously tripped off her tongue; maybe she was hungover, she didn't push it. Catherine would say what she wanted to. Her downcast eyes and her finger intently pushing around a cigarette in the ashtray, her glass held tightly by her other hand seemed to say that her mind was there but nothing else would come near. Then she lifted her head with a jolt and a smile towards Honor and said, 'I hope Sarah Jane has some vague inkling of what she's letting herself in for. I try to tell her but she won't take it from me, bossy big sister and all that. She never tells me anything of what she's doing at the moment. Do you speak to her much?'

'Not when her mouth's full. Sorry, that was unnecessary. You can't be so fatalistic, Sarah Jane's party's just beginning.'

'I guess so Honor. It's just a feeling, you know me I'm a natural optimist.' Catherine stubbed out her cigarette and lit another.

'What's Josh, the man behind the beautiful screen persona, like?' Honor asked, genuinely curious.

'What do I think of Josh? Well apart from all the obvious traits you pick up on first meeting – vain, egotistical, American, lazy, dumb – he is devastatingly good looking. And there's no way of getting around that charm and charisma that beckons across a room whether you're interested or not. I don't think he's a good man, I suppose that's what worries me. Gets my protective elder-sister streak going. But hell, who's perfect around here, I wouldn't say I was necessarily qualified for God's right-hand girl either.' Taking up an American wild west twang she added, 'Besides, a girl's got to live and we do it the best way we can, ain't that right sister?' She finished a last gulp of her wine, emptying the glass with a flourish; leaving only an unhappy smile.

'Of course we do,' Honor said, and patted her hand to comfort Catherine. 'Talking of which, I haven't told you, have I?'

'What?'

'Jeremy called.'

'Not Jeremy, scoundrel Jeremy?'

'Yup, that very same one. Father of my child, disaster of my life.'

'Well what did he have to say?' Catherine leant forward, connected again, fully engrossed with the long-running saga that had dominated so much of the girls' conversations concerning Honor, with Honor, for the first few years of Jack's life. 'That Bastard Jeremy' as he was so fondly known. Honor's prince who had gallantly offered her a semen-stained insole to infect her Cinderella feet and then galloped off into the sunset with some blonde, bosomy *Carry On* nurse. That Bastard Jeremy.

'He rang to apologise. Believe it? Said he wanted to make it up to me and Jack!'

'My God, what's happened to him? Did he get re-born, re-birthed or re-married? What did you say?'

'You mean apart from the stunned silence. I kind of ummed and ahhed a bit and then agreed to have dinner with him on Sunday. I don't know what's happened to him, I'm sure I'll find out and be able to tell all by Monday morning. I thought I'd ask Gem to baby-sit, if she promises not to glare too much at him. What do you reckon?'

'You're not inviting him to your flat are you? I'm not sure you could guarantee that any of us wouldn't embark on some gentle grievous bodily harm towards The Bastard. You know how a lioness reacts towards anyone that harms her cubs . . . a mild shredding through the blender perhaps?'

'Okay, I get the picture, you're not keen.'

'We might, however, be placated by a large lump of alimony regularly deposited at your feet, it's the least he could do for Jack. Wasn't he a trust-fund baby as well?'

'I don't know, takes one to know one, Catherine. Look I'm not supposing or hoping for anything until I've spoken to him. Right now, I'm just intrigued. So much time has passed that I suppose the venom has all been spent. Look, I'd be grateful if you could keep the claws away from him until it's really necessary to get at his wallet. I wonder if he ever did tell his parents about Jack, or his drug habits?'

'You mean you think they didn't know? Why didn't you tell them? They do have a right to know.'

'Quite frankly, I didn't feel his family had any right to anything. I only ever met them once. The mother was quite nice, warm but everything-in-its-place type. Very Italian aristocratic beauty. The father was a typical English public schoolboy, totally fucked up and anally-retentive. You know the type, boardroom portrait of himself over the family dining table.'

'Oh you mean just like his son, or my husband and my father. Why do we do it to ourselves, marry the same men we were brought up with and loathed?'

'I blame it on J. M. Barrie, if he hadn't written *Peter Pan* we wouldn't all still be trying to get to Never Never Land to escape our parents with some untreatable boy.'

'Who on the stage is usually played by a girl. By that theory it's amazing we're not all gay.'

'I don't know. I know nothing, except how to cook a soufflé that nobody in my house wants to eat.'

'You're cooking them in the wrong house Honor, that's the trouble. Come and cook them here, they'll be appreciated.'

'Okay, what do you want me to cook for your dinner tonight, madam?' said Honor, genuinely offering.

'I'm going out tonight to a thing at the Serpentine but it would be brilliant if you could cook something for David and the kids. Of course you and Jack can stay for dinner, as long as you're not too choosy about your dining companions.'

'Never let it be said, Catherine, that you have a problem with receiving.'

'Sorry, did I misread your offer Honor?'

'No of course not, I'm only joking. Spinach, anchovy and stilton soufflé? I'm very happy to make them but I think I'm going to get Jack home early, so that I can get a tub of Ben & Jerry's Rain Forest Crunch, a hot bath, pyjamas and the Saturday night movie. Serious sugar withdrawals.'

'Thanks Honor, you're a brick. I can't blame you turning down the chance of a *Bouquet of Barbed Wire* scenario, if I don't want to stay for dinner I don't see why you should. Stick to plain cheese, they wouldn't appreciate any delicacies.'

'Honestly, it's nothing to do with your family, you know I'd love to run off with your husband, adopt your children, live in your house, in fact swap lives. It's just you don't have the real in-house necessities.'

'I can't placate you with Vienetto? I admit it, I married a man who can't tell the difference between Walls and Häagen-Dazs and reared two children to the same standard. I think his taste buds were sanded down at birth, or maybe it's years of my . . .'

'Tender loving care?'

'I was going to say cooking, but maybe TLC's more accurate.'

'Was it really love at first sight with you and David?' Honor was only half-joking, drawing Catherine back round to the subject that she wanted to discuss. Like a stung teenager, her mind kept returning to the bite, the image of Harry's mocking smile, eyes bright and . . . in the end, sex. And once she started thinking about sex, in this vulnerable state, even Jeremy would've done.

'More a case of "Strangers in the Night", drunkenly fumbling through each other's underwear and flesh. In the morning we looked at each other and decided, it wasn't such a ghastly mistake after all. Like winning the fruit machine without pulling the handle, surprising but not entirely unwelcome.'

'But do you think that it's such a rare thing that you have to leap at it each time it happens, or that it's such a common occurrence that if you just manage to keep your eyes open, it appears?'

'I think it happens when you're ready but not waiting and the unexpected takes you in another direction, that's what I've read.'

'Somebody at work said it's a sign you've known that person in another life.'

'Or you just want to know him in this one, with his clothes off.'

'Catherine! Married women are so coarse, I don't know if I could ever be one.'

'You don't have to lose a sense of desire when you get married, there's always the option of keeping it. What you really want to talk about is Mr Lift, isn't it? You can't fool me, Miss Hon, Missh on, Mission Possible.'

Honor blushed from her knees to her hairline.

'Give it a go Honor, you deserve something good.' Catherine squeezed Honor's shoulder and laughing, they hugged. 'Be brave and go for what you want. People who stand and queue waiting to be chosen just get left behind. I've seen it a million times, outside nightclubs in New York.'

'Thanks Catherine. The problem with being on your own is you never get real hugs apart from small people's ones.'

'You mean man-sized, timber-style hugs.' Catherine attempted a deep Scottish accent that made Honor laugh.

'I suppose a hug's not enough to keep an affair going.'

'Nope, nor a marriage.' Catherine didn't like to mention that she couldn't remember when she and David had last hugged.

'What was that you were giving your fulsome advice about, darling?' David walked in through from the hall, feigning preoccupation whilst reading his post. He'd been listening at the door, fascinated yet pained. It was like pulling at a scab listening to Catherine talk about their marriage, wondering if there was any hope of it healing the river of septic puss flowing beneath the fragile surface.

'Life, that kind of thing. You are staying in tonight, aren't you?' added Catherine, glazing over into a different person. She had an ability to move from soft intimacy to a formica-edged surface in moments. It was her knack for switching in the opposite direction that made her so good at dealing and selling, good at her job.

'I don't expect you are?' David raised his eyebrow to her, quizzically, Simon Templar style.

'You know I'm going to this very important Serpentine thing, I told you ages ago. Anyway Honor has kindly agreed to do surgery on our fridge and whip you and the children up a soufflé.'

'Oh, hello Honor.' He hadn't found the energy to acknowledge her before. 'That really is very kind of you. We've learnt to live with a bad mother and a worse cook, haven't we darling?'

'You may have, but I haven't. What I always say about parenting, better bad and there, than good and absent.' Catherine finished with a flourish of a smile that bore more resemblance to a winner's grimace at the end of a tough first set.

'I'm sure, Catherine, that Honor hasn't come to watch the petty banter we fill our lives with, dear.' And he went to stand behind her, handcuffing her slim wrist and squeezing it rather too tightly for affection, so that her bones crushed against each other.

'Oh don't worry about me. I'm hardly here anyway, most of me's still in hangover land. If you want me to make you something I'm on automatic pilot, but don't expect conversation.'

'David wouldn't, he likes to do all the talking around here, isn't that right darling?' She smiled up at her husband and watched his jaw twitch. 'You'd just be required to listen.'

'I don't require anything, thank you Catherine. The children and I will get something from Pizza Express along with some exciting war videos,' David returned. He was unwilling to be portrayed as a baddie, even in Honor's eyes, so he added, 'That way it'll feel like a night in with Catherine. Honor you're welcome to join us. I'd even let you choose one of the videos, how about it?' he asked, gracing her with his slit-eyed, thin-lipped smile.

'Another time, thanks. I think I'm safer nursing my head and early to bed.'

'Hair of the dog, medicinal reasons, can I tempt either of you? I see you've already got to the bottle Catherine.'

'Thanks for asking David. Good day?'

'Tiring, I was working, but I achieved a few things.' A wash of satisfaction wiped his face. 'I suppose you've been doing nothing?'

'We've been hard at pissing about. It's not an easy life for us girls surviving that kind of hen night.'

'I dare say. I expect Josh's to hold some untold excitements too. And now if you'll excuse me, I'm disappearing upstairs, to study the papers. *Bon nuit mon ami.*' He left with his clinking glass of iced Scotch, feeling like he'd held his own in an uncomfortable rally.

Catherine shrugged and raised an eyebrow at her friend behind David's disappearing back, when really she felt like jumping up and sticking her tongue out to his pathetic face. *Mon ami* indeed!

CHAPTER SIX

Sod it! Gem thought. They can have it like this. They don't know what they want anyway and they'd probably cock up printing the colour properly, or crop it short. This can do them!

That was the way Gem was feeling these days, resentful. It was Saturday afternoon, a working day like any other usually to Gem, except for the tail-end of a hangover she was carrying. She left her picture for the magazine not totally unfinished but ragged around the edges, something she wouldn't have dreamt of doing at one stage. She would have thought it unprofessional to send a piece of work off like this but she was tired of it, illustrating pointless articles about things she wasn't interested in. She had until Monday morning, maybe she'd feel differently then.

Once again she'd been seduced by the easy seeming money of it, but it never was so easy drawing things you had no desire to.

Gem didn't know what she wanted any more, she was as successful as she could be as an illustrator but she knew it wasn't really her, pandering to the Sunday magazine market. She wasn't ready to face up to the question of what she should be spending her life doing, apart from making money. Doing jobs.

Gem recognised she was becoming slapdash and didn't care, she'd go down to Solde Rosso, the new club in Soho, and meet Janine, or not. No, she'd go on her own and see what she could find. After the last two nights of anonymous sex, she was on a roll.

She dressed in a very skimpy tight all-in-one with no bra, that shadowed her breasts and accentuated her nipples in lemon silk-stretch jersey. Over it she wore a flowing floral-chiffon micro mini-skirt, that pretended to cover her bum. At least her suede-stacked boots covered her calves. It was a fuck-me outfit, no pretence. She belted on a leather jacket that was longer than the skirt and walked out daringly to catch the tube.

Gem fixed her eyes on some unattainable middle distance ahead, hard and strong. She wrapped herself in with protective zeal, like a fence of electric cling-film about her. Only the stupid would dare crash through, the drunk and the drugged lying heaped around the tube entrance saw it clearly. That was the problem with living in Camden. 'Look at my legs, admire my outrageous sex-on-display, look but don't touch and if you dare to comment, I am unapproachable because it's only fashion.'

There was always somebody who couldn't read.

'What you need is a good fuck, darling.' An aggressive pin-stripe drunk whispered threateningly in her ear on the stairway down. She trotted guiltily away and read the tube map on the platform.

The paranoia disappeared once she walked through the heavy swingdoors of the club. The darkness lent itself to anonymity, eye contact was the thing here. Checking in her jacket, she made her way straight to the bar, skirt flouncing with her hip swing, to order a double vodka on the rocks. Only once it was in her hand could she lean her slim, muscled body against the bar and relax. Time to take in the scene, slip into the beat, survey the other bodies that jostled for attention.

She saw immediately the one she wanted. He looked familiar, Gem couldn't quite place him but maybe it was his Alain Delon look that she recognised – deliciously dark.

He looked good enough to eat and that was all Gem could focus on. She ordered another vodka to fill her glass and give her the necessary courage to get up on the dance floor alone to the 'Harlem Shuffle'. Soon she had 'hitch hiked baby across the floor' in front of him. Of course she started to bump into people she knew, and she danced, now unselfconscious, with this transient group of friends that only occupied the dark hours. She wasn't sure she'd even recognise them in the broad light of day and she knew she didn't want them in her other life.

By the time James Brown was gettin' on up with 'Sex Machine', she'd almost forgotten the lone, moody smoulder that had been her target on arrival. She was enjoying herself, having a laugh and a dance, shaking her bottom, twisting her top, kicking her legs in the air and proving to anyone who cared to look that she had shaved her armpits this afternoon; a nick stung uncomfortably as proof, dancing-sweat and deodorant dribbling into it, burning it pink.

He was looking at her now, his turn to read her dress and

signals and he thought, why not. She was slim and pretty and had this contagious laugh that rang across the floor and she danced with humour, he liked that. He'd have that tonight, why not? He'd only just flown in, nobody knew he was in town, besides it might help his jet lag. He'd ask her for a drink when she came off the floor; he was stationed in front of the johns, she had to go sometime. That was his well-worn nightclub policy, they all had to come past you at some point. Until she did, he'd look, stare, be seduced by her movements. She looked like she'd work hard in bed, that had its plus points when you were tired.

It worked. Gem felt the heat of his stare drill through her back to her gut like a sardine on a barbecue. She turned and he smiled. Connection. But she didn't stop dancing, she kept on in a bid for chase. Sensual flirtation. You couldn't be too certain of success until they were lying underneath you. A smile could mean anything. After the next dance, she thought, she'd get her drink as an excuse to pass him. He didn't look the dancing type. She might be wrong, she'd try to beckon him on if the next song was any good.

The next song was hers, 'Voulez-vous Coucher Avec Moi, Ce Soir', Patti LaBelle. Good. Gem beckoned. He shook his head, no, but smiled and narrowed his eyes to a look and jerked his head to signal her over. But not that easy, she thought and shook her head 'no' back, but danced towards him slowly, dancing away again as he leaned forward. Cat and mouse slamming up bright little sparks that if kindled would've turned into a forest fire. They both knew this game, old hands at it, neither was toting for virgins.

The song ended and Gem picked up her purse and walked towards him, and then passed to the loo. He'd wait, she knew. He did.

'So you want a drink first?' he asked in his drawling Texan accent, surprising Gem. The comment didn't, they knew what they were talking about, why muck about?

'But you're American? I thought you were French.'

'Gee I'm sorry, would you like a refund?'

'No I'm sorry, it's just you look French. I didn't expect you to be American.'

'But I am allowed to be.'

'Of course.'

'And am I allowed to buy you a drink even though I'm not French?'

'Of course, a vodka on the rocks, please.'

He led her to the bar through the crush of people, holding her arm. She liked that. And once he'd got their drinks he led her to a table at the back of the room where it was quieter and darker.

'So what makes me look like a frog? I ain't wearing a goddamn beret!' he demanded, when they sat down.

She feigned coy embarrassment, excited by the encounter. There was something so familiar about this boy/man, cute, but different from the others, something she wouldn't mind having around for longer than a night. She knew that instinctively and it wasn't a common feeling.

Her alarm bells were ringing.

'Well you look like a young Alain Delon for starters and these days Parisian boys all go around wearing cowboy boots and trying to look like Texans.'

'So you're saying because I look American I must be French?'

Gem nodded.

'So they finally caught on to the finest kind of boot made. Who's this Alain Delon, sounds like a queer's name?'

'No of course not!' Gem laughed in response. 'He was one of France's great lovers, the biggest sex symbol film star of the sixties.'

'Well I was only born in the sixties, but I don't mind the comparisons as long as he was a sex symbol.'

'He was definitely that.'

There was an awkward silence as they smirked at each other over their drinks. She let his jean knee rub at her leg. Why not. She liked the feeling of the rough denim against her bare skin. The smirks disappeared, but sex hung as heavy as the damp cigarette smoke. He pulled his chair in to the table and his leg pushed her knees apart.

He was glad now he'd hired the convertible Mercedes at the airport, she'd like that, he thought. 'She'd go for that.'

The hotel Gem ended up in that night was a brown and bronze concept of swish. She awoke in the morning covered by grey and beige silk sheets, her head lay upon embroidered pillows and Billy was naked by her side softly snoring.

God, he was good.

Gem felt her heart slip, she thought she was in love. I must be in love, she thought. Didn't I give him a blow job? I never do that, I hate doing that, but I enjoyed it last night, and she giggled to herself remembering her orgasm that the rest of the hotel, the world, must have been woken by last night. Billy had reached up into parts of her that had been unexplored territory. Not once, but again and again, and then once more when she'd been drifting off to sleep, slowly and tenderly, as though they were one.

Her bladder bulged and insisted she get out of the delicious warmth and the smell of perfumed five-star sex, to the bathroom.

The marble floor was cold on her feet, so she rested them on the side of the bidet as she sat on the loo, ecstatically dizzy. Her jaw held a dull ache from the wide smile she'd woken up with, perhaps along with too much drink and too little sleep, plus the other activity and the snort of coke. Now she was comfy on the loo she didn't want to get off. She hugged her knees to her in an uneasy balance, congratulated herself on last night's findings.

'Clever girl, Gem.' She whispered out loud. Partially because she wanted to mark the occasion and half because she wanted to stop and tell the first tadpole thought of disturbance to bugger off. Dark thoughts were even now pushing forward, all the things that were wrong, that could go wrong. She would have to run back to the bed sharpish if the floodgates weren't to sweep open. Jump into bed and begin again. A nice way to take your mind off nasty thoughts. Nasty horrid thoughts trying to spoil all her fun.

'Hi gorgeous,' he said sleepily, not remembering her name. 'How are you doing?'

'Floating through bliss. I don't think I'll ever walk again,' Gem said climbing in beside him, slipping her body down to spoon his. He kissed her neck and wrapped her over with his muscled brown limbs. His fingers moved to a nipple, teasing it with a smudge of pressure, his tongue ran the length of her back and settled tickling, delving and blowing into her ear. His other hand slowly stroked down Gem's flat worked tummy muscles, playing pleasure upon her nerve endings. Gem felt herself being dragged back into another world where brain didn't work, intellect was worthless – tactile-land. She let go of any hold as she felt him hardening and insistent behind her. A gush of expectation poured through her brain of him filling her again; her innards were pulsating putty.

It was gone eleven by the time they ordered food from the incomprehensibly posh-voiced waiter on room service. Gem still didn't know who Billy was, except rich. She'd got that message well enough, and as she lay amongst the bubbles floating in the tub she tried to decide where it all came from. Private income, poor boy made rich from hard labour, lucky entrepreneur, heir to an oil well? He couldn't be older than thirty-two say. A badly preserved thirty or a well preserved thirty-five. She felt she knew every part of his body but nothing about his person – Billy what? This was the first time she had wanted to know. She heard the sharp knock of breakfast arriving, but for once she wasn't in a rush to get out. She wasn't being her normal Gem at all. She'd be happy to spend the day there sucking his toes, massaging his body in oil, chewing Ben & Jerry's Chunky Monkey from his belly button. She'd suggest it to him.

Gem wrapped her hair in a towel and put on one of those extra-thick robes you only find in posh hotels, not permitted to mere mortals. She opened the bathroom door and saw Billy, phone in hand, gesticulating to the waiter, pointing to a table to place it on that wasn't strewn with last night's debris. The scene looked like one of those awful English stage farces, all covered in bras and panties for when the husband walks in. Gem was struck by a rush of fear that maybe Billy was married, that somewhere he had a wife and children he was being unfaithful to, and she cared, unbeliev-ably she really cared as his lopsided smile showed his perfect teeth.

His smile shook that picture from her mind like an etch-a-sketch being wiped.

Poor bugger on the phone, only listening while I get to watch the real treat, she thought. There was only one way to stop these horrible thoughts, she'd have to be a big grown-up girl and ask. Face her fears. She could tell he was cutting short the caller and he finished it with, 'I'll see you tonight sweetheart.'

Obviously a sister, Americans use 'sweetheart' for everyone, don't they? Gem hoped, pouring out some coffee for herself and this stranger, Billy, who sat opposite, a towel around his waist.

'Black or white?' she asked.

'White and three sugars. I like things sweet,' he smiled.

She smiled back but it wasn't the same as before, suddenly

there was this gulf as though something had been unplugged, now their skin was no longer touching.

'Look, er, it was great last night wasn't it?'

'Yes, brilliant, but don't tell me . . . You're married and you'd like me to leave the hotel via the wardrobe very quickly.'

'It's not quite that bad, it's just I'm kinda busy at the moment. I've got a lunch thing and some work stuff to catch up on, but relax and have breakfast.'

'Sure, I understand.' She had to, she'd said those lines and harsher, many times to others. Excuses and delays, sometimes real reasons, but she'd never said it to fucks that good.

Gem had a horrid suspicion that some of the disappointment she'd doled out in the past was boomeranging its way back. 'It's a pity, I thought there was something there,' she said with a sad smile back to him, but his eyes remained blank.

'There was sweetheart, really there was. Look can I call you, maybe we can do this again sometime?' he said so unconvincingly that she had to look away, she hated to see the spell evaporate.

'Well if you're not too busy and I'm not too busy, maybe we can,' she replied as though making a doctor's appointment.

She wrote her number on the pad by the phone and was tempted to sign it Mickey Mouse to match the charade.

Gem went to dress. Breakfast didn't seem too appetising now, she wanted to get out. She walked about the room gathering her clothes, trying to avoid stepping on the used condoms that scattered the thick-pile carpet. She pulled on her clothes, conscious of his gaze on her body, zipped up her boots and pinned back her mess of straggled hair. She wanted out fast, she wasn't going to spend hours making up to look half-decent for the final 'goodbye, nice fucking you' ceremony. At the bathroom mirror she conceded by sealing up her mouth with some 'sticky plum' lipstick.

Gem took a last look around the room that she had come to love, for all its hideous beigeness and air of synthetic luxury, and saw it for what it was. Then her eyes settled on Billy. He was even standing by the door, though he hadn't opened it yet, holding her jacket for her, she half felt she knew him, he looked so familiar. Ah well, appearances can be deceptive. She crossed to him to put on her jacket but his hands didn't stop and she felt the familiar signal rubbing at her skirt, unsheathing itself from his towel.

'I've got one last condom left, would you like to share it?'

'You'll have to call me a cab to get me home afterwards.'

As though that was some kind of hard-struck bargain. A cab ride in exchange for her body. The animal in Gem enthralled to her flesh, was unkind to her heart; once again she accepted sex as a substitute for love.

CHAPTER SEVEN

The dull pace of Honor's life had finally been disrupted. She didn't know what she had done to light the volcano. Her simple existence consisted of Jack, her job, a few friends, family at Christmas and Easter, a bookshelf stuffed with well-read novels, a worn library card and the TV most nights. The phone was stubbornly silent as far as men were concerned, and there seemed little point in ever leaving the answerphone on. Dissatisfaction didn't nibble irritatingly in her corners, it just gathered dust.

Honor accepted her situation for what it was as she listened to her self-help tapes with forced enthusiasm each night, hoping for a different kind of life, the life she thought her friends lived. Sarah Jane's dangerously exciting party-girl exploits, Catherine's sophisticated existence of shopping and restaurant, Gem's money, career and freedom.

Honor wasn't jealous; she loved her friends and wished them the best of everything, but she couldn't see beyond the faces they presented to her. She lived vicariously through their tales with a naive optimism. At night, after she put Jack to bed, she would talk to the mirror on her sitting-room wall and say, 'Honor, you might be a mother and a cook today, and tomorrow still be a sexless wage earner but one day you will metamorphose into an elegant beauty, thrumming with passion that men will desire and yearn for, "Honor I love you, won't you marry me".' And she would pout her lips as if to kiss her own image and either burst into laughter or take it to bed to tie to an erotic dream.

Now she was having notes pushed under her door and messages left on her answerphone by men, not boys. Boys like the kitchen staff or waiters she worked with, other chefs that she'd have flings with that began at a leaving or birthday party, fuelled by the alcohol. They would lapse into embarrassed laziness, friendships that had been confused in a hazy excitement with something more.

Adrian had been one of those. Honor couldn't refer to him as her last boyfriend – there had been no love involved – but they were fond of each other and had had a kind of sex life. Meaning he arrived at her flat after work in time to be served dinner on his nights off. They would eat and watch telly or a video, and if he wasn't too exhausted he would roll on top of her in a poor imitation of arousal, tired and friendly lovemaking that by the end was totally un-climactic for either of them. More of a sleep inducing muscle relaxant; a cup of camomile tea would have done the same. Afterwards Honor would feel more lonely and frustrated than if she had been in bed alone. She wondered if this was what marriages felt like ten years on with the silent shadow of a mistress. What she really wanted to know was, why were men always so tired, when all they had to do was look after themselves?

When she could no longer stand the waste of these shuttered relationships, she would make her exit, jumping ship to be left alone again with Jack. Better her love and energy go to him, she thought.

On meeting his mum's so called 'friends', Jack was usually as uninterested in them as they were in him. There was little pretence in the situation, he could scent them at the door and only ever growled a 'hello' as a territorial defence in protection of his hearth. Any amateur anthropologist could have pointed out the ancient rituals between competing males, of whatever age. Jack knew straight away from the tone of his mum's voice that there was something more complex than simple friendship going on. He wasn't some dumb kid that got fooled with a packet of crisps and a bar of chocolate as an easy bribe on a long-term agreement. What kid ever was?

Jack liked it best when it was just him and Mum, when Honor wasn't distracted by somebody else to cook dinner for, pay attention to. Saturday night bliss was being cosied-up on the yellow rug-covered sofa, sharing take-away pizza from the box, staying up late watching a movie and digging into a carton of ice-cream with two spoons clinking in competition.

Jack was noticing his mum's new excitement, she laughed out loud, talked too fast, too much, and all the fuss about a note – anybody would think the Spice Girls had asked her to join them! He wasn't going to ask which slimy snogger it was from. That's what grown-ups did together, Gussy had told him so.

'Snoggin' is when they put their tongues in each other's mouths, that's also a French kiss,' she told him with an expert's casualness. 'Then they shag. Do you know what shaggin' is?'

Jack shook his head, bug-eyed, fascinated by these adult secrets that Gus was letting him into.

'Duh Dumbo! Don't you know nothing?' Augusta shook her head at Jack's six-year-old ignorance and realised she had to divest him of it. 'Shaggin' is when a boy does it to a girl not to have a baby, only sometimes they forget to use a condom and then the sperm swim out of the willy and up into the eggs and then they get pregnant. See?'

Jack didn't see, he'd always thought it was the woman who got pregnant, but he didn't dare ask her anything else. 'Uh, oh,' he replied.

The note was under Honor's door when she and Jack had returned from Catherine and David's disagreeable meowing. She was just thinking how pleased she was to get away to a cosy Saturday night special, with no soufflé to cook for the miserable condescending git her friend had married. A soufflé probably wouldn't have risen for him anyway. She and Jack had stopped by the store on the way home from the bus stop, buying two Italian-style pizzas to quell Honor's hangover hunger and a Coke to quell Jack's impatience at having to wait for the cooking time and a tub of chocolate fudge ice-cream. Then they'd popped into the video store and after much debate between Schwarzenegger and Renoir chose a movie called *Groundhog Day*, Honor and the video boy convincing Jack that it was the same guy in it who'd been in *Ghostbusters* (an endlessly repeated favourite). Honor slyly thanked the video boy for his assistance, until reading the plot line in the lift, which said it was a comedy about a man stuck in the same day for the rest of his life. A bit too close to her own life for comfort: some weeks only a crisis at work marked the difference between one day and the next. Resigned to their choice and Jack's excitement, she crossed mental fingers, as she jangled the keys in the lock, that it would be dull enough to send Jack quickly off to sleep and she would be able to watch *The Lady Vanishes* on the telly and imagine herself lost on a train adventure with Robert Donat.

The note crunched as the door opened. Honor picked it up and said – "Oh look Jack we've got a note, I wonder who that's from?" Jack's obvious uninterest left the note on the side un-read until she'd put the pizzas in the oven, the ice-cream in the freezer and the kettle on for tea. Jackets were flung over a chair, shoes flipped off by the door, curtains drawn (for real cinematic effect), tape in the video and the table covered with cutlery and a roll of paper towel. The kettle clicked off to the boil as Honor pulled on her favourite ugly grey cardigan and poured the water into a peppermint tea. She read the note –

> To Honor Summers,
>   I called by to borrow some sugar as an excuse to talk to you, but you are not in so I don't need an excuse, do I? I have to work tonight but tomorrow (Sunday) I'm free for coffee, porridge or brunch like an American, are you? I hope your leg is better – I will bring my healing powers. Your new neighbour at number eleven above you – the lift, remember?
>   Harry

A date with porridge! Honor was ecstatic and her first thought was how she could get rid of Jack for the day; after all, you could never tell where porridge might lead. Then she remembered she had promised to spend the day with Jack in Holland Park – lunch and the adventure playground. She was stuck so firmly in her own guilt that she couldn't welch on any deal with Jack, imagining him to be as bad at dealing with disappointment as she was.

If this man Harry wants to see me, she thought, he must jolly well fit around me and my son. That's how it must be! Just because he sent my hormone level rocketing through the top of the lift, there is no reason to be unusually compromised, her brain said.

Later, as the film rolled on and the pizza got eaten and Jack had picked all the peppers off his and left them on the side, she thought again, Am I trying to sabotage this chance of romance? Making conditions for a man I don't even know, who only wants to have coffee with me for goodness' sake! Does it make me feel better to have him sign the Happy Family agreement pact? Where the hell have I put my identity, I'm sure I saw it lying on the sofa yesterday maybe it's fallen down the back, or I've left it sewn into my apron at work or attached like a nametag to a piece of my child? Where's Honor gone? Is this any time to have an identity crisis – the one time a man asks me out? For God's sake woman pull yourself together!

As the video went round, the reel of her brain projected its own movie, personal in-house entertainment with all the excitement, tragedy and tension she could stand. It might as well have been *Terminator 2* or *Bambi*.

The credits came up and the ice-cream happily melted around Jack's solitary spoon, the pizza lay a soggy reject – a couple of slices attacked, the crusts abandoned. Jack slept soundly with his head upon her lap, curling up in his pyjamas beneath a patchwork cover that Honor had made for him when he was a baby. She looked down at him, stroking his silk-black hair away from his heavy-lashed eyes. The bump of his freckled nose and the tilt of his lips parted by breath made her heart bulge within the walls of her chest, the physical expanse of her love. If only all love could be as simple and pure as this, she sighed to herself. My son, my Jack. 'Oh how I love you Jack,' she spoke softly and had to bite hard on her lip to stop the tears constricting her throat, for everything she wanted for Jack.

How could she ever feel this for a man? To love enough to be unconditional, as she did with Jack. Delicately scooping her hands beneath his heavy sleepy head, she moved her lap from under him so that she might slide both her hands beneath his body. Cradling him up, his head flopped into her breast, she carried him to his room and jumbled the mess of his limbs into the snug of his bed.

Returning to the living room she noticed the light of the answerphone flashing silent messages. It's probably just Mum, she thought and distractedly played it back whilst putting the kettle on for some camomile tea before bed.

'Look Jeremy here, are you ever at home Honor? I'm just ringing to make sure you're still on for tomorrow evening. I thought it might be easier to meet at the restaurant, Dominic's, along the Embankment opposite the Foster building, you can't miss it. I'm booking for eight thirty, okay? Great, good, see you there then, no? I mean, yes. Yes?'

Honor laughed at his confusion.

'Your old mum here. Just ringing to see that you and Jack are all right. Give us a ring sometime, lots of hugs and kisses from your dad and me.'

She smiled inside and out, flooded with all the love pouring towards her and jumped to click her heels, bugger the camomile. But maybe she needed some calm, to slow up the hormones tingling through her bloodstream. Hell! She'd been calm all her life, now where was a pen and paper to reply to Harry?

Honor decided to say 'yes' to brunch, they could meet in the park once she'd signed Jack into the playground and she'd take Roger along too, Jack's older friend from across the street, that way he'd be happy and occupied. She'd fit everything in, that's what she'd do. See Harry during the day, it was only a cup of coffee and a bite to eat, she tried to play it down but her guts were whoopying biological somersaults and she could feel a gleam of mischief dart across her eyes. In the evening dinner with Jeremy, father of her child, love of her life. Gem was baby-sitting. Everything was possible. And if she managed it all tomorrow, she'd apply for a diplomacy job with the United Nations next week.

Honor rang Paolo, Roger's mum, and agreed to pick him up around eleven thirty and deliver him back at four. Paolo was delighted and agreed to do the same next weekend for Honor, she said she was going to spend the whole day in bed with her new young lover, Bob. Honor laughed at the extravagance of the notion, before thinking that maybe she too would do that again, one day. Not with Bob perhaps, but maybe with somebody else.

Clearing a space amongst the milk and juice cartons, Honor placed a clean piece of paper on the kitchen table and sat down to write.

Dear Harry,
Sorry you're out of sugar, I'd love to give you some . . .

No that's awful, I can't put that, he'll think I'm a sex-obsessed harlot, or an ex-script writer for *Carry On* films, she thought, before scrunching up the paper and throwing it towards the blue bin where it bounced neatly off the swing lid and fell predictably to the floor. New piece of paper. Start again.

Dear Harry,
  I'd love to have porridge, brunch and coffee with you tomorrow.
This is my number, 342-0523, call me in the morning before eleven
or I'll see you in the Holland Park Café at midday.
  Flat 9, Honor Summers

She couldn't decide whether it was too forward, over-enthusiastic, but what the hell, she couldn't find another piece of unscribbled-upon paper so that would have to do. She crept out her door, note in hand, no shoes, and up the stairs – a fugitive. Then she started to worry. She was giving her phone number to someone she'd only met once, she knew nothing about him, not even what he did: he could be a mass murderer for all she knew, hiding his victims' bodies in the lift shaft! She'd left the light off and was beginning to regret it. Had she written herself a suicide note? Maybe he was recruiting for a demonic religious cult . . . On the other hand – how did he know she wasn't a mass murderer, a castrator of men with a kitchen full of sex slaves tied to the chopping board? Honor sniggered at her own silliness and quick-ened her pace to his door.

Number eleven faced her with an unexpected bright slice of light gleaming beneath the door. She hadn't imagined for a minute that he'd be in, after all he'd written that he was working. She wanted to be anonymous, to appear tomorrow as a fresh new radiant sexy sunbeam, not be caught in her old cardi and ripped jeans pushing notes of filthy invitation through strangers' doors. She held her breath, bit her lip, crouched down and slid the note quietly under. A minute rasp on the carpet made the muscles in her neck stand out tight from her jaw and sent her muttering inside her head, 'dearlorddearlorddearlord', eyes screwed tight with wishing. She slowly stood back up, oh so slowly, in case the man behind the door might hear her jeans rumpling back into place, her hair brushing her shoulders, her breath exhaling or the tom-tom beat of her exploding heart.

Luckily she'd studied creeping for childhood fridge raids and midnight feasts, and in moments she was back downstairs to the safety of her room. Honor closed the door behind her, let out a screech of naughty relief, childish hysteria, giggling without her hand clamped firmly across her mouth, enjoying her deranged hyena behaviour, when the knock came. She realised it was real as it came again. Honor stopped; caught in the mirror, a frightened rabbit stared back.

'Hello, Honor?'

His voice. She pulled her cardigan off and used her fingers like a giant comb through her hair.

'Hello, who is it?' she asked to give herself more time, straighten her eyebrows and tuck in her T-shirt. Oh Christ, I look crap!

'It's me, Harry,' he replied from the other side of the door whilst she sped about the room picking up the rubbish, drying clothes and scattered shoes, throwing them into the bin of her bedroom.

'Oh. Okay just a minute,' she said closing the bedroom and bathroom doors. Finally she opened her front door.

'Hi,' she said coolly, as though he was always calling at her door.

'Hi, it's me, Harry.'

'Yes,' she said, not moving. Her body leaned against the door blocking the way in, she was caught again by his eyes.

'I just got your note under my door,' Harry said.

'Yes? Good. I mean I thought you might. I put it there.'

'I just found it. I hope I'm not disturbing you too late?'

'No, no that's fine,' but Honor still couldn't move, she just stood there soppily smiling back at him.

'Are you sure you wouldn't like me to ring you tomorrow morning instead? I mean if you have company. I heard you laughing . . .'

'No it's fine honestly. I'm sorry, I mean come in. It must have been the TV.' The words had finally formed themselves in her mouth and tripped out like something foreign. This strange tongue might not have seemed like hers, but then standing in front of her was the man that she'd been in the lift with this morning, and now he was inside her flat! Suddenly the mess didn't matter.

He smiled back at her and said, 'Was the pizza good?'

'Oh yes thanks, Somerfields' best! Sorry about the mess, Jack and I were slobbing out, he's in bed now.' She smiled back. 'I was just about to clear up.' You lying cow, she thought to herself.

'Oh, so that's who you were laughing with?'

'No, God no. Absolutely not! No . . .' Honor couldn't stop herself laughing thinking that he thought she was obviously howling away with some man. 'No Jack's been asleep for about an hour, he's my son, he's six. I was laughing to myself,' she coyly admitted.

'Ahha! I was trying to work out the obsession with loud early morning cartoons and the football I could hear up through my floorboards. You see you have me here under false pretences, I was thinking you were a single woman after my own heart,' he said in a way that felt like open heart surgery, to Honor.

There was one of those pauses, the embarrassing ones that need cement-filling, but poor Honor's mouth suddenly seemed to be full of polyfiller. Harry had no option but to continue. 'So you're telling me the young man I've seen you with is not your husband and I suppose you expect me to believe this toy is not yours?' Harry picked up a gratuitously ugly sick-green monster with red protruding eyes, tongues and detachable intestines.

The hideous tension was broken. Honor could speak. 'No, but he lets me play with them if I'm good.'

'And are you?' Harry dared, crossing a line again, his eyes mischievously twinkling back at her, but she surprised herself by not simpering and playing the pawn. She turned from where they'd both been standing in the middle of the only bit of space in the room.

'Of course I'm good, when I'm not I'm . . . horrid. Would you like some tea?'

'I don't know if I dare. I'm terrified that if I'm on the wrong side of you I'll be poisoned with a single gulp. Perhaps it would be safer if I got a bottle of wine from upstairs. Would you like some wine?'

'Any other night I would say yes, but I'm afraid I went out last night to a hen party, so I feel safer on the tea, clean out the system from the overload.'

'I understand, feeling tender huh?' And the way he said it with his Scottish intonation upon the word 'tender' made Honor's toes curl upon the carpet. She knew because she was looking at them, wishing she had shoes on.

'*Tender is the Night*,' she said. He looked back questioningly. 'Sorry, don't worry, it's the title of an F. Scott Fitzgerald novel, *Tender is the Night*.'

'Sorry, I don't read.'

'A matter of principle?'

'Dyslexia. Letters tend to jump around the pages, so I stick to those talking books. At school they just call it being stupid.'

'I got called Silly Summers, ordinary stupid, not interesting dyslexia.'

'I'm sure that's not true. Anyway I should let you get some sleep. I'll call on you at eleven and you can tell me where you and Jack need to go.'

Honor listened to him, looking at that wide fine face, she heard her own voice whispering to her. Let him be a friend, he wants to and he is offering. You don't have to spend your whole life struggling to prove something about independence and female strength. It doesn't mean you have to sleep with him just because you accept a lift to the park, but another voice within her replied indignantly, But I want to!

'All right,' she said tentatively, 'about eleven then, and if we can pick Roger, Jack's friend, up on the way, that's great. You're right I need some sleep, I must look a wreck,' she said, self-consciously leaning against the kitchen sink full of dirty dishes, knowing he would have been fully justified in agreeing.

Instead he stepped towards her. 'Not at all. You're a good-looking woman.'

Honor was glad of the support behind her as she felt all her innards going squadgy, caving in towards her backbone as their eyes were unable to disengage, locked upon a tightrope of sexual tension. He placed his large hands upon the top of her arms and lightly squeezed them whilst bending to kiss one side of her cheek, his firm lips sinking warm on her flushed skin; it was bliss. Then he was gone, the door closed after him, and Honor wondered what had happened.

Her first thought was she must have had a seizure, cemented to the spot unable to move. A stretcher would be needed to carry her to bed, she felt like Tom's Jerry blown up with dynamite, Laurel's Hardy hit over the head, Scooby Doo or Muttley. Life appeared like a technicolour cartoon. Just because Harry was gorgeous and roused feelings in her that she hadn't felt since . . . since Jeremy.

'Oh yes, Jeremy, I'd almost forgotten about him, I guess I'll just have to ring him in the morning. This bloody weather! It doesn't rain for years but then it pours. I'd better book myself a place on the ark the way things are going,' she thought out loud, laughed, stopped and remembered. Harry can hear everything. He'll think I'm mad, he'll think I talk to myself.

CHAPTER EIGHT

'Oh hi David, it's Sarah Jane here. How are you?'

'Fine, fine. I take it you've rung to speak to your sister, she's out. I'd call back in the morning if I were you.'

'Okay cool. Where's she gone?'

'Some art dinner or something, I'm not sure.'

'How are the kids?'

'Fine. Busy looking at some video I think. Look, I'm just in the middle of something, I'll tell Catherine you rang when she gets in. See you soon.'

'Bye then,' but David had already hung up the phone in his abrupt manner.

'Oh Catherine hi! Did David tell you I'd rung?'

'Yes, when I got in last night but it was late. How was he with you?'

'I wouldn't say overly friendly but it's Not Unusual, as Tom J. would say. Why?'

'Same here. Nightmare in Elm Park Square. Don't ask me why, he stormed off in a terrific temper this morning to work. Thank God for the refuge of Monday mornings. Enough. How's everything going?'

'Oh wonderful, Josh has just arrived in town and booked into Bolton's Hotel so I'm lying here in swishland – silk sheets, dark velvets and sunken marble baths.'

'Wow!'

'Why don't you come over for lunch and we can run up some room service from the Jacuzzi? Josh won't be back until this afternoon. He's got a meeting with his agent and a producer about some new project. Besides I've got a few things about my hen night I want to discuss with you.'

'As long as there's a bribe involved in keeping stumm, I take it we're talking nudge, nudge, tinkywinky? I've been trying to call you, you're never in.'

'What do you mean Catherine? I just wanted to say thank you for such a brilliant night! It was a real laugh wasn't it? I didn't do anything did I, Catherine? No, you're pulling my leg? I did have some very strange dreams that night, but I woke up alone. I definitely woke up alone. I swear!'

'I'm sorry Sarah Jane, and I thought we'd paid for the whole night, now I'll have to ring and ask for my money back!'

'Oh stop it. Wheeling the axe over my head because you're my big sister. Come over, go on it'll be fun and you're not going to see me for another ten years.'

'Okay, okay. I should be working but fuck it. I'll finish this bit off. I'll be over in the hour.'

'Well done Honor, you remembered to put your answerphone on. I'm desperate to know what happened with you and Jeremy on Sunday night. Give us a call when you come in and by the way are you free on Friday night? I'm giving a "Meet a famous moviestar" dinner. Josh is in town so we're going to have a meal for Sarah Jane. All hen night conversations are strictly forbidden! Bring a date. Jeremy had better change his name if you bring him, we don't care if he is the father of your child! Wouldn't the neighbour be more exciting? Would be for us. I'm organising someone else to cook the dinner so you'll be able to eat it. Saturday at eight, did I say Friday I meant Saturday, Saturday at eight and if you can't find a baby-sitter you can always bung Jack upstairs with the kids. Loads of love to you and Jack, by the way it's Catherine calling if you didn't recognise the voice, Wednesday afternoon.'

'Catherine? It's Gem here, how are you?'

'I'm fine, how are you surreptitious one? How did you survive the hen night?'

'I survived it, that's all you need to know. In fact if anybody asks you what to put on my tombstone, "I will survive" will do nicely.'

'It's got that bad that your best lines are nicked off seventies disco divas?'

'Oh I don't know, the ups and downs of modern living. Single girl, big city stuff. Boring work that no amount of money is enough to compensate for. But as you can tell I'm trying to view it all positively.'

'Why don't you get back to your painting Gem? Doing all this illustrating always gets you down. I'm sure I could get you a show. Somewhere.'

'I know, I know you're right Catherine. But I put it down for a while and it just gets harder to climb back in, you forget where you were and end up pretending, doing some crappy portrait.'

'Ahh well . . .'

'You don't have to tell me it's because I'm not willing to suffer enough to be a poverty-stricken artist lying in some garret. I know that! Oh I'm sorry, Catherine, it sounds like I just rang up to moan and I didn't mean to. I actually rang up for your advice.'

'What can I tell you, apart from keep away from men in fancy-dress builders' outfits because some of *us* would like a chance.'

'Don't. I'm totally humiliated, especially now that I've met this gorgeous man. He's American and looks like Alain Delon and makes love like a god and is staying at that really swish hotel Bolton's and since we've had this night of passion he hasn't called me and I wonder whether you think I should call him. I usually never do.'

'Really?'

'Okay that's not true but most of the time I don't. I'm dying to see him again and I'm afraid if I call him he'll sense it over the phone and that'll be that.'

'I think he could probably sense it from here sweetheart, without you calling him. Get rid of the desperation, resign yourself to never seeing him again and once you're certain that it doesn't matter call him. He'll probably have already called you, of course, and by then you won't care. That, as they say, is life.'

'But he might have left the country in that time!'

'It's up to you how long the process takes. Where did you meet him? You weren't hanging around hotel lobbies again Gem!' Catherine teased, she sensed Gem needed to laugh.

'How did you guess? How's a poor starving artist meant to make her way? It's all prostitution in the end. No, I went to this club and our eyes met and . . .'

'And then your bodies, don't tell me. Gem, I don't mean to be harsh but whoever found anything other than a fuck in a club? It's not really where people go looking for relationships. Well they might go looking for them, but they won't find them. It's like taking a blind man to a silent movie and telling him to guess the leads.'

'Well, I know that. Anyway, who said I was looking for a relationship?'

'Sorry. It was just the way you were talking. We all, I mean Honor and I, assumed you were still in your celibate stage but after the hen night we weren't so sure.'

'Oh no, I stopped that ages ago. Up until now I was doing pretty good research into the perfect zipless fuck, à la Erica Jong, but this beautiful specimen – I mean this man I don't care whether I ever see again or not – seems to have buggered it all up, but as you see Catherine I'm back on course again. Anyway, when were you gossiping with Honor?'

'That's my girl. Honor came around the day after the hen night and we played at feeling sorry for each other's hangovers whilst our kids kept each other amused with political debate, you know the usual. I had the hair of the dog and Honor had the biscuit tin.'

'How come I wasn't invited?'

'I think you were, hmm, busy. Hey, big-time gossip. I haven't told you, Jeremy's back in town sniffing after old Honor again by the sound of it, he took her out to dinner on Sunday.'

'She asked me to baby-sit, and then cancelled last minute, so I don't know what's going on. All I pray is they didn't decide to stay in instead, she's looking so brilliant at the moment he's bound to take advantage.'

'But it doesn't mean she'd let him, she seems to have changed recently.'

'I definitely noticed something the other night.'

'All those books on self-discovery and therapy she's always recommending?'

'Don't. I know I should lie in a flotation tank full of them, have the texts massaged into my body, acupunctured into my brain, but I'm too busy.'

'Do you want to bring a pretty boy to dinner on Saturday night? I was about to ring you to ask you to come. I'm giving a dinner for Sarah Jane since the beloved Josh has arrived in town.

Hey he's staying in Bolton's Hotel, did you bump into him in the corridor?'

'No! So we're going to be privileged enough to meet the real Josh Todd. If I'd known he was in the next-door room we could have had breakfast together, that's assuming Sarah Jane was there? I'm surprised your sister's allowing him out before the wedding?'

'Well, she is and we are. So Saturday night it is, at eight, I've got to get on with some work and if I were you, I'd do the same, it's a better place to get your self-esteem than men. I should know. See you Saturday, and if you strike lucky with your date give me a call.'

'Thanks Catherine. I'll let you know about numbers. Bye, see you Saturday.'

'Catherine, this is a message from Honor Summers on Thursday morning. I'd be delighted to accept your invitation for Saturday night plus date. I don't know if it's the wisest decision to have invited Harry the neighbour, but at least I'll have door-to-door lifts! I'll tell you about the Jeremy saga later. Bye. Oh and about the Harry one too if you call me tonight. Isn't life exciting?'

'Hi, Honor, I've got half an hour before the theatre, can you spare the time to give me only the most intimate and gruesome details of your couplings?'

'Is that Catherine by any chance?'

'Of course. So?'

'Just a minute. I'll take this in the other room so I can watch if Jack's trying to hang any of the neighbours' kids out on the swing. Okay, got my window seat, are you ready?'

'Yes, yes, yes.'

'After I got home on Saturday there was this note shoved under my door from my lift man asking if I wanted to have porridge or brunch with him the next day.'

'What did you say? Forget the food it's you I want?'

'So of course I said I wanted everything, smartie pants. So we all went to Holland Park the next day.'

'Well-known porridge restaurant.'

'Yes, and I signed the kids into the adventure playground, Jack and a mate to keep him occupied. Then Harry and I disappeared into the back of the café for the next couple of hours. You'll never guess what he does?'

'I'm on tenterhooks, don't tell me, he's a chef?'

'Well almost, how did you know? He used to be, now he owns his own restaurant, The Blue Room? I think I've heard of it. He used to work with Peter at The Café and then he worked at a few other snotty ones. French, you know.'

'I know The Blue Room, it's behind the church off Notting Hill, terribly chi chi darling, I went there just the other week and had the most brilliant piece of fish and the best lemon tart. Oh you lucky thing, he'll be seducing you with delicious food. It's too unfair that two brilliant cooks get together when I end up with the clot who can't boil an egg, not that I'm any better but at least I know how to get taken out to dinner. I can see the restaurant now, Harry & Honor's or Harry's Honor. And then what happened?'

'Ha ha. You may find it hard to believe Catherine, but we just talked and it's really brilliant because we got on instantly. You know how it is with some people when you just meet them and it's easy, but he's really gorgeous too. In a way he's so nice it doesn't matter what happens, does that make any sense?'

'No, but they do say "truth is stranger than fiction", so I'm prepared to believe you.'

'I don't think I could lie about anything at the moment.'

'Sweet! You have my blessing and jubilation on this strange union. What's the matter with the world, call me old-fashioned but does nobody fuck any more?'

'I'm sure you're more than making up for the rest of the world's abstinence.'

'So what about Jeremy. You haven't told me about Jeremy?'

'Guess what? He cancelled, couldn't get a flight over from Paris and the restaurant that he'd supposedly booked, I knew was closed on a Sunday.'

'What you're saying is the bull-shitter doesn't change.'

'It's one way of putting it, still it's been re-scheduled for Wednesday. Fun week, huh?'

'Can't wait darling. Bring a bit of excitement into my dull housewife's life, before I start redecorating. The painting market's absolutely dead, I don't know why I pretend some days. I should just stick to fridges in formaldehyde. Actually I do, he's about six foot two, twenty-four years old and a brilliant abstract painter, I'll show you some of his work when figurative Gem's not looking on Saturday, she'll only get miffy. By the way she's not celibate any more, she's been shagging her way around the clubs!'

'NO!'

'Yup! You don't know that and if you do you didn't hear it from me.'

'You are an awful gossip.'

'I know and would you love me any other way?'

'Yes Catherine, we would. Although of course we'd drop you like a hot potato if you gave up being a prestigious art dealer!'

'Don't you mean pretentious? I thought that was the basis of our friendship. Hey, the time, must dash.'

'See you Saturday, Catherine.'

CHAPTER NINE

'What's that frightful music you've put on David?' Catherine shouted at her husband. 'Can't we have something a bit more upbeat? We're not holding a bloody funeral tonight.'

These days they often talked to each other from separate rooms, through doors and walls, across tables and, since they didn't have an intercom system, they shouted. Neither felt the need to be any closer to the other.

'It's Boccherini. I thought you would have recognised it, dear,' he spat venomously whilst securing his cufflinks.

'Boccheroni, sounds like some Spanish fish stew. It'll make a dreadful mess of the CD player if you don't get it out now. I bought some new CDs. They're on the bookcase, can't you put on one of those?'

'Catherine, you're so dull when you play at stupid. You know very well Boccherini is an Italian contemporary of Haydn. We went to see Edward Heath conduct at . . .'

'I know no such thing and if we're talking about dull I slept through that concert for the Tory lawyers' conglomerate. Surprising with such riveting company.'

'It's your choice, Catherine, if you want to die with the same measure of ignorance that you were born with.' He'd crept into the bedroom without her noticing, ostensibly to change his tie.

'And my choice to live with the intellectual snob of the year, too,' Catherine said to her make-up mirror as her wand of mascara brushed her lashes with black wishes, assuming he was still in the other room.

'What was that?' David was suddenly whispering at her side, his cheek placed menacingly close to hers. 'I didn't quite hear you.'

'No? I said, "A little learning is a dangerous thing", so they say.' Sometimes Catherine would venture provocatively close to the cliffside until they both could feel the crumbling precipice beneath her toes. A little push and . . .

'And what is that supposed to mean!' David's voice had

dropped to a familiar growl of barely suppressed anger. His hands now were upon her shoulders, bearing down with the whole weight of his body.

'Just that I suppose it's better for me to die as I was born, just in case I only learnt a little.' Catherine smiled charmingly back at her husband as though nothing else was happening. She was good at pretending. Steady and cool on the outside, only a slight twitch on her upper lip gave her away as she finished applying her lipstick. Inside her stomach had tightened like a draw-string purse and the silent pulse of anger beat a little deeper, sending messages to all the veins threading her body.

These days she was always taking back what she couldn't say, what she couldn't afford to feel. Catherine suppressed her desire to turn around and slap him in the face with a wet shark, to shout, 'Just fuck off my back you pathetic little bully!' Once again she choked back her fear of this gut rage. One day, brave enough, she'd unleash it at a family occasion and do something she couldn't take back. No returns of any sort.

David withdrew to the bathroom, a disappointed bull who'd been on the point of charging, abated but confused.

'Have you finished rowing yet?' A gum-chewing Augusta casually entered the abandoned battlefield and jumped tummy down to lie splayed across her parents' bed.

'Only Mummy, I think the woman who's doing your cooking is at the door and it doesn't do to row in front of strangers. What will they think of us?' Augusta precociously mimicked her grand-mother.

'Well don't lie there, go and let her in,' Catherine replied whilst softly massaging her own red-marked shoulders with crossed arms, giving herself a comforting crook to bury her nose in.

'Don't worry, I'll get it,' David barked, adding a sigh as though once again he was expected to do everything in the house and these women were incapable of even opening a door with any efficiency. It needed a man's ability.

He disappeared from the room, at last purposeful. He looked elegant in his navy linen suit, his glossy fine hair falling easy from his crown. Catherine stole a glance in the mirror at his retreating form and almost felt something like a pang of pity that the packaging was still so right. For a moment, looking at the wrapping even made you want to keep the contents. Only for a moment, exteriors can be so deceptive. The sound of his stout step on the stairs hammered some sense back to her brain.

'So Mummy, when are they arriving and is my little slave coming?'

'I do wish, darling Gus, that you'd stop referring to Jack as your slave. I don't think Honor would like to think she endured all that pain and hardship to raise a domestic for your casual commands.'

'I'll call him something else but I don't expect that'll stop him grovelling after me.'

'I don't expect it will. Some men are just born like that, but you'll find a little sensitivity towards the mothers can be a great bonus in securing their co-operation for their son's downfall.'

'But Granny Herbert never liked you, you've always said.'

'Unfortunately I've learnt that little bit of my own advice the hard way. You see how lucky you are getting the tips early?'

'I'd prefer make-up lessons.'

'When you're older.'

'Mummy! I am practically eleven! Do I have to wait until I'm in my grave for everything! Why don't I get a video and go around to Catrina's? Eggman Ben's gone over to Jules'.'

'I know. It's a bit late to be organising all this with Catrina?'

'No. Catrina's mum says I can come around any time. They like me,' she stabbed.

Catherine ignored the jibe. 'As long as you don't drink their vintage champagne again.'

'It was just a joke Mummy. Honestly! The sofa got more than we did!'

'I know that. I had to pay for it.'

'So, you're rich. Anyway Dad paid for it not you!'

'We're not rich, just well off. Don't say rich, it's vulgar. Anyway that isn't the point.'

'Okay, okay. We won't drink any champagne, I promise. Now can I ring Catrina?'

Augusta sneered a nose-wrinkling smile to her mother, the phone already pressed to her ear after record speed-dialling.

Even to Catherine, Augusta seemed overly mature for her age. She watched her daughter's able manipulation with something almost like admiration. She'd be a smart businesswoman one day, so clued in, had she been like that at her age? She couldn't imagine so. Her step-father had initiated her into an early physical sophistication so that she was still unwilling to remember whole chunks of her childhood.

Augusta hung up the phone and smiled sickly sweet to her mother.

'Mummy darling, can I have twenty quid for tonight? To get some videos and ice-cream and stuff.'

'All of that does not cost twenty quid. You can have ten if you get it from my handbag.'

'But Mum!' she said jumping off the bed in annoyance. 'Catrina and I want to go and have a hamburger from Ed's delivered and things. Please Mummy, don't be a meanie. I'll be on your side for the next argument you have with Daddy. Please Mummy, pretty pleeeeze.'

Augusta wrapped herself around her mother with a cloying display of affection you'd easily pay twenty pounds to get rid of. Drippy kisses and grabby clawing.

'Okay, okay. Take the money Augusta, and don't tell Daddy. Now get out of here, before I change my mind!'

'Thanks Mummy, you're the greatest!'

Augusta went straight to her bag, took the twenty and slipped an extra five in her pocket, just in case, before bounding back to give Catherine an enthusiastic kiss-hug. 'I'll remember you in my will. We might come by to see Josh Todd later. Okay, okay, don't give me that look. We won't embarrass you.' Augusta waved her way out with the note.

Catherine returned to powdering her cheeks.

She knew her daughter was up to no good, the plotting and planning of the young should never be investigated too thoroughly, she believed, otherwise the little things started to lose their excitement. The parent's fear is the lure of ever more dangerous and illicit thrills. Catherine had no idea what Augusta was up to with her older friend Catrina, but what was a little champagne and a few cigarettes going to do to the healthy robustness of her daughter, much older in mind and more sensible than her brother? What can happen when you're not yet eleven, your innocence protects you, doesn't it?

Upstairs, Augusta packed her disco bag goodies: new silver stacked trainers, tasselled hot pants, a packet of menthol cigarettes, gold nail-varnish and matching eyeliner and some of her mother's lipstick, rouge and eye shadow. Why shouldn't she be out enjoying herself, she wasn't going to end up like her father having a miserable time or Boring Ben watching football and growing spots, holding wanking competitions with his friends. Boys were so pathetic. Groan-ups, don't mention them! Dumb clots can't see a thing going on in their own miserable lives, let alone mine, Augusta thought. Serves them right if I don't do as I say.

Catrina and Augusta will do themselves up drinking Catrina's mother's vodka diluted with fresh orange juice, that way it doesn't taste so horrible. They will fill the vodka back up to the pencil mark (that the mother now places on it) with water, before placing it back in the cupboard. It's all right, the mother won't know, can't tell. Catrina, who's twelve, almost thirteen, says so. She's gone out with a boyfriend and won't be back until lunch-time the following day. Catrina knows everything, Catrina sleeps with Tim the lodger and Sebastian, one of her mother's boyfriends. Her mother doesn't know but parents don't know anything, do they?

By eleven thirty, tall Augusta and leggy Catrina might be paying their eight pounds each on the door at Blues Baby's, a new club on the King's Road. Catrina is a schoolgirl but she is also a catwalk model and can bluff them in free most of the time. Then they will be dancing with the rest of the gang at the far end of the club. They try to dance away from the older crowd, but it doesn't stop the old men shifting around their corner like starved bees around the honeypot, just waiting for the lid to be lifted. Pockets full of illicit presents, offering pills like playground bribes of chocolate and friendship, champagne, fizzy drinks for kisses and feels of their pubescent breasts. This is Saturday night Chelsea, just like anywhere else, where teenagers stuff their beds with pillows and shin out the back window whilst parents downstairs watch television.

'Hello Catherine. Harry, this is Catherine our hostess and one of my best friends,' was Honor's nervous introduction on the door-step.

'Hello there. It's good to meet you. Honor was telling me a little bit about you.' As Harry said her name he turned to catch her eye reassuringly.

'Oh, only a little bit? Honor I'm going to have to sack you as my PR! Do come in, it's lovely to meet you Harry. I love having my hand kissed. He's gorgeous Honor,' Catherine added in an audible whisper.

'Notice how unerringly on time we are,' Honor said proudly pointing her finger at the diamanté evening watch her granny had recently given her.

'Beautiful! In fact Gem has been incredibly rude and arrived three minutes early. Beaten again I'm afraid, by Gem's lack of etiquette. Come through, we're in the conservatory. David's show-ing off his orchid collection that he brought yesterday from Rassels, to amaze us all with his taste and green fingers. They've only been in the house for twenty-four hours, so he hasn't given them a proper chance to die yet. Next week it'll be a different story, invitations to the poor things' funerals, I expect,' she said, leading them through.

'What would you like to drink, can I tempt you with a little champagne?'

Harry was looking bewildered at the machine-gun fire of Catherine's conversation and Honor smiled at him conspiratorially, quite used to her, quite at home.

'That would be wonderful, thank you.'

'I have to say, Harry, that is the sexiest accent I've heard for a long time, but I'm sure women everywhere tell you that.' Catherine handed him some champagne and looked him straight in the eye. She didn't feel comfortable in a room unless she was sure she could seduce every man in it, just in case. Harry understood the Cather-ines of the world, he'd recognised her type the moment he saw her, playing at being seduced to make her feel at ease, that way she wouldn't be after him for the rest of the evening. He would be left alone with Honor which was what he wanted.

'No. Most of the time people say they canna understand what I'm saying.'

'I'm sure Honor will agree, it's not what you say, it's the way you say it.'

She introduced Harry to David and, leaving the two men talking, turned back to Honor.

'Honor, champagne should help your indigestion. By the way, whilst we're still out here, have you ever seen this Gregorio that Gem's brought along? I think it's the only proper man I've ever seen her with. They go quite well together. I think he might even be straight!'

'Gregorio, Gregorio Jonski, hasn't he got the same agent as her? Isn't it Gregorio that she says is "half-Russian, half a painter and a whole bore"? I always think he's quite funny, but her confidence must be at a low ebb to bring him as a date.'

'Why?'

'Because she knows he's besotted and she doesn't want him.'

'Knowing Gem, that's why she doesn't want him. Ho hum, it means her American didn't call back.' Catherine lowered her voice as she looked in the mirror to see the others approaching and heard the click clack of Gem's heels across the tiles.

'Is that you lot sniggering out there in the living room? Aren't you going to come out here, so we can join the party . . .' Gem interrupted their gossiping.

'And enjoy the floral arrangements. Of course we are, and I'm bringing the bottle for top-ups,' added Catherine, leading them through to the conservatory.

'Hello Honor, good to see you again,' said David, today smiling warmly and disarmingly at her. With the public face of the gracious host with buckets of charm fully in place, he managed to look quite attractive. This had to be what had kept him and Catherine together, Honor imagined. Perhaps Catherine exaggerated his bullying tactics but then who wouldn't fight back with Catherine steamrollering, flirting and laughing at forty miles an hour? Honor thought, If this is marriage, it makes you appreciate being single.

'So, Honor, great to see you. How you doin'? That's such a great dress you've got on, it really suits you, that Venetian Red. Aren't you going to introduce me?'

'Thanks Gem. You're looking wonderful as usual, love your hair. I'll introduce you when he finishes talking to David. You're Gregorio aren't you? I'm Honor, we met ages ago at some lunch.'

'Of course I remember. We discussed the pluses and minuses of fine art cleaning.'

'God you can remember that! Oh look, Gem has managed to introduce herself to Harry, I knew she didn't really need my help.'

'Wonderful isn't she,' Gregorio sighed, entranced. Gem's silken flowered crepe clung to her firm slender body. Her hair was flattened to her scalp, shiny with hair oil, a strict parting and a rigid set of kiss curls cemented to her forehead, the rest in a blonde chignon at the nape of her long elegant neck. Her prettiness had become beauty, her part-child, part-woman aligned.

Honor watched Gregorio's stare, then David's. She caught his eye and looked quickly away to Harry's; she hoped his eyes were more admiring than desiring. Why shouldn't he, Gem is my friend and she is beautiful? Honor thought.

But then so is Honor, with her mass of black curls, olive skin and a face always on the edge of a smile.

A brass knock stops the buzz.

'I'll get the door, that must be my sister, regulation half an hour late,' said Catherine, and the talk began again.

'Sarah Jane! What's the matter darling?'

Catherine folds her weeping sister in her arms on the doorstep, mindless of the snotty tear-stained face trailing distraught slime across her Miyake-covered shoulder.

'It's nothing, I've had a row with Josh, I'm sorry I've ruined the whole of your dinner,' Sarah Jane cried and snuffled, not noticing the damage to her sister's dress.

'Is he back at the hotel, can I give him a ring?'

'Oh no he's driven me here. He's in the Mercedes just across the street but he refuses to come in. He says I humiliated him over lunch. I just had a bit too much to drink, he says I took my top off and he doesn't need that kind of publicity. It was only for a minute, only a joke. I'm sorry, now I'm ruining your evening too.' She cried a little more before snorting it all back in and calmed the shudders with some deep breaths. Semi-reclaimed she stuttered, 'Can I go to the loo now? Fix myself up then I'll go back out and apologise on bended knees. It'll be all right, honest Cath. I'm so sorry. I'll make everything right again.' Her eyes pleaded like a chastised child.

'Sarah Jane there's nothing to be sorry for. Are you sure you want to come? It doesn't matter, if you're feeling miserable. It was only meant to be casual. Are you sure you're all right, you'd tell me wouldn't you, sweetheart, you would tell me?'

'Of course. It's nothing. Don't worry I'm fine, really I am. You've gone to all this trouble and I . . . You know what a pain in the arse I can be sometimes. You know, Josh is right, he says I do it for attention. I'll just go to the loo, I'll be straight back. It's nothing Catherine. Honest. Believe me?'

'Yes, of course.' They exchanged unbelieving smiles, props of the game that they'd now both agreed to keep in place; parallel lies.

From the doorway Catherine watches her patched up little sister retreat back into the car, her willowy body bowed in contrition for her sins, her nose still sniffing at a powdery reviver. She can just make out Josh's hard cross form, telling off, making straight and sure Sarah Jane knows she is wrong.

Josh is right, Sarah Jane is wrong.

The sermon is followed by the enfolding arms of forgiveness and the final act of submission on Sarah Jane's part; her head lowers beneath the windscreen. Josh pulls a jacket over her head; suckling penance.

I can't look any more, she thinks. Catherine turns away half-sick in her stomach from the ritual humiliation, backs into the hall at the sight of his hand firmly lowering her little sister's head down into his bully lap, whilst he relaxes back on to the leather seat. The firm and immovable push of male strength upon female flesh. Somehow it was bearable that she did it, but not her sister. 'Please, not little Sarah Jane too, why does she have to put up with it?' she pleaded to empty space, in the closest way she had to a prayer.

Catherine wondered how men managed to trust women they pushed and held. She toyed with the idea of buying sets of steel razor dentures for her close girlfriends at Christmas, but it was she who would appreciate them most. Imagine what David would think! Her mouth widened in a sadistic smile at the thought of saying, 'Darling, I've got a pressy for you.'

No, sweet Honor would have no use for them.

Sarah Jane was resolving the situation in the same way they had watched their mother handle their step-father, as children. Their mother had always told them that they held a key in their girls' bodies, that men wanted women's sexuality so bad it would open any bank balance, steal any diamond. Men will crawl through a river of shit for it, as Valerie Solaris (Andy Warhol's failed assassin) so adroitly put it in her S.C.U.M. Manifesto – Society for Cutting Up Men. Catherine left the door ajar for Josh and Sarah

Jane to make their entrance in their own time, and wandered back down the hallway. She wondered if anyone would spot them in the quiet of the evening. A sardonic smile sat upon her lips remembering the lessons learnt at their mother's lap.

Their mother dispensed her pearls of wisdom nightly from the giddy heights of her dressing table, along with clouds of powder and sprays of perfume. It was the only time they saw her. Sarah Jane and Catherine would gather cross-legged on the floor in their nighties and woolly dressing gowns, either side of their mother's stool, both mesmerised by her evening making-up ritual. There she extolled her worldly knowledge, how to climb into a sports car in a skirt without revealing too much of your legs, that Crystal was the finest and therefore the only champagne to drink, and that too much make-up was as bad as none at all. Cultivating society was important and these were its rituals.

Just when they seemed to be getting on, a nanny would come and haul them back up to the cold nursery. There they would listen for the click of their mother's departing heels on the marble hallway floor, the heavy shut of the carved oak door and the Porsche crunching away down the gravel drive. Catherine and Sarah Jane would stand at the top of the banisters, their cries of, 'Please don't go Mummy, don't leave us. Please don't go, not tonight,' dismissed with a glove-waved kiss thrown to the air for either to catch and then fight over; for there was only ever one.

'Silly girls, you know I have to meet Kenneth.'

Kenneth was their step-father who provided all the beauty, wealth and secrets that surrounded them in this diamond luxury. Mummy said they must be grateful, they were very lucky girls. They must always do as Kenneth said.

Tiptoe yearning, they would sniff for the remains of Mummy's scent, Joy, floating from the soft, warm, lying promises of her cashmere coat.

'The most expensive and the only perfume worth having,' she would tell them. The little girls would try to hold on to that smell, take it to their beds and sniff it into their hands until they were washed over by sleep.

Catherine had always done as Kenneth said but when she saw Sarah Jane was being initiated into his rituals too, she had to protect her when her mother wouldn't listen.

If Catherine nowadays recognised the smell of Joy, left hanging in some dress shop, she would be stirred, an unrequited longing would jump at her, for something she could no longer remember wanting, not, at least, from her mother. These days Catherine never smelt Joy on her mother, who had now taken to wearing 'the queen's perfume, Bal de Versailles', so much more expensive, more appropriate. The other name was never right; not for her mother.

CHAPTER TEN

Everybody was seated around the dining table. Under it, Josh gave a bruising kick to Sarah Jane's shin as warning. Looks would keep her in order for the rest of dinner.

The first course was laid out in front of them, covering the settings before they even sat down. Catherine hated that. Pure laziness on the girl's part not to wait until they were ready, settled into the table; she made a mental note not to employ her again. She looked over to Sarah Jane's pinched face and hoped she didn't feel too insecure about not being put right next to Josh.

Sarah Jane didn't look happy, Honor could see that, she could've sworn she saw her wince with pain and bite her lower lip. Maybe she was pre-menstrual, that was what was making her so manic and emotional with pre-wedding nerves. Even so, she looked a damn sight happier than Gem. What had got into Gem?

As soon as Gem saw Sarah Jane and Josh arrive, she had dropped her glass of champagne and stood there gawping with her mouth open like a dead-eyed fish, surrounded by broken glass. Strange, Honor thought Gem would have been easier than the rest of them with Josh's fame.

Gem still didn't look much better, gaunt and frozen, silently spaced.

Rather rude, thought David, she'd barely raised a hello to Sarah Jane and her chap, he didn't seem that bad, quite friendly considering. Catherine should do something with her friend Gemma, tell her to go sort herself out.

Gem got up and excused herself in the direction of the loo.

'He said his name was Billy,' Gem insisted to a mirror. 'He said his name was Billy!' She was safe to speak once locked behind the bathroom door. The night that she had so exulted in, re-lived countless times since, on continual replay so that she knew all the actions and all the lines off by heart, she could now barely distinguish from her imaginings.

'I love you Gem, you're the first girl I've felt like this about. You're not a girl, you're a woman and I love you from your perfect toes to the tip of your cute lil' nose.' Gem had the whole thing rewritten.

Josh's appearance had been a winding punch in Gem's solar plexus. Everything dropped, not only a glass – smash! She stood amongst the debris, thinking NO. Catherine fussed, clearing up, but there was no doubt, couldn't be any doubt that it was him. The body that she had licked in its most intimate places, the skin that she had kissed with such passion, the hips that had pinned her to the bed, the lips that she had drunk champagne from, the arms that had held her against the hotel wall as he filled the inside of her, only the week before, stood in front of her covered in dark denim – shirt, trousers, jacket.

No wonder he had been so familiar. How had she been so stupid? He looked different from in the movies – obviously.

With the bravado of a smile covering his boyish Texan face, Josh politely accepted the greetings. His grin only faltered for a moment with Gem. A cloud of a frown drifted across his brow and unsteadied his straight gaze, but he never forgot his profession: acting.

'And this is one of my bestest friends ever, Gem, meet Josh my fiancé, isn't he wonderful? I'm sure you'll get on brilliantly, you know Josh paints too but usually he's busy filming, aren't you, darling?' Sarah Jane continued oblivious, jumping like a ball between bats, her hair flying with the laughter, her gleaming teeth matching the shine of sequins scattered across her tiny dress.

'Hi there, good meeting you Gem. Have we . . . I'm sorry, you just look so much like Gwyneth Paltrow . . .' Josh trailed off suddenly recognising the differently and more elegantly bedecked Gem.

'Gem's gorgeous and a brilliant painter, aren't you Gem? Now don't be modest.' Sarah Jane kept on and draped her arm about Gem's shoulder and hugged her cheek to hers. 'It's so nice to see you, we'll catch up over dinner.'

'You're looking beautiful Sarah Jane. Josh is a lucky man.'

'I sure am.'

In the bathroom, Gem couldn't stomach it any longer, the pain forced through her like a trumpeting exhortation to expel any champagne or peanuts temporarily lodged. There she was, for once throwing up without the aid of her fingers on her tonsils. The force of expulsion threw the acid vomit into and over the lavatory bowl. The warm liquid rushed up her throat and through her nose, leaving it stinging and sore as though it had been whooshed through with Domestos. Still her stomach continued to heave in nervous contractions, with nothing left to bring up but a pale lemon/lime slime that slid down the side of the bowl to float as the final topping on the ice-cream mess. She heaved a sigh that closed her eyes, felt her temples pulsate. Holding on to the wooden towel rack, her fingers sinking into the soft pale cottons, she pulled herself up, straightening her back, righting her dizzy, crowded head. Gem deep-breathed herself across the room to the sink, turned the cold tap full on and plunged her hour-long make-up under the freezing flow to dissipate the blotches that had sprung up over her skin. She patted her face dry with tissues and found a lipstick in her pocket to re-apply some of the mask.

That will have to do for the rest of the meal, she thought, pushing down the disappointment of another wrecked dream, the guilt of betraying her best friend, the whole damn fucking-men thing. She smoothed her hair back into place, puckered her lips in the mirror and cleaned up, flushing the evidence of her disappoint-ment away. That was it, bye, bye, baby. Get your head around this one Gem and get it right – sucker. Aware of her breath she looked frantically for mouthwash and settled for eating a blob of tooth-paste before unlocking the bathroom door.

All the way down the stairs, Gem held on to the wall and tried to think happy thoughts but none came to her. Back at the table, who had she been placed next to but Josh, the little shit. Charming.

The grilled oiled peppers lay in a bright mess amongst the clean lumps of squid, scattered across burgundy-and-veridian crinkled leaves. The guests sat down silent and unsure at how to start eating, embarrassed in front of a real genuine no-holds moviestar who beaconed charisma like a lighthouse. How to pretend to act normal before such fame, plastic glamour, American beauty?

Josh Todd currently had Hollywood in the palm of his hand, let alone a dinner party in London. He was shockingly handsome. His smooth, dark, smouldering but boyish looks were better than

Alain Delon. He was Dean and Brando's successor, a contender with Gable. He played characters who hid their vulnerability with a tough exterior, shy behind their lowered eyes, a hairless boy on the outside with a man's heart and soul. What woman wouldn't fall, he was a 'do the right thing' man? The studios had set him straight, with projects lined up for him.

Josh was in his element. Quite used to making people feel awkward with the power of his magnetism, he also had the power of putting them at their ease when it suited him. Catherine was her usual charming, disarming self and got the chat flowing, passing the bread, making jokes about the food and her own cooking ability, lauding praise upon Honor's gifts and exaggerating her sister's talents to ever greater heights. The consummate hostess.

Once the table was cleared of the first set of plates, everybody was talking or listening, groups settled in, digging for common ground. More wine was poured and drunk, drunk and poured, white, red, separate glasses, spilt and mopped with the linen napkins so as not to soil the linen tablecloth.

Josh turned away from the bruised Gem to Catherine on his other side, all sleek in her command like a Greek Diana, the huntress.

'So Catherine, what are you doing with that jerk of a husband?' was his first whisper of intimacy to his sister-in-law to be. You had to be up-front, an aggressor with the English, but it was the way he said it that really counted.

'I'll pretend for decency's sake that I didn't hear that. It's the way we English are, all uptight repression. Besides what goes on between two people once the bedroom door is closed is anybody's guess. Isn't it?'

'You're right about that. So Catherine, what do you like to do in bedrooms?'

'I think you're trying to be deliberately naughty Josh,' and she half-closed her eyes at him and slid him a smile of delicious danger.

How was he to know this was her house speciality in her private realm of artworld pick-ups? Another girl's secret, like Gem and her body servicing.

Josh chose to see Catherine's look as an open invitation, a come-on just for him. It was, but only in the lamest terms; she would do nothing in front of her sister until her plot was firm and riveted in place, secure as a Chubb. His leg pushed hard and firmly against her, rubbing against the back of her calf, just as it had done with Gem in the club only a few nights before. Catherine was amazed at how easy it could be to re-route an idle river. Now a plan was beginning to form.

On the other side of the table, nicer conversation, genuine laughter was going on. They had reached the topic of cabinet members' sexuality and wanted to get to the bottom of why Gem's date, Gregorio, should know so much about Timothy Crowbridge's comings and goings from the male brothels in South Kensington. All except David, notable in his uninterest.

The main course was heralded. Steaming bowls of new potatoes arrived comfy in their skins and dripping with Greek oil, criss-crossed with brown shoe laces of anchovies and dotted with squidgy green capers and the glistening crystals of sea salt. There was a bowl of Julienne orange and green stripes, courgettes and carrots with sesame seeds and oil, then the sea bass, *loup de la mer*, was brought in and shown off, portioned on to the beautiful turquoise glass plates.

'This is so delicious Catherine. The garlic and lemongrass are perfect.'

'Why thank you Honor, it was nothing, just a little something I ran up in moments on my machine. It's all packets, tins and microwave, easy when you've got my advanced knowledge of tin opening,' Catherine joked. 'Do pass the potatoes over.'

'You keep busy in Hollywood I imagine, Josh?' David took the bull by the horns. Fame is only relative, he thought, justifying his condescension. I'm on first name terms with really important people, like judges and MPs, honourable men who've done something worthwhile to attain their status.

'You could say I'm in demand, so I'm not a petrol pump attendant any more.'

'So was that your other career? Interesting. I suppose that was when you were "resting" – that's what they call it, isn't it? – you've done all sorts of things, no doubt.'

'I guess you could say that but usually I work. There was a lean time when I was at college but I've been lucky, right place, right time.' Josh smiled back easily, he was used to husbands' aggression.

'I read a fascinating thing in the paper, which amazed me. Did you know, apparently Henry Fonda and Katharine Hepburn had never met before they made *On Golden Pond*? I mean you'd imagine wouldn't you, since they were both in the profession for so long, living in the same place, that they must have bumped into each other, at Oscar parties and the like.'

'LA's a big place. Just because we all work together, we don't always play together. We don't have famous-actors-only parties all the time. Most of my friends are writers and painters.'

'Interesting. In my profession, the law, we do see quite a lot of each other, for business and social reasons. Of course I'm not married to a lawyer but many are. Take Tony Blair and Cherie, they tutored in the same chambers, though of course he's prime minister now. It's a bit like the world of medicine really.'

Josh gave a severe glance over to Sarah Jane who was sitting next to David, it interrupted her conversation with Harry and willed her to talk to her brother-in-law. 'Get this son-of-a-bitch bore offa my back now!' his piercing look screamed, and she did as she was told with an apologetic glance, as though it was all her fault.

Josh got up and left the table heading for the loo, really in search of Catherine; now she was much more interesting – plus the loo smelt revoltingly of vomit. There was something about her he hadn't absorbed until now; like an addictive scent. Strange how that girl that he'd made out with last week should be here out of all London. Small-town living. He hoped she wouldn't spill to Sarah Jane, he didn't need that kind of hassle; it had been exercise, flossing, physically expelling an excess build-up.

Sarah Jane would understand. If she found out he'd cry sorry, she'd weep forgiveness, he'd played the scene before, knew the lines. Perhaps she could get a threesome going, now that would be fun, two blonde playmates. He'd tell her that she was the only one he'd ever love, and then ask her later.

Honor had been terrified. Ten minutes before Harry knocked on her door she was still doing her deep-breathing exercises, reading passages from *You Are The Key*, trying to calm herself down when she really felt she was a hairpin battling to open a Yale. Perhaps she could be ill, come down with some horrible contagious flu, cancel him at the last minute. He could probably hear the tell-tale signs through the floorboards that Jack wasn't home, silence. She must have been mad, in a state of life-blindness, to have asked him to Catherine's in front of all her friends. She didn't even know him, how could she be sure he'd get on with any of her friends? He was handsome and fascinating and sweet and generous to her, but he might just seem dull and stupid to them. Worse still, why would he be interested in any of them? They were brilliant and funny and loving to her, but they might seem just pretentious and silly to him.

'Ssh, ssh,' she said to herself. 'Calm down,' and she lay on the floor, shutting the door on her last ridiculous thought that she was being unfaithful to Jeremy, Jack's father. She even made herself laugh with that one, how much of a bad time can you give yourself? Calm down, deep breath, let it go.

The door bell went and she jumped off the floor, she must have fallen asleep but instead of going to the door and answering it, she went, trance-like, back to the mirror and finished her half-done lipstick. Then she answered it.

Harry was there, smelling all delicious, pressed, polished and shining. What was I wasting my time thinking about? she asked herself immediately. They kissed hello on both cheeks, his lips lingering on the last, his hands holding her shoulders and slowly he kissed towards her mouth, nibbling the corners and then they were kissing full on the lips with such urgency bodies began pressing hard upon the other and the front door. Honor forgot herself until Harry pulled away, leaving her panting. He smiled mischievously at her, tapping his watch. Fuck dinner, Honor thought crossly.

'Com'on now Honor, we can't be late for your friend, and maybe it's better we wait. Like the Taoist belief.'

What? God, don't do this to me, Taoist? What's he going on about? Taoist, oh Taoist, yes men save their ejaculations and they can go on for hours pleasuring the women. Honor had heard of it but never knew a man who'd be willing. It sounded like an excuse for men who couldn't come. Where was the pleasure for her in panting with frustration?

'It might be good for you Harry, but it's not doing me any good.' She took a deep breath. 'But you're right, it is rude to be late for dinner. Christ! I look like Coco the clown,' she laughed, catching her reflection, an overflowing, smudged red river. Harry too. She handed him the tissues and went to make herself up again. Harry followed her to the mirror and whispered to her hair.

'Relax, we'll have plenty of time later,' and he blew on her neck giving her a rash of goose-pimpling shivers, running his finger down her spine.

'We will?' Honor nervously tittered at his whispers of promise. 'Then how do you expect me to leave this empty flat and go to a houseful of people for dinner with those thoughts in my head? I'll have to take up nail biting.'

'Surely no, not on these beautiful hands?' He took her rough working hands and kissed them, his face wiped clean of lipstick.

'No, not my nails! They're far too hideous and I know where they've been. I meant yours,' and she growled at him.

'Down tiger, no, down.'

'Please, not on the first date, Harry! I think we had better go.' And she smirked at his face, covered in confusion at her implications.

Honor was feeling relaxed, sure now of her sexuality after Wednesday night.

On Wednesday night she had said no to Jeremy. She had batted her eyelids, licked her lips and said no, and how proud was she? Very!

Jeremy had taken Honor, mother of his child, out to a screamingly expensive restaurant for dinner. He had put his plan to her across the realm of white damask tablecloths, napkins and excess cutlery.

The plan was this – he would buy a house in London, move Jack and Honor into it, so that the three of them would play at happy families together. Honor would stop working of course and be mother to Jack, wife to Jeremy. How about it, huh?

Honor had shocked herself by spoiling the game and said no. Jeremy wasn't the giving-up type and he could feel the electricity as surely as Honor must have, the buzz of a sexual current remained between them, stronger than he'd remembered it, though Honor had always told him it was there.

Jeremy was surprised. How she'd flowered with motherhood, he had imagined she would have gone to rack and ruin; increasing his noble act of sacrifice. Still no matter, looks weren't important where atonement was concerned; in sacrificing himself to her he would be redeemed.

Jeremy had been in therapy for two years and now he was grown up enough to make amends. He had kicked his habit, closed the door on Narnia for good, he'd had his last adventure. He was a new Jeremy, a reputable doctor, a specialist who was ready for a warm nest; he wanted his family. He wanted the uniform and props, the responsibility and kudos of fatherhood. He wanted Honor for his home.

'Don't worry about your mess and clutter, we'll get a cleaner in every day,' Jeremy had said reassuringly to Honor as he'd told her his intentions in his considered monologue. Explained how his magic wand of happiness would bring money and privilege.

Honor had sat before him, her eyes lowered to the table, watching her fingers crumbling a bread roll over the once-immaculate tablecloth. She'd let her mind wander remembering the dreams and prayers in which she had begged Jeremy to come back and say all that he was saying now. She would have gift-wrapped her soul to whoever could've given her this in the past. Lucky the devil hadn't been passing. She remembered at the time laughing at the so-called power of prayer, sneering at God and his lack of results. She couldn't accept his decision, her own condition. The prayers had worked, just five years too late.

'Dear sweet Honor, such beautiful intelligent eyes.' Jeremy put his arm across the table and warmly clasped her hand with his hairless pianist's fingers and looked up, thoughtfully handsome, through his tortoiseshell glasses.

'You never used to wear glasses, but somehow they suit you Jeremy.'

'Call me Dr Harris, if you please.' And he looked back at her with mock sternness. 'You may now undress and wait for me in the examining room.'

Honor laughed, the idea of taking off her clothes with Jeremy, she couldn't imagine being naked and lying in bed with him, making love with him.

'How can you tell a doctor at the scene of an accident in holiday traffic? He's the one speeding past. You're not supposed to laugh, only doctors are allowed to. Do you want to hear any more fresh from Emergency?'

'That's terrible Jeremy.'

'You try keeping sane in the geriatric unit.'

He was the same but a stranger, his words, his manner had been remoulded and she couldn't connect him with the Jeremy Harris of the past, father of her child, maker of her dreams, object of her obsessions. He was gentle now, softer, she was sure, kinder, or was it the drink talking? After all he was Jack's father, maybe it would be possible . . . and what about Harry?

'I've got to get back. Baby-sitter, work tomorrow . . .'

'Stay for just a small Grappa? No? You never were one for late nights Honor. We'd better have the bill please.' He motioned and smiled to the waiter.

'Nothing to beat a nice warm bed tucked up in your 'jamas with a good book and a cup of tea. Old before my time, aren't I?'

'Your descriptions aren't exactly the height of eroticism, but what are you reading, Anais Nin?' he asked, opening his wallet and flourishing notes like a fan upon the bill with a careless glance.

Honor tried not to look at the bill but couldn't stop herself glancing at the ninety-five pound total. Ninety-five pounds! It was an outrage for the food they were served. Of course she could've cooked better, the sauce had too much lemon in it, the fish was overdone but it was worth it for not doing the washing up.

'*The Debt to Pleasure*,' she answered smugly. He looked like he was trying to remember if it was a de Sade title; she put him out of his misery. 'It's by John Lanchester, it's about a man obsessed with food, but primarily with himself. You'd like it.' He looked disappointed. 'It's funny,' she softened.

He had asked to come up for a nightcap. No. Asked when he'd see her again. Don't know. Would she call him later on? Perhaps. Would she reconsider?

'You think about what I've said, you know it's the right thing to do, for Jack's sake,' he had pleaded manipulatively.

'I will think about it. Thank you, I appreciate it, even past its sell-by date.'

'I'm sorry. I wish I could have offered sooner.' She had looked in his eyes; he meant it.

'I know. I do know.' And they had kissed in the most tender and intimate way. It had pulled at Honor's heart but still she got out of the cab and didn't look back.

Honor had climbed into bed that night happily alone, thinking, how things change, I must have changed, how peculiar, I've been so caught up in my whole living of life I don't think I'd noticed. I used to yearn to have his body cupped close to me during all those months when he rolled over and slept on the edge of the bed. Couldn't bear the heat I gave off, he said. All I wanted was to feel, to smell, his skin on mine. I didn't even care that he shouted at me. Thank God, things change.

Honor had rolled to her side, trying to forget the kiss and that she still loved him. She'd given herself a hug and as she'd drifted off to sleep she'd forgotten to do her tummy exercises, again.

CHAPTER ELEVEN

'Pudding, coffee and brandy time. Everybody ready?' Hostess Catherine immaculately asked.

'Ahh. That's where you'd gone to Catherine. We were beginning to think you'd run away from your own party,' was David's dry comment.

'Just busy entertaining darling.' Catherine threw her husband a dismissive sneer of a smile, all scrunched up eyes and tight mouth. She turned to the rest of the guests with a warm centre-page of a smile and put the lemon tart on the table with such pride, it could have been her own baby. The same quality that made her so efficient at selling art. Catherine was able to sell anything, so long as it was by somebody else. Anything she might have produced wouldn't have been worth the flour it was made from. She always judged herself harshly, except where men were concerned.

Everybody gobbled the lemon tart down except Gem. Gem could hardly keep her bum on the seat, let alone think about putting more food into her mouth. Gregorio had her plate and, encouraged by the whoosh of a brandy charting his veins, went to the kitchen and hauled out the girl who had cooked it all to receive their congratulations, much to her embarrassment.

David was filling up with moroseness as quickly as brandy, he felt sickened at the sight of all these people pretending to have a good time. Catherine laughing too loud, whose jokes were that good? He couldn't join in, couldn't compete. He took his glass up and sidled away to his study, didn't even bother with the coffee or saying goodbye, they weren't his friends anyway. He'd smoke a good Cuban, relish it alone, treat himself.

Harry was bemused by funny, sexy Honor; to find himself in the middle of her most intimate friendships was a little different to simply fancying her. Not that he was trying to get her straight into bed. She was single, had a kid, it wasn't like you could do that so casually. Besides, she was his neighbour. Everyone seemed nice enough but his eyes kept coming back to Honor, she was sweet and he liked the way she was always smiling and her eyes twinkled, lit from inside. It had been a while since he had willingly taken a weekend off work, that must be something. Work, where he was surrounded by women like Catherine, elegant escorts of dull or powerful husbands, thrusting their phone numbers into his hand with some make-believe catering needs that required intimate urgent discussion. He knew Catherine, her type, he was fed up with them.

Harry had sworn to give up married women as soon as he moved flats and had only succumbed once since, with Lady Caroline; she was hard to resist with more humour and flesh than the rest.

Friends at work had started to tease him, noticed he must be looking for his own wife, rather than somebody else's. He supposed he was tired of endlessly checking his watch, always parking his car for an easy exit, always wearing loafers. Once excitement had lain there. Now it was just more of the same old stuff, like watching continuous repeats of *Home and Away*.

Harry was bored. So many eighteen-year-olds trying to look thirty-five, so many fifty-year-olds trying to look eighteen. Everybody wanting to have others' lives, bodies, minds. Harry came from a Scottish island, Scalpay in the Outer Hebrides, and he intended to go back or at least move away from England. What good would a woman like Catherine be there? A fully qualified magazine flicker, good at filing her nails and shopping in Sloane Street and Brompton Cross, what would she be in a croft? What would his granny have made of women like that? Och, it didn't bear thinking about.

He could choose some young girl, somebody's daughter with a degree in fashion and gossip and a part-time job modelling. Perhaps it was time to stop playing with women as toys, stop being one himself, for he could see it all as clearly as a chess game, only as he got older it was changing to chequers.

What would replace it? Would I want it? I don't know it. I'm more comfortable with what I know, even if I don't like it. How to chance it? All fears, only the anticipation of the unknown. We think safe is what we know. Harry had been brave once before, had stepped from a simple sea village life to find the world. First Edinburgh, then Glasgow and then again to London in search of

what? Fame, money, reputation, a different life? Acknowledgement, recognition from somebody other than his mother and
father that he was as clever, as brilliant, as beautiful, as strong as
they had always told him. Or not as stupid as his teachers had
always told him. He had proved all of that.

Why can't we just believe our mothers and be done with the
journeys? What? And miss out on the adventures of life? Besides,
sometimes mothers lie. Some mothers tell their children they are
ugly, stupid, bad and wicked, just repeating what was told to them.
Some mothers say their children are already with the devil. Some
mothers don't like children, some children don't have mothers.
What then are they to believe about women, about themselves,
about men?

Across from Harry sat the successful Josh Todd. Who
would've guessed that Josh's mother had disappeared from his life
when he was five? Just upped and gone like that. Reappeared
every couple of years or so, to try and work things out, to stay with
him and his brother, but she never could hack it for longer than a
year. Off again to Las Vegas or Hollywood, New York or Nashville
with her unfulfilled need for recognition in lights and affairs that
might promise untold riches, leaving her penniless and grieving
again and again.

Josh and Tommy were brought up by their grandma, between
their mother's experiments. A moral and judgmental woman, Annie
Jespers would stand, watching her only daughter Annette fail,
waiting to catch the falling baby of her life. To Josh's grandmother,
her daughter wasn't 'capable of fixing a peanut butter sandwich
without screwing up, let alone looking after two boys'. She was 'too
pretty and she didn't get it from our side of the family! 'Course she
couldn't keep that husband of hers, who was a no good nothin'
anyway, mostly foreign too.'

A small, strong, shrew-like creature, Annie had vivid eyes and
looked like she could bring hellfire to heaven if that was her wish.
Josh had left home when he was fifteen in search of his mom with
her dark hair and pale skin. Worked his way around Hollywood
and Los Angeles, even a spell in Malibu, in the only way a
good-looking boy can, without getting his hands dirty with a
regular job. He never found her but plenty found him. Josh was
attractive but only Mikey was prepared to keep him.

What Josh had told David over dinner wasn't completely untrue, he had got work as soon as he'd finished college, a private drama college that his antique dealer 'benefactor' had paid his way through. Fifty-year-old Mikey Bezzlson had even arranged his agent for him and practically paid for him to get his first role. Mikey had loved him, had known in his heart that when Josh achieved stardom he would be abandoned, yet he loved him all the same. He knew that Josh's agent would want him to marry a young starlet whose skirts were too short and cleavage so low that they'd always be photographed coming out of any restaurant or premiere. Gay still wasn't a mainstream cinematic attraction. You could get by being gay on television but Josh wanted the movies. Josh Todd gay? No way. Leave your girl alone in a room with Josh Todd? You gotta be kiddin'. The studios realised he was prime 'throb' material for boys and girls, an acceptable poster to have in either sex dorm without being labelled, like the one of James Dean in his leathers in *Rebel Without a Cause*: all misunderstood, lip-slouching sex appeal.

Poor Josh, he'd set off too early in his search for Mom, just as she had been wandering back again, determined to do right, too late; she was always too late. Once again they had missed each other. By the time she had tracked him down, written to countless TV stations that he'd appeared on, film companies and finally his agent, he didn't want to know. Josh had found the stardom she'd always wanted, wanted so badly that she'd left him to fight, dance, sing, act, sleep her way to it. He felt she'd only ever come back because of her failure, not because of her children. Not out of love of them, never for him. It didn't matter how much her almond eyes had pleaded to Josh, her 'big boy', and 'lil' Tommy', that she loved them, that she was doin' this for them, as she packed herself up off to that mystery part in the sky, promising that it would reunite them, make their dreams come true. She always left, no matter what she said, in the end they were only words.

Now Josh had what his mother had always wanted, he wasn't sharing any of it with her, after all she hadn't stayed when he'd begged her to. Begged, cried and clung to her skirt, hidden her suitcase and followed her to the bus station, she telling them all the while she had to go, that it was going to be good for them. He didn't believe her. It was good for them her being there, but she had never been able to see that.

Josh Todd was now a man, a grown-up, thirty years old. He didn't have to give anything to nobody that he didn't want to, these days, and why the heck should he? He'd worked for it all himself. His brother had died in a motorcycle accident bombed out of his mescal worm-soaked brain, squashed across some nowhere highway. His grandmother had died from the shock of the news, not that Josh had cared for her or her beatings. He didn't like his mother, but he liked his mean grandmother even less. Now there was just his mother left, alone in the house he'd grown up in. Josh knew that, she'd written to tell him so, another moanin' self-pityin' letter. He'd replied once, sent a postcard from Paris, a place his mom used to tell them they'd go to some day. 'When I'm rich and famous, it'll be Paris one day, London the next. How'd ya like that, boys!' and her face would light up with the imaginary wonder of it all, before growing dull, focusing back on their dirt poor reality.

The postcard he sent was a black and white 1950s photograph of a busy Parisian street with a handsome boy and girl caught in a moment of passion, kissing. Josh had bought it outside the Pompidou Centre with Sarah Jane, and had secretly posted it after writing in bold handwriting on the back in a gold pen – 'SUCK IT! Yours as ever, Josh.'

He hadn't finished punishing her. He wanted to send her a wedding photo too.

Josh had told Sarah Jane that he was an orphan, that his family had died in a car crash and that he'd been brought up alone by his grandmother, now also sadly dead. It made life less complicated, more sympathetic. She never touched on the subject since Josh had first told her, it was too embarrassing, like talking about cancer or AIDS to sufferers. At least Sarah Jane wouldn't have her own family back in LA, thought Josh. That was the advantage of a foreign wife. She could always go home alone and visit and they would wish he had come too, he'd always be so charming. But how could he? He was a moviestar, a busy man.

Josh was keen that everybody should like him. He made it his business to win everybody around. It was part of his job and he was good at it, even if it meant he had to talk to David again. He didn't need to talk to Sarah Jane, Sarah Jane was his. He got no response from the girl he'd slept with, though he'd put in an effort – halfway through dinner he'd asked her about her paintings and all he got was this kind of blank, dead response. Weird, you sleep with someone, you'd at least expect they'd be able to talk to you a week later!

He hadn't got that response from Catherine when he'd asked to make a long-distance call, 'somewhere quiet, to do with work'. Of course he didn't need to make the call, but she knew that. She'd led him up alone to her small study at the top of the house where nothing could be heard from the party. As they stepped inside the room the opportunity was there, so he pressed her to the back of the door, lifted her dress with his hand and felt up the smoothness of her stockinged leg to the naked flesh of her thigh and kissed her everywhere but her mouth. The lipstick had to stay intact. He was sure she could feel his erection pressing hard in his jeans when he rubbed against her hip bone for some small relief, but it only brought greater discomfort when she said, 'No.'

'Waddaya mean, "No"!' Josh replied in disbelief, but persisted. 'Are you sure?'

Firmly and finally, Catherine pushed his tongue from her ear. 'No more. Not for now. We can save it for another day, per-haps . . .' Then she left him teasingly, slipped back downstairs, unruffling herself, suppressing her amusement in the hall mirror as she went past.

Josh was left with the phone and his desire to get her back, her smell was in his nose and he wanted more. He rang his assistant who called the Portobello Hotel and booked a room for the next day and then called his agent in LA, for a chat.

David, alone in his study with his Cuban cigar and full brandy glass, was hiding away from the party. He switched off his computer and pulled out his school photo album, until he couldn't stand the worst of the memories leaping up at him. He closed one book and opened the next. His university days were better and the photos were in colour. Photos of girls in floral dresses with blonde hair, drawn like net curtains across their faces, eyes enticingly wide-lashed peeping through to the glint of sunlight. Pictures of picnics down the river. Henry Montague stuck mid-punt as the boat drifted away with only the water left as his fate, always made

David chuckle. 'Classic,' he murmured. Henry was a QC now. Sally and Lucinda uniformly Laura Ashley-ed into a field of wild flowers. Later drunk, half-naked pictures of them taken in the name of art and Sam Haskin's, breasts and hands and half-bitten apples in a blur of his own sensual confusion.

Going to Cambridge at the age of eighteen after fourteen years of boys-only boarding was like being put into a free chocolate factory at the age of seven with no rules. His hands weren't slapped away in rebuke each time he felt for a breast, like Nanny did when he grabbed for cake at tea-time during the holidays. Holidays full of empty cold houses in Scotland, summer and winter, no different from school. At least at school when you wet the bed Nanny wasn't there to tie you to the wet mattress for the rest of the night, and when you told Mummy she shouted and didn't believe you.

At least at school there were boys you could jump into bed with when the overwhelming cold sadness swept over you. When even Teddy was not enough to cry against, badly missing something to cling to in the dark. The need for physical warmth and a full belly when all you could feel were iced toes and the empty rumbling of your stomach growling in rebuke. Pretending the growls were Teddy talking, turning pain into comfort with all the courage needed to stop the tears rolling. David had tried to be brave from the age of four. Brave in the way they taught you at school. He had bullied as he'd been bullied, shown compassion in the way he comforted the younger boys, stopped himself up from showing any other emotion apart from the rallying cry of comradeship.

David was brave, as brave as they come. By the age of six he was calling his mummy 'Mother' and shaking her smartly by the hand on departing at the station – look no tears – stepping into the train carriage back to school for another long term away where they would make him a real man along with the other short-trousered recruits, used to waking on winter mornings with frost over their grey bed blankets.

University was different. University had been wonderful. Full of frightening excitements with girls. Lucinda had placed his hand into her unknown pocket of damp warmth that had made him want to run and squeal and never touch a woman again. When she had pressed her nipple into his mouth, he had spat it out with disgust and had had to placate her by saying he had a hair in his mouth.

Even with all her kindness and availability Lucinda had too much flesh for David, was too ripe and pink and round. Worse, she was demanding and coarse and laughed at his erections, more still at his inability to keep one, made fun of his accent when she'd already down-graded hers. He wasn't surprised she became a Labour activist. He'd never been good at accents, not even his own.

Sally had been easier, quieter, shy. He could control Sally, put her face to the pillow and reach ecstasy whilst clutching at her bony shoulders, his hairy rugby stomach collapsing upon her skinny back and mewing cries. David could be a man to Sally, but he couldn't love her. Cruel Lucinda held his heart in her tiger's mouth and lipstick smile, but he couldn't fuck her.

When David had met Catherine there was a flash of recognition, something of the Lucinda about her, but she was passive when they made love. When he was buried inside her he could believe that he was king in her land, that he wasn't borrowing her body, she was giving it to him. Of course, they had both been very drunk the first time and he wasn't completely sure she'd been conscious, but it had been good for him, he knew that. Later when she had tried to assert herself in the bedroom he had held her down and shouted, 'Don't,' so she hadn't. Their intimacy was all unspoken. He was afraid that if he told her his feelings it would be like snitching on your birthday wishes before they had a chance to come true. He was afraid of being laughed at, he was too brave not to be scared. He told her he loved her, that was as far as he could go. 'Catherine, I love you,' he'd said on the day he proposed and it was true, as much as he could, but he could never tell her why, he didn't know. Now he couldn't say it to anyone any more, not to his wife Catherine, not to his son Benjamin, not to his daughter Augusta, and certainly not to himself. Things had gone bad somewhere among the tangled knotted tackle of his life, or perhaps they had always been that way.

He flipped the album closed, puffed on the expensive fatness between his lips and took another gulp of brandy down to hit the spot, to warm his heart. 'Ahh, that's better,' he said, and shut his eyes on the empty room. Brandy was the only thing that could fill the mysterious sense of loss, full to forgetting.

CHAPTER TWELVE

'You can't go now. It's too early Honor, stay and have another drink,' Catherine said adding in a conspiratorial whisper, 'and you haven't told me anything about Jeremy. What happened?'

They drifted away from the table together, Catherine's lean arm linked through Honor's, a bony shoulder pressed to fleshiness, heads conspiratorially bowed in whispered giggles.

'So there's nothing much to tell I'm afraid. I mean, no juicy bits of gossip to salivate over.' But once again Honor had ended up telling her all about her dinner date of expensive doom, although she didn't tell her about the kiss.

'What do you mean? I think that's very juicy, Jeremy's finally proposed to set you up in style and you didn't jump into bed with him. Just not jumping into bed with him would merit gossip. Can't you hear it now, "Extra, extra, Honor went out with a man and didn't date-rape him, shock horror." '

'Oh stop it, Catherine. You make me sound like some voracious sex vampire. That reputation's ancient history. For God's sake it's pre-Jack, a man's tool is a screwdriver in our flat, and the closest I get to "hot and steamy" is a bath, if the boiler's working.'

'Ahh poor old Honor, my heart bleeds for you. You really do get a rough deal don't you, only leaving with the most gorgeous man in the place. And if you try to tell me that the simmering pot of sex isn't going to get to boiling point . . . either you're a far sadder case than we realised, or I don't believe you. I want full reports in the morning, on my desk in an essay not less than five hundred words on "why the highland fling is more than just a dance and what's traditionally worn under a kilt", Miss Summers!'

'Ha ha ha, wouldn't you like to know. What about the new young Picasso?'

'Here, quick, come up to my study and have a look at these before you leave.' Catherine hustled Honor up the stairs and brought out a couple of paintings for her to look at.

'Aren't they great. I just love his use of colour.'

'Erhuh? And what else? I thought you were smuggling me up the stairs to show me a picture of him!'

'Okay, okay. I thought I'd show you my "I'm a serious art dealer" mode first but since you insist, Philistine, I think I might have a Polaroid of him in his studio. There, how d'you like that huh! Serious beefcake, eight-pack as Gussy would say!'

'Catherine I only wanted to see his face! Very serious beefcake. I'm sure you'll be able to make a huge amount of money out of his wares, with or without the painting. Have you ever thought about running a male brothel? You seem to have a natural eye for it.'

'I'm obviously not selling any of his stuff to you am I? The plus of being a good-looking artist is you get to personally show to the wives of your clients. A certain dealer I know does all his deals via the wives' bedrooms, it's all selling in the end, sex, art, crockery. And being his dealer I've got to test the goods first. The problem is when the husbands have the final say.'

'Of course. Married sex getting a bit dull these days is it? I hope you've warned your sister. On the other hand she looked like she already found out this evening. What was up with her?'

Catherine shrugged her shoulders and started to move back down the stairs towards the front door as she listened to Honor prattling on.

'But Josh is gorgeous, I didn't think he'd be so nice, easy to talk to, I mean genuinely sweet. I'm sure they'll be happy together; maybe she's just PMT-ing.'

'Oh I don't know, the whole thing's beyond me,' Catherine responded because she felt it was expected. 'Anyway Honor, thanks for coming, I'll speak to you soon, okay.' Catherine brushed the conversation to a close and kissed a perplexed Honor goodbye in the hall.

'Thanks for a great evening and for making it all so easy with Harry. Talking of which, I'll fax the essay.' She winked at Catherine and laughed.

Catherine turned, only just managing a smile. She didn't want anyone analysing her sister's predicament, knowing herself was humiliating enough, yet another warped relationship for the family album. How could any relationship be normal and happy? But then wasn't it only ever a matter of perception: what was joyous for one could be hell for the other? Pay your price, take your ticket.

Catherine had married during the Thatcher years with their obsession with choice; the higher the price the better the ride, the happier you would feel. That was the idea that Catherine had bought, but now she often felt cheated at the high cost of this arrangement.

Even Honor seems happier than all the rest of us these days, even before Harry... I must ask Gem what's up. Catherine thought her way back to the dining room, busying her mind, preoccupying herself with others' lives.

'Ah ha Honor, here you are. I was afraid I'd lost you in this big house or you'd left without me.'

'But Harry you're my chauffeur, I couldn't leave without you.'

'It's sad to think that's all I am to you, but what a kind employer you are to invite your staff to sit with you at dinner. I see I'm in no position to complain.'

'I should certainly hope not!' Honor replied, her face wreathed with happiness. They stood looking at each other, standing by the front door, eyes linked, holding hands, smiles bouncing between them.

'Shall we go, madam?' Harry asked formally, head bowing, eyes lowering as he opened the door.

'Yes, I don't see why not. Home James,' she instructed and as they walked to the car she clicked her heels in the air Gene Kelly-style, heliumed with the wine and attention. Life was grand.

Harry opened the car door for her and she slid into the shiny leather of his old Jaguar. He waited to close the door before getting into the car himself. A proper chauffeur.

'Really I should be sitting in the back, if you are to have any respect for me.'

'But I have already Honor. With a name like that, who couldn't?' He lifted her hand to his lips.

That moment. If she could freeze-frame that moment of feeling and being, bottle it to sell, she could be a millionaire in moments. For dreams can be as thick with the scent of longing as the leather seating in an old car. Brimful with anticipation, excitement, goose-pimply shivers, erotic quivers and butterfly-stomach joy. Expectation of the wonderful. 'Connected Intimacy', the concentrated essence. A new aromatherapy perfume by Honor Summers. Who wouldn't pay over the odds for that feeling?

Harry was slowly kissing with his warm dry mouth, gently up her bare arm, to the top of her shoulder, along her collar bone, through to her ear, across her jaw bone before landing to nibble the corner of her mouth.

'Mmmmm,' she giggled. 'I feel like a tray of hors d'oeuvres you can't decide upon.'

'That is because I haven't tasted the most delicious delicacy yet.' He grabbed her tongue with his teeth, sucking it deep into his mouth. She could feel her muscles straining, she could feel his fingers rubbing at her nipple and all her pleasure.

'Where's Honor and Harry? Have they disappeared already for an "early night" by any chance?'

'Yes, she tried to find you Gem, you must have been in the loo. She said bye to me.'

'Oh well I guess I should be going home too, work and all that in the morning.'

'Don't be a spoilsport, it's not even twelve and look what Josh brought which I've just discovered in the fridge. Vintage Dom Perignon, we can't let that go to waste.'

'But Catherine, whenever you drink it, it won't be going to waste,' said Josh, suddenly behind her.

'Brother-in-laws say the nicest things. It's almost worth losing a sister for.' There must be no suspicion before she had executed her plan.

'Oh my dearest sister, how could I leave you? You'll be able to come and stay whenever you like, I'll have the best sofa permanently made up for you,' said Sarah Jane drunkenly.

'That's a good enough reason for opening the bottle, someone get the glasses. Let's hear it for "the sofa". May I always deserve the best.'

'What about to the bride and groom?' added Gregorio.

'To the bride and groom, otherwise known as Sarah Jane and Josh, may they languish in the pool of happiness for always without creasing up like prunes.'

'Getting a bit purple aren't we?'

'Thank you, Gem. I thought you appreciated me, but now I can tell. I give a dinner and all I get is a sofa and lit-chick-crit on my aspirations. Charming.'

'Talking of appreciation, where's David appreciating?' said Sarah Jane.

'David doesn't and won't! Probably calling a credit card sex line for kicks.'

'Yeah, that sounds fun. Let's go join him?' said Gregorio enthusiastically, rising from his chair, glass unsteadily in his hand.

'You poor sad fuck. You would wouldn't you?' Gem unleashed some of her vitriol on to Gregorio.

'Why else do you think I'm such an impoverished scenic painter? Men of my status are rich when not tied to the chains of the sex telephone line, addicted to heavy breathing. Call me Camilla, call me Camilla.'

'Okay, Camilla. What a date!'

'Do you know that wonderful romantic Righteous Brothers' song, "You've lost that flat in Ealing, ohohwo with the leaky ceiling, bring back that flat in Ealing. Now it's gone gone gone ohwowo.'

'What are you talking about, I can't call it singing?'

'Do you really think I'm looking manly tonight, Gem? I rather hoped that the pink flowers on my dress rather showed up the feminine in me,' he said fingering his black velvet jacket.

'Of course it does. I'm just talking about the way your hair pokes through your lace tights, have you heard of Immac, from one girl to another.'

The drunken banter continued defusing the nastiness that Gem had been cultivating internally. Easy laughter at last circulated around the table until the interruption of the CD's boom, extra-loud opening bars of 'Hey, Big Spender'. And Sarah Jane was up, dancing on the chairs and climbing over the table, unzipping, flinging and singing, bare flesh to the wind, the evening's cabaret unleashed.

Josh sat there, an amused mask upon his pursed lips, Gregorio was wide-eyed in hope. Catherine and Gem, well used to the display, joined in the singing and drank another glass, Gem's annoyance fizzling away with the champagne bubbles.

'For Christ's sake! Can't you turn this noise down?'

'David! Just in time for the cabaret. A little champagne?'

He wavered towards Catherine, his hair flopped down his forehead, his eyelids at half-mast. Another glass of champagne was something he didn't look like he needed, but he cocked his almost empty brandy glass in anticipation and heavily plonked his hand down on his wife's knee, to steady his collapse to a chair.

'Been at the study supplies, dear?'

'Your sister showing off her tired old minge again, dear?'

Catherine gave his smiling face a withering glance that Gem had the misfortune to turn around and catch, but David didn't even notice. The gold stars glinted on the dining-room ceiling in a pretence of heaven but it wasn't worth staying in. What price the hand-crafted table and individually made chairs with the quiet aggression that raged across them?

The number finished and Gem got up. It was making her depressed. This scene of drunken jollity suddenly seemed forced. Gregorio regretfully followed. He was having fun, male bonding with Josh, moviestar, mate for a night, let's pretend a lifetime's friendship.

'Spread your wings and fly to Daddy . . .' The music went on.

Sarah Jane squirmed on Josh's lap in delight, half-naked and visibly G-stringed. 'Time to go home. Get your clothes on babe,' he said brusquely, noticing that Catherine didn't strip in public.

'Oh Daddy!' She wriggled back, unwilling to leave his lap without knowing she provoked his hardness. A hardness he'd prefer to use on Catherine.

'Bye all. Thanks for a great dinner, Catherine, Sarah Jane, David. Nice to meet you Josh. See you at the weeding,' Gem said in as normal a voice as she could manage then. She couldn't get out of the house fast enough. Gregorio on her tail, she ran down the hall and out the door.

'Wait for me Gem. You're not training for the Olympics are you? Share a cab?'

She was on the Fulham Road by the time Gregorio caught up with her. She'd run down the street, hair flying, heels clicking, breath panting. Her mind was a mess of contradictions, what she should have done, what she wished she had. Gem wanted to lie down in the street, preferably under a passing car. She felt stained with shame, full up with disgust. Then Gregorio was at her side, solid and smiling concern, his glasses tipped too far down his nose, his arm pulled through hers, steadying him, slowing her.

Gregorio was drunk, Gem was mad, a perfect couple in their crazed states.

They walked along silently, joined in their isolation. Gregorio, because he didn't know what to say, waited with worried glances for Gem to speak. He knew he couldn't talk until she did. He could've said a million things, comments on the cafés, bars, supermarkets and restaurants still open. Clubs just getting going for the trust-fund babies slumming it from Notting Hill, back to the 'burbs of Chelsea, or just home for the weekend from school. Gold spike heels and sugar-pink mini-skirts, angora sweaters with bare brown tummies, leather jeans in biker boots, hot pants and floppy hats, the boys all in jeans.

Gem's attention was drawn to a girl just like Gussy – it couldn't be.

'Makes you feel old, doesn't it?' she said.

'Gives you an appetite too.'

'Gregorio Humbert Humbert!'

'What? Did he feel the same way about walking? I'm starving. I think it's time to get a cab, these legs of mine won't go the distance, not to Kentish Town at least. I'll drop you off in Camden. Are we going in the right direction?'

As the cab got near to Gem's road, Gregorio leaned over to Gem in readiness to kiss her, but all she offered was a polite peck.

'I suppose a fuck's out of the question then?'

'Sorry Greggy babe. Nice try, wrong night. Maybe another time, huh?'

'You mean you don't want to take me home?' he self-mocked pitifully.

'Nope, I know I'll regret it but . . .'

'What was going on there tonight?' he asked, serious for a moment.

'Oh, nothing, everything. Another boring long story.' She reached to hold his hand, squeezing it. 'Maybe I'll tell. I need to be alone to get stuff straight.'

'I vant to be alone. I don't know that feeling. Can I call you?'

'Sure. Go to the pictures sometime. Night, night. Thanks for coming.' Gem jumped out of the cab and offered some money to Gregorio.

'No need. Thanks for inviting me. I'll have to go home and ring up all my friends to tell them how I asked myself to stay at Josh Todd's place in LA. And since you won't sleep with me, I'll tell them it's your fault I've woken them. Sleep tight gorgeous.'

She smiled sadly back at him and waved. At last I can cry, sniffed Gem sifting her bag for keys and a hankie.

CHAPTER THIRTEEN

Gem spent the night sleeping in her tears. The following day she wept from one room to the next, so consumed with grief she never even thought about food. If somebody had mentioned a Triple Brownie Overload to her, she wouldn't have known what they were talking about, almost like a normal person.

Looking at her sleep-fraught face and her wealed cheeks in the bathroom mirror, she didn't hold a clue how she was supposed to get out of the house and meet the world. Her exterior might have looked hideous, but inside she felt a little better; calmer, stronger.

The last two nights had been an all-time gutter low, she was amazed that she had survived the ordeal of Catherine's dinner, but she had had no other choice than to bury the secret. Getting home had been a wonderful relief of sodden indulgence, more grief-stricken than the day of Princess Diana's funeral. What was she mourning for? Everything, and by the end of the next day everyone, including her mother and father. She had a grain of compassion for even their sad lives, as compared to a bucketful for her own. Then she had slept one of those heavy unmoving sleeps of sedative quiet for the whole night.

It felt to Gem as though she'd been on one of those EST courses, confronting all her miseries, followed by a colonic irrigation to rid herself of the shit and toxins that had been poisoning her system. Light-headed with relief, her thoughts still darted back to the bed with its familiar, warm comfort, the blankets dampened by despair, but now the passages were unblocked she couldn't go back. Besides the sun was shining and she had too many things to do on this Monday morning, and she was a responsible professional. However much she'd let herself down she couldn't do it to others. Appointments and work beckoned.

The light streamed through the long rectangular windows of her living/workroom. Her wooden floorboards gleamed and the dust danced and glided in its spotlight. It was one of those mornings that was rushing towards the sun, too warm too soon but filled with possibilities. No day to remain inactive and self-obsessed, even Gem couldn't resist it. Did that mean she wasn't really a manic depressive, if she couldn't sustain her misery in the face of just one sunny day? Not trying hard enough, slacking on the job of her sorrow.

Gem laughed at the thoughts that meandered through her brain as she filled the kettle up, always a reassuring sound, thundering water against the metal like a mini hydro-electric plant. She got a clean cup out of the cupboard, an oversize *café au lait* cup for dipping forbidden croissants in, and instead put in one camomile and one peppermint tea bag, winding the annoying tags and string around the handle so they wouldn't jump in when she poured the water on top. Then she turned to her music deck, she felt ready for something uplifting, and pressed play on the CD already installed – bad move, she didn't look first and the mournful strings of *Ella sings Cole*, 'I've got you under my skin', hit her.

'. . . Don't you know little fool you never can win . . .' She certainly didn't need to be reminded of that! She switched it to tape and Mama Cass.

'Worn-out phrases and longing gazes won't get you where you want to go, NO . . .' And by the time she'd showered and was plastering the foundation across her face she was jauntily singing along to 'I'm in with the in-crowd'. It didn't do much for the make-up around her eyes, but perhaps being outside with a large pair of dark glasses would even things out. She went and checked in her *Beauty Bible* what to do about the dark purplish-green bags. Fresh air seemed to be the only answer when walking around with wet teabags in place wasn't convenient. An extra spray of Mitsuko by Guerlain; now that always helped.

Schlepping around the West End with her portfolio, Gem was seeing magazines for illustrating work, film art directors for backdrops and, last on her list, something Gem had been daring herself to do for ages, a gallery. A real live art gallery. She'd been picky about who she'd approach, she wasn't going to show her work to just anyone! She had to approve of the work they exhibited first. It was all fear and trepidation really. How to be stolid enough to bear criticism, how to cope with rejection, not take it personally. With backdrops and illustration it didn't matter, it wasn't close to her heart, but her painting, that felt like she'd used her blood and moved it around the canvas with her organs. They were her babies, not experiments in colour and form, patterns to ease the eye or things to fill up a wall. Sometimes she looked back through them huddled behind the sofa – the ones she most cared about she couldn't bear to have on display – and they would take her back, like time-pockets, to how she had been when she was painting them. Gem was always sensitive about her paintings.

She chose Hal Gums behind Carnaby Street. There was a brilliant exhibition of distortedly surreal naked human sculpture that she was happy to look at whilst waiting.

The receptionist swivelled her chair away from Gem's gaze and whispering audibly, wound up her call holding on to the tight string of pearls about her neck. Gem looked away and tried not to listen to the smooching giggles.

'Yes? Can I help you?' Suddenly the efficient sugar-pink lipsticked mouth spoke.

'Yes, I hope so. I've an appointment with Mr Gums, my name's Gem Daley.'

The receptionist gave Gemma a look up and down, her knee-high boots, lederhosen hot pants and wide-collared shirt with Heidi plaits didn't impress. How hard these poor art students try, she thought.

'Well, there's nothing in the book, of course he might have forgotten to tell me, but anyway he's out for lunch. You could always wait, what was it about?'

'I was bringing some of my slides over to show him.'

'You could leave them here if you don't want to wait.'

'Well I don't know. I don't like leaving my work . . .'

'I'll make sure he sees them. You can call in the morning and speak to him.'

For the first time Gem left something precious in the hands of someone she didn't know. She often left her body in the hands of unknown strangers but never her paintings. She was in a more intimate relationship with this receptionist than she was with most sexual partners.

'You don't think I could leave the whole of my portfolio here and come back in an hour, I know it's an awful lot to ask but my arm's almost breaking off.'

'I don't see why not if you put it at the back there.' The receptionist liked being asked for such small favours, it made her feel good saying yes.

'Thank you, you're so kind.'

'Don't mention it,' the receptionist said and smiled such a lovely warm smile, that Gem felt cruel for silently judging her velvet hairband.

'I'll see you later then, and thanks again.' Gem smiled back and even waved as she passed around the outside.

Unshackled from her portfolio she felt strangely self-conscious without her purpose, her prop shield in hand, and nothing to do but window shop, maybe have a coffee. She wasn't buying anything, not unless her work got accepted, and then she would reward herself with a new dress and some sunglasses. Though the day had already given her two commissions and one maybe, all she now demanded was the cherry on the top. Trolling down New-burgh Street, John Richmond, The Dispensary, Jess James' jewel-lery, Liberty in the distance, maybe she'd go and buy something for her mum. Gem was just pushing through the doors when she felt a heavy hand descend upon her shoulders.

'Modom I have reason to believe you've been selling yourself around our premises . . . How are you, you old tart?'

Gem turned around to see Honor smirking in front of her. 'Honor, how lovely to see you, are you going in here?'

'That was the general idea.'

'Will they let bag women into this exclusive store? When was the last time you had a bath, you shag bucket? I can smell the heavy mysterious scent of sex on your skin,' she smiled back giving her a hug.

'Oh shut up. That's rubbish. Can you?' Honor felt suddenly insecure, she'd always wondered if people could smell and tell. Bus conductors or hall porters who saw you every day must notice the difference. Was that how milkmen got lucky?

'You say you not sex with the Scotsman, woman?' said Gem in a silly badgering Eastern accent, linking her arm with Honor's as they walked through the bustling foyer of jewellery and scarves.

'With the newspaper? Neither with it or with him; everything but. I think we're saving it for the wedding night so we can trail the streets with the newly bloodied sheets – Moroccan style.'

'Will you be requiring a handmaiden to daub ketchup, otherwise I hate to think about his penetration techniques where you're concerned. Has he got spikes on it? Where are we going woman? To the glassware dept. Why we go here?' Gem was playing the irate foreigner, perplexed to have found herself led down the stairs to an avenue of fancy-shaped glass.

'Aren't we here to buy the happy couple due to be wed, a pressy?'

'You might be doing that, I'd completely forgotten. I was just here to kill an hour whilst my portfolio's being perused for a major West End exhibition,' Gem replied subtly, her confidence crisis over. 'I thought I'd buy Mother a gift, you know, anything with Liberty written on it will impress.'

'Hey Gem, well done on braving the gallery! I'd be impressed if Jack ever bought me anything written on, let alone Liberty. Be careful, your daughters might say the same about you one day.'

'Nothing definite but it's worth a go. They've got to show and sell somebody's pictures this year so why shouldn't they be mine? Anyway, I'm not having a daughter, only great big hulking sons to carry my basket from the laundromat. They will guard, care for and revere me, as well as my canvases.'

'What, you mean like Jack does for me? Get a life Gem.'

'Hhmm nice idea, do they sell them here?'

'I remember once seeing some in the hardware department.'

'Do you think they ever come up as sale items?'

'Most definitely, mine was from the reject department, up until this month – now I feel like I've upgraded to Fortnum's!' It was Honor's turn to be smug.

'Lucky you! Honor, just a thought but do you think we should be buying glass as a wedding gift for people who'll be living in America?'

They had walked through the hall of handmade glasses and were rounding the corner into the beautiful bright swirls of the Venetian section.

'No, but everyone who lives in LA loves Liberty and I couldn't see a scarf that Josh and Sarah Jane wouldn't fight over. Is your mum from there?'

'Richmond actually. LA, and I might want to go home. I think

I'm going to give them a painting as a wedding present, a Gem original.'

'You see you're so lucky you can do that, I can't exactly make a Lancashire hot pot for them to take on the plane. Anyway, what do you buy the couple who have everything? It's futile, battling to keep up with the Todds.'

'And that from the lips of someone who's got twenty-four-hour drape-a-man!'

'I think the grapevine's turned into an intercom service.'

'Always was. Are you going to tell us the story of when Jerry met Harry?'

'It's not worth discussing the muddle at the moment. For the record Jeremy hasn't met Harry and won't. Anyway the number of men hanging about is no measure of a woman's happiness, is it Gem?'

'Spoken like a true *Spare Rib* girl, that's the spirit. Let's go and have a coffee and discuss getting the vote. And you can't get them that vase. It's hideous and costs a fortune!' Gem didn't mean it but she could see the road Honor was on, and knew she couldn't afford it. Things were always so tight for her and Jack, it would mean them going without for a present that might break or not be appreciated. Gem had a plan.

'Got any better ideas?' Honor felt miserably poor.

'Yes, I've one. You get the table, I'll get the coffee and I'll tell you.'

They made a strange pair in their arty clothes, Lederhosen Gem attracting wandering glances, and Honor in jeans, cowboy boots and Tammy Wynette tie-at-the-waist gingham shirt; the Hollywood/Austria alliance. What the making of *The Sound of Music* must have looked like, the antithesis of the current Camden look, druggy waifs straining in their spiked stilettos. They were eighties art-student leftovers.

Gem brought the coffee over to Honor sitting at one of the tasteful wipe-clean floral-covered tables. She neoned out amongst the Nicole Fahri-clad women meeting for shop and tea, all this season's colours beautifully in place, not a drop-hem between them, in fact not so different from Catherine. No safety pins hiding unsightly holes or hastily patched garments like those Honor wore.

'What's the idea then? It's got to be quick. I haven't got all day,

I've got to go and collect Jack from judo at five,' said Honor, watching Gem get her manic health nibbles out, some creased and worn dried apricots. 'No thanks, I'll go get some chocolate cake.'

'Are you sure?' she offered. 'You've got loads of time, it's only half past three. Listen this is what we do for Sarah Jane. We buy a posh leather-bound large blank notebook here and we do a personal cookbook, you provide the recipes and I do the illustrations.'

'Sarah Jane's never known how to boil an egg and won't they have a cook there?'

'So, she'll be able to give it to the cook to remind her of home and the delights of Modern British.'

'You're right, brilliant. Great, I can use my evening course calligraphic technique!'

'Is that a new way to make soup? They'll have to be tried and tested.'

'I try and test them every day Gem. Strange to think people pay to be my guinea pigs, but I am a bit rusty on boiling eggs, as if you ever eat anyway. It's good to see you happier than the other night, weren't you feeling well?'

'Not terrific, out of sorts with the world. Did I spoil it all?' asked Gem sadly.

'Poor you. No, it was fine, nobody noticed you were there, honestly.'

'Thanks a bunch. Gregorio noticed. Well he noticed in the cab on the way home, unless he mistook me for you, actually that's possible. He did say, "I suppose a fuck's out of the question?"' Gem imitated a drunken, slurring Gregorio.

Honor laughed, spluttering into her coffee. 'He didn't really, did he? What did you say?'

'What do you think! No, of course.'

'Ahh you can't fool me, I hear Gem's wild woman of wonga's come out.'

'Oh yeah sure. I said to Gregorio, "Gregorio," I said, "fancy me vomiting over you tonight darling," and he said, "Love it doll." Anyway I had my period.'

'Gem, I don't know if you noticed but you're not talking to your mother or a man, it's Honor here and we all know having your period makes no difference, except it makes you hornier, and it can be messier than a butcher's shop.'

They both broke into girlish laughter, exaggerated by the looks from the next table, who were trying to edge their seats away from the distasteful conversation. Not what they wanted to listen to while sipping their Earl Grey. Not the ticket at all. The girls sighed back in their chairs, legs stretched out before them.

'So when are we going to start on the great manuscript?'

'Tomorrow night, when you're back from work?'

'I could do it for a bit, I've got to go out for dinner. Fancy baby-sitting?'

'Yeah, don't see why not if we do a couple of hours first and I get to watch Jack's Disney video collection. It'll be good exercise for me, cycling Camden to Bayswater and back. Got to get some new ideas for paintings from somewhere for my show. Who are you dating, anyone I can be jealous about? Not that I'm not already, anyway you don't need to date, you've got a kid already.'

'It's true I only ever date to get pregnant! I'm embarrassed to tell you in case you refuse to baby-sit on moral grounds.'

'Oh you mean you're seeing Jeremy. Again?'

'How did you know? That ratbag Catherine's intercom service, huh?'

'And you know I think she did a mail-out special for that bit, I tried to get her to buy a full page ad in *The Sunday Times* to announce it but she said David was being a bit tight this month. It's not my business I know, but why? With the nice Celt drooling after you?'

'No, I haven't done the business but even if I do it's not committing me to anything other than a night of sensual delight and a chance to throw him out of my bed at three in the morning so Jack doesn't see him there.'

'God forbid Honor,' said Gem vehemently, raising her voice, 'that your son should find out you're sleeping with his father, where would it all end?'

'Where indeed! Can you keep your voice down? Let us say I'm perusing the contract of an offer. It's difficult. Everything says I should make a stab at patching it up with Jeremy because he's Jack's dad and we never made a proper try at it. He seems changed. I guess I am too. It wouldn't be the same as last time. He was stressed out from exams and the baby. It wasn't all his fault, I was a mess too!'

'Stand by your man! You can't seriously believe that you could forgive somebody who walked out on you when Jack was just a baby, and never even offered to help you. He was an out and out shit, sleeping with other women, and he used to hit you, have you forgotten all that?'

'What do you mean sleeping with other women? Gem, what do you mean?' Honor was truly shocked.

Gem had always assumed that Honor must have known about Jeremy's infidelities; he'd been so blatant. Honor only had to go into the loo and his hand would be on your breast. 'You know, Honor, that he slept with Helen and Basia and that other small blonde friend of yours. You knew that, come on you knew!'

But it was becoming quickly clear to a panicking Gem that Honor hadn't known anything of the sort and that Gem had just opened a ripe tin of maggots for their afternoon tea; as good a time as any to let the truth hatch and fly.

CHAPTER FOURTEEN

Catherine was in a cab sailing through the park past the Serpentine towards Notting Hill, not the most direct route but it was a sunny day and she was early. It was Tuesday morning, hitting lunch-time, she knew her destination held treats and her stomach gurgled with excitement. Lunch had been ordered, Beluga caviar, blinis, Scotch smoked salmon, cream cheese, rye bagels and champagne. The champagne sat in an ice bucket waiting to be popped, a small jug of lemon juice and some thickly frozen Stolichnaya vodka sat at its side. For pudding there would be Baccis, little Italian chocolate kisses with hazelnuts buried within and messages of love written in four languages snug in the foil that wrapped them.

Sarah Jane had got on the train to Hampshire that morning, to stay with her mother to discuss final wedding plans and iron out the last-minute panics. All of her mother's making but it seemed as if Sarah Jane was the only one whose presence would placate her; besides she had been summoned by her step-father: 'If we're paying for the bloody thing you can damn well turn up when your mother says so!' No such thing as a free wedding, not from He-Who-Must-Be-Obeyed. She was hungover from last night, bored on the train, she'd ring Josh on her new mobile, that he insisted she always have with her so he could get hold of her.

She'd left him only a couple of hours before after a night of frenzied passion, but an unease suggested it was all hers. She'd tentatively asked if there was anything wrong and he'd used the usual excuse of drugs, too much coke. There was no answer, the desk said he had left half an hour before. She'd ring on his mobile.

Catherine had decided not to take the car, she had told David that she was going on the train out of town, somewhere near Guildford and wanted to do some work on the way; besides she was taking an artist out to lunch, she didn't want to drink and drive. She hoped he wouldn't ask about it later, pushing her to make up some rural lie about leaves on the line.

The truth was, she didn't want to drink and drive, or have her car spotted parked outside the Portobello Hotel. Taxis were anonymous, and sexy, thought Catherine running her hand along the long length of her thigh, she could feel the bump of her suspenders beneath the silk jersey knit of her dress, could feel their tautness across the back of her thighs. She was concentrating her thoughts, making herself thrum with sexual energy, even the taxi driver sensed something. Must be a hooker in the back, he thought.

The taxi pulled to a slammed halt that jolted Catherine back to daylight. They were there. She found her bag, the money within it and gave a generous tip, saying, 'Keep the change.'

Predictably generous, the cabby thought, well you wouldn't want to keep hold of that kind of dirty money when you're the local posh bike. Guilt tip, she knew I knew.

Catherine was thinking, I must get rid of this irritating loose change rattling around my bag. Looking for condoms amongst it wouldn't be very sexy. Giving the cabby an ingratiating smile, she sailed forth into the foyer.

'I believe Mr Smith has booked a room?'

'Of course Mrs Smith, he hasn't arrived yet, but he rang and said you should go up. Can I show you the way?'

'Thank you, that's very kind of you,' she smiled walking up the stairs feeling her skin tingle with anticipation and her assiduously flat stomach wobble within.

It felt like she was on the start of a roll, at last caught up by the big wave that she hadn't even known was coming, the thrill of easing up and riding high, being swept in and on to another place, through to another plane, where you give up your control at the door, cling on to your board and hope the surf will see you safe. The excitement of danger.

Catherine couldn't think of Sarah Jane, wouldn't think of her. She was doing this for the best of reasons, but the clickety-clack of a railway rhythm was stubbornly stuck on her brain – Sarah Jane was on a train. Sarah Jane was on a train. Sarah Jane was on a train . . . back home to Mummy's.

'Thank you, the room's perfect. Please tell Mr Smith I've arrived,' she said to the handsome, twinkly young receptionist. Was it her state, she wondered, that made everyone so attractive?

Catherine looked into the bathroom and started running steaming hot water and bubbles into the round translucent tub, then she took off her jacket, hung it in the steel and glass wardrobe and made herself comfortable with a magazine on the metallic satin *chaise-longue*. Her suede spiked shoes draped off the end, her stockinged painted toes like delicate Christmas-scented goodies.

After two minutes she was restless. She got up and turned the bath off. She lay back down again, arranged her dress, looked at her nails, looked at her magazine, looked out the window, lit a cigarette, examined her watch. The beautiful Cartier watch David had bought her last birthday (from a pub near his office for a hundred quid) ticked steadily on with its Hong Kong interior.

Catherine had been early, two minutes, and now it was three minutes past. A moment of doubt as insubstantial as chiffon wavered before her mind, but she closed her eyes and blinked it away, just like the other thought she'd had to get rid of that morning, the big one, WHY?

Catherine had gone through it all in her mind again, justifying it to herself before she could cast it aside. She was sure and set now, resolute that this was for the best, the right thing. Saint Catherine atoned for her loveless marriage and disrespectful children, given a purpose, to save her sister, to give her a way out without a long-term sentence. Catherine was older, she thought she knew better, things her sister still had not learnt.

She got up again to check her face, her hair, not a smudge or a split end in sight, then she opened the champagne and sniffed at the jug beside it before tipping a little into the glass to make her favourite, a French 75. Really it should be made with gin but Catherine didn't like gin, it was another reminder of her loathsome mother.

'Hhmm delicious,' she smiled, licking her lips and perusing the smoked salmon like a cat, but deciding against because of the cat's breath it brought.

Catherine thought about her next course of action if he for some reason shouldn't appear. There was always Laurie to call, though Tom was sweet, or even Vic. Standbys for an altered schedule, always be prepared. She'd sold a piece of Vic's yesterday to a major collector from Germany, a free-standing bronze-coated dialysis machine hooked to a bottle of vodka, deeply tasteful for the right interior. The client had bought it as a gentle reminder for his alcoholic English wife and intended it to go next to the drinks cabinet. She lay back on the *chaise-longue* with her drink and imagined making love to Vic. Hideous name, but great pecs, she thought and ran her mind's eye down the rest of his lean sculptor's body and savagely sexy shaved head.

'Have I got the right room for Mrs Smith? They told me at the desk she'd already arrived.' Josh was in, replacing her toy fantasy with a real grown-up version, shrugging off his leather jacket and tossing it on to the chair. He fixed himself a drink, questioning Catherine with a look and raising his eyebrow awaiting her answer.

'Oh Mrs Smith had to go out but she told me to look after you, I mean make sure you were comfortable, keep you amused,' she said, proffering her glass. He was taller than she remembered, broader, more ruggedly handsome.

'It looks like you're the one busy being comfortable, can I ease you out of the pain of your shoes, perhaps a foot massage with my tongue?' There wasn't much subtlety in Josh's approach, they both knew why they were there, what use pussyfooting around?

He was kneeling at her side, looking unblinking into her eyes, unstrapping her ankles, first one then the other, brushing away the discarded shoes to the floor like crumbs from the table. He laid his head assuredly upon her calves and slowly blew up Catherine's dress and then stronger until it wavered and billowed with the wind. Catherine heard a bus in the distance rumble by, felt the tingle of goose pimples appear on her inner thighs above her stocking tops and felt the warmth within her tickle to wetness. She closed her eyes waiting for the pleasure to continue. His hands soon followed his breath, warm, heavy and large, softly grabbing at her flesh, stroking, feeling, kneading.

My that feels good, Catherine thought dreamily, totally relaxed into her sense of physical pleasure. But just as her mind was vacating her body's motel, she checked herself back in and locked the door. She had to be in control; for this, she had to be.

Josh pulled himself upon her, straddled the couch with one of her legs under him and put her other foot in his mouth. He pushed her dress off her silky shoulders revealing a ridiculously ornate lace bra. Their gaze was still locked as his hand plunged into her breast's packaging, adeptly finding her hard brown nipple. The softness of her breast fell warm against his hard hand whilst his other hand was between her legs till she wanted him to stop. He was making her stockings wet, sucking at her toes.

Just a few more minutes of this divine state then I'll surprise him, she thought. Let him think he's in control of the bliss-giving. She could feel his hardness upon her right thigh and moved her hand upon it where it magically grew to fill her grasp. Her toes fell from his mouth and his eyelids began to fall against his will, narrowing his eyes to slits and pursing his lips; she was doing something right. She started to undo the buckle of his belt with her other hand, slowly, deliberate. She unbuttoned his suede jeans till she reached the predictable soft-grey cotton designer shorts beneath. She plunged her hand down into them, gently manipulating his balls until his breath grew short and his scrotum taut. He held on to her shoulder thinking it would give him support but she held his hand and with her teeth undid his poppered shirt, licking and biting at his nipple until the moans made him wobble impatiently.

Now Catherine was in control, catching his beautiful face in a moment of blissful strain, listening to his sighs, feeling the rise and fall of his muscled body. There was no talking, no kissing – it didn't seem necessary with the amount of raw passion that rode between them. Invisible conversation. Kissing could come later. Their bodies were on automatic pilot, able to communicate their requirements telepathically. Catherine and Josh were much the same animal.

She manoeuvred him to lie down whilst she slipped out of her dress; she didn't want stains all over her new Jasper Conran. She placed a condom over his erection, before mounting him, her hand holding him firmly in place, so he wouldn't rush into her, instead she slowly let him slip in until he filled her and they both made involuntary gasps, she could feel him touching her cervix as he felt totally engulfed. Her muscles tightened about him as she moved up and down, firm and regular. He wanted her to speed up, go faster, he couldn't stand the slow pain thrill. He started to move his hips towards hers.

'Sshh slowly,' she whispered.

'No faster, faster bitch, fuck me.'

'I'll fuck you, but I'll fuck you slow. Can you stand it?' she purred back. But he grabbed her buttocks like a cushion and pumped her as if she was a tyre until they were both screaming in ecstasy. The only difference between them was that Josh's cries were real.

Drring dring, drring dring . . .

'Josh I think you left your mobile on,' Catherine murmured, flopping on top of him, her cheek upon his chest, happy for an interruption of her empty state.

'Oh fuck, let it ring. Can you take this rubber thing offa me. I can't move.'

Catherine sat up and pulled off the sagging rubber casing from the limp flesh of his dick and held up the contents to the light.

'Imagine the amount of money you could sell this for, all your doting fans wanting Josh Todd babies out there,' Catherine teased, tying a knot at the top and tossing it into a bin.

Drring dring, drring dring, drring dring . . .

'Imagine the paternity suits!' he answered dryly.

There was an awkward silence. The phone stopped ringing. Once the sex was over, what to say when you hadn't spoken except in the most intimate way? Catherine felt strangely overdressed in the company of her brother-in-law to be. One breast hanging over her bra, her suspenders and stockings still in place, G-string flung to the floor. She didn't feel sexy any more, another drink had to be the answer, maybe a bath, before beginning again. She was lying back down on his chest, at least covering one side of her vulnerability. She could feel his limp mound of spent stickiness nestling into the curve of her hip.

'Would you like another drink?'

'Yeah that would be great, do that for me hon.' He seemed dozy, his words lost in the post-coital neverland men dive into, slow to surface.

Catherine got up, put her breast back into place and went to the bathroom. She took the bathrobe from the back of the door and put it on for comfort, looked in the mirror to smooth down her hair. Everything else was still in place, just the flush of her cheeks showed a pretty natural pink through her foundation.

Now what to do with the caviar and sour cream, I think some licking's in order. I shall decorate this gorgeous plate like a buffet and feast from him, she thought, whilst pouring the champagne. She topped up the glasses from the jug until they fizzed over, fraught with bubbles. She turned towards him and stopped to look at the loveliness of his casual limbs, displayed upon the *chaise-longue*, the image of a Maplethorpe photograph. His eyes were closed and a half-smirk played upon his pretty mouth.

Catherine took a sip from one of the glasses, the drip of the overflow falling upon her toe a cold contrast to the warmth of the soft carpet. She took a larger gulp and held it in her mouth and took the bowl of caviar with her. She approached him with all her feline grace, putting only her lips to his as she kneeled beside him and placed the bowl on the floor. As she kissed him she let out little seeps of liquid until his tongue lunged into her mouth to be awash with the cocktail. She finished the kiss when he wanted to go on, withdrew herself, as his arms went about her, sealed his mouth with a last kiss and calmed his face with a stroke before lipsticking him with the caviar from her finger. Later he would lick it off her nipples, glean it from her labia, lap it out of her belly button but for now he would suck her finger clean before she filled her mouth with more champagne. One gulp for her, one for him. This time she didn't move towards his mouth but his hardening cock, which she placed in her mouth like a cork for the champagne that bubbled around it.

'Wow. You're amazing!' was all that Josh could say as he licked the caviar from his lips and felt the Jacuzzi around his cock transport him.

The day had been set like a perfectly moulded blancmange.

CHAPTER FIFTEEN

Honor was crinkling up in the bath thinking that she had slept with Harry.

Not on the first night after Sarah Jane's. They'd snogged endlessly in the car. He'd said goodnight to her at her door. She'd looked momentarily baffled but put a good-natured smile upon her face as he kissed her upon both cheeks. He said he hoped she'd have dinner with him soon. She wanted to reply churlishly, 'But I thought I was going to have the rest of the menu now, torrid, steamy pudding. Do I have to wait whilst it marinates before I can even put it in the oven!' Instead she said, 'Yes, that would be nice,' like some programmed Stepford Barbie girl-next-door.

Honor had started to wonder if the whole thing was a fantasy. She knew they'd kissed, but what did a kiss prove? What was she expecting, a full-blown love affair with roses at her door and notes of adoration? That would be nice. Yet other times she just didn't know, she knew she felt frustrated as though she'd been led up the garden path and given the key to the wrong door. Her Cinderella Syndrome had been confused by Germaine Greer, Erica Jong, Fay Weldon: her body yearned for one thing and her brain for something quite different. The politics of female supremacy went bad in the heart.

Maybe Harry was meeting another woman later on, Mrs Somebody Else upstairs. Honor thought about calling a cab and going back to Catherine's for the rest of the party, she hadn't left early for an extra dose of beauty sleep, she'd had years of that and it hadn't made any difference. Maybe Harry had a few others, why shouldn't he? There were no rules to this game where everything was left unspoken and you tried to feel your way around a Braille romance when you'd just learnt signing!

The only way was to be clear. Ask questions you wanted answering, state the facts you wanted to know, but it took away the mystery, the delicious excitement of the unexpected bumps and floats. Honor had just hit a bump and she was wondering if it wasn't easier to skip over the fence and forget the rest of the course, before another tripped her into a trough. Or was she supposed to just stick it out and enjoy being with him and not mention the hidden agenda, her expectations? God, sex made life complicated. Was it really worth the bother? Her mind and body had argued through the night in her dreams and she'd woken at four in the morning, wrestling her duvet.

The next morning she had felt more herself. Luxuriously spread over her bed, cosseted by pillows and snug in her covers she'd called him. If he was with another woman, she'd just have to listen.

'Harry, good morning. It's Honor giving you an early morning Sunday wake-up call.'

'Of course it's you! I'm afraid I'm already awake and I've been out to buy the papers and I'm busy making coffee and croissants.'

'I can almost smell them. Can't you bring me some in bed?' she'd said coquettishly.

'But of course. Does Jack want some too?'

'No, he's with his granny and I'm luxuriating in silence.'

'I didn't realise.' Honor'd thought he sounded surprised, but there was no point in regretting lost opportunities with a new day ahead.

'Well, do I get breakfast in bed, or do I have to schlep to the shops myself?'

'*Madame*, breakfast awaits you, five minutes and I'll be down.'

'Can't wait. I love this new home-delivery service. Do all the residents get it?'

'Modom, I don't know what you mean, you'll have to ask them yourselves,' he'd said with an inadequate English accent, and put the phone down.

YIPPEE!

Quick, jump out of bed, change into your nice sexy nightie, pyjamas aren't so attractive are they? Where are my silk ones, can't find them, bugger! Do your hair and a bit of hoovering, shove all the clothes off the floor and into the wardrobe and hope the door stays closed. And last, leave the front door open so that I'm lying in bed waiting for room-service.

Oh, Harry, I'm in here, coooeee. Prepared and dressed for consumption – just like Zola's Nana.

Don't be so ridiculous Honor. Harry is a friend, he is bringing you breakfast not a personal condom demonstration. Just in case, where are the condoms? Pick up a book and read. Which book? Shakespeare's collected works, too pretentious? *The Brothers Kara-mazov*, half-read, too heavy. Laurie Foos' *Ex Utero*, funny but emasculating, Pablo Neruda's *Selected Poems*? Is this why people read Jilly Cooper? *Riders* would never look intellectually threaten-ing on your bedside table. Honor rooted around for a blokish old Martin Amis to display. What do you do in bed when you're not sleeping. The radio, Radio 3, Jazz FM? Decisions, decisions. It all felt too contrived, not relaxed and fun like when she'd suggested it. She was wishing she'd accepted breakfast at the kitchen table like some old married couple reading the Sunday papers, relieved not to have to talk, when she'd heard a soft knock. Honor had turned the radio down beside her bed and heard him call her name. She'd desperately pulled up her covers, embarrassed.

'Honor, *Mademoiselle, le petit déjeuner*?'

'Oh room-service, come in. How nice, just put it on the side thank you.'

That had all been on Sunday. Leisurely languid and loving but no toe-curling passion against the wall. Caressing chats, kissing and cuddling but not the full monty.

They had even dozed off in mid-morning ease. Sleeping together for about ten minutes . . .

By Tuesday she hadn't heard a thing. This was both good and bad for Honor. Good because it made her feel better about dating Jeremy, bad because she'd spent the last days going through possible explanations – personal hygiene (a day's leg growth, hair not limb); inability to perform; worse, bad performance; joking inappropriately ('You don't expect me to fit all of that in, do you?' More distressingly, he hadn't). By the end of her personal interrog-ation session she couldn't even find a reason why he'd made breakfast for her. Plenty of reasons why he hadn't made passion-ate love to her. Perhaps if she hadn't had to go and collect Jack . . . Dinner hadn't been mentioned again, though he'd seemed attentive. Honor was confused. It was like trying to decipher hieroglyphics.

That's why she'd kept quiet with Gem in Liberty's. Her mind

was in turmoil. She'd even spent an evening with the door ajar waiting to hear the lift arriving, or footsteps walking past but nothing, only false alarms. She had finished the bottle of wine that she'd only meant to have a glass from and then, seeing the bottom was in sight, had searched for an old joint that Sarah Jane had left in a jar for emergencies. Finding it, she had puffed herself to sleepy oblivion and crawled her way to bed.

Honor hadn't wanted to tell Gem that Harry had slept with her, but that they had not made love. On the other hand, she didn't want to sound boastful when Gem had . . . what did she have? Nothing. At least Honor had Jack, had Jack for life. Gem only had a mother who clung to her, oh and her work. If Gem hadn't her career prospects, the best body in the world, a great sense of humour, her own money, a dream flat, and the beautiful nature and face that she undoubtedly possessed – she'd have had nothing. Honor was kidding herself, who was she to start feeling sorry for Gem. 'Let she who is without sin cast the first stone.' Wasn't that something from the Bible: roughly translated into modern parlance as, 'She who isn't sad herself, wouldn't even say it.'

'Mum where's my dinner,' Jack interrupted her thoughts, 'and how long are you going to stay in the bath? You're always in the bath. Can you inside-out my pyjamas, I can't do it, Mum. Is there any juice?'

All Gem lacked was a child, or a man. That was all. And it wasn't exactly difficult to find the two in one these days. In fact the problem was decoding the labels on the packaging to make sure you got enough man ingredients. Honor read Sarah Jane's Josh as 100 per cent boy.

Catherine's David had found the nursery dressing-up box before the tin soldiers. Jeremy too, when she'd met him. Now she was confused. Was Harry any different, was he playing games, or was this what normal men did? What was a normal man? And if you found him would you ever want him? And were they all carbon copies of her father?

Gem seemed like the winner out of all of them. At least she only had herself to reckon with, didn't qualify herself in the world or find her co-ordinates linked to a man's position. Didn't require one permanently at her side. Didn't expend all her energy getting het up about the other women in a ridiculous past, as Honor had done with Jeremy. Her self-worth had been determined by the amount of patronising acknowledgement he threw her way, but that wasn't his responsibility, it was hers. She'd leapt on Gem for letting slip about Jeremy, had found herself seething with rage at the girls who had betrayed her, as though he was blameless. Ridiculous, still to respond like that, dredging up the same emotions.

From now on she would react differently. If Harry had other women, that was up to him; if she had other men, that was up to her. If she chose to have Jeremy she had to forget the past. Hell, she had to forget it anyway.

Maybe the ability to commit to intimate relationships is exaggerated into a big deal by those too afraid to stand alone. So many half-empty people waiting to be filled by another, hoping two half-people will make a whole, but anybody with GCSE maths knows they only ever make two halves. Honor sighed, hauling herself out of the bath. But then even two halves can multiply into millions, she was sure of that.

'I'm coming Jack, just give me a sec to dry off before I see to . . . What are you eating?'

She could see through the slit in the bathroom door rummaging in progress and the fridge open, with Jack's Taz boxer-covered bottom protruding. 'Not before dinner Jack. I was just about to make you an omelette or kedgeree.'

'Ugh, kedgeree! I'm starving now Mum and you never get out of your bath, I could've starved to death. There's nothing in the fridge Mum. Where's the chocolate spread?'

'You can't have chocolate sandwiches for supper. Let me make you something.'

'I won't eat omelette. I don't like omelette.'

'Well what would you like?' she found herself weakly obliging.

'What have we got?' he petulantly pouted out.

'Kedgeree, or boiled eggs and hot buttered toast or Welsh rabbit with bacon,' Honor replied cheerily, hoping to make it sound inviting by her tone.

'Why can't we have pizzarollas and micro chips like everyone else at school?'

'Because it's not good for you. I don't like giving you processed food.'

'Why not?'

'Because you'd turn into a processed person, and besides you won't grow properly.'

'What's a processed person?'

A bureaucrat, she thought of answering but saw it causing more questions. Instead she said, 'How about french toast, real maple syrup and crispy bacon?'

Honor knew she'd won when she heard the familiar, 'Yummy. Can I have it now, and this whilst I'm waiting?' He held up the last fig in the fridge that Honor had been saving as a treat for herself, waiting till it was ripe and cold.

'Yeah sure. Now put your pyjamas on before you Mr Freeze. Food in five.'

She watched her son savagely bite into the delicacy with some tiny regret. But he ran towards his bedroom with a skip. If it was doing him good surely that was better. She loved to watch him eat good food, to know he was growing tall and healthy, like watering a favourite plant and delighting in its flowers.

The Canadian-cured bacon sizzled enticingly under the grill whilst the butter bubbled on top of the stove. A towel slipped over her eyes and the other escaped from under her arms whilst she tried to cut slices of wholemeal bread. She put the slices to soak in the whisked egg and nutmeg before being caught in the boiling butter to be turned brown and crunchy on the outside, the inside squadgy and delicious, with the savoury bacon and sweetness of the maple syrup seeping through.

'Tatatataaaa. Meal One is served,' she quoted from one of her favourite books of Jack's. The buzz of the front door went. 'Hello, come up, is the buzzer working? Good.'

'This is delicious Mum! You're the best french toast maker in the whole world.'

'Not just the best mum?' she said and wished she hadn't fished so obviously for compliments.

'Well I think you'd be better if you didn't make me clear up and do my teeth, but it doesn't stop me loving you 'cos you're the only mum I've got, so you must be my best.'

'Well you're my best son,' she smiled back at him.

'But I'm your only one!' he replied peevishly.

'True, but it doesn't stop you being the best.' She gave him a hug from behind his chair and kissed his full and munching cheek.

'No lipstick?' He was firmly installed in his six-year-old misogynist phase.

'No lipstick Jack, I've just got out of the bath. And here is the gorgeous Gem?'

'Hello, you divine human beings. How are you, Jack?' She made the lipstick kiss mistake and he sneered in reply at her, wrinkling up his nose whilst smearing it off with his sleeve-covered palm. 'Next time I'll have to put it all over your face, big boy,' she joked.

'Ugh, girls!' he responded, taking away the bad taste with a big gulp of orange juice.

'So how are we doing on the recipe stakes, Honor?' Then she whispered apologetically, 'About yesterday. I'm really sorry, I thought you must have known.'

'Don't whisper, it's rude!' full-mouthed Jack pointed out helpfully with his finger.

'Like everyone else did? Don't worry, it was a different life. There's some wise old saying isn't there about not raking over old coals. Let's leave it. Doesn't mean I won't use it for blackmail purposes, watch a worm squirm. No I'm joking. I've let it all go now. Dropped, see, no hands.'

'I don't see why, I'd rub his face in it if I was you. Dog dirt could only improve his complexion,' said Gem spitefully.

'That's why we're different.'

'Mum, whose face, what are you talking about?'

'Just a friend of Gem's and mine who you haven't met since you were a baby.'

'Oh. If Gem rubs dog-do in his face he'll get blind eyes. It's dangerous you know? Can we get *Jurassic Park* out from the video shop? Pleeeze Mum, special treat.' Jack tugged at his mum, standing on her foot and pulling at her arm, wavering like a sail.

'Vintage whine Jack, and don't stick your tongue out at me. What do you want me to answer first: yes, no?' said Honor, establishing authority, rather too late, she suspected.

'So we can watch *Jurassic Park*, goodie,' he purposefully contradicted her.

Honor sighed and took a deep breath before laying down the boundaries again. 'No you can't watch *Jurassic Park*, it's too frightening for Gem, she's of a nervous disposition and I don't have a mobile phone so you couldn't phone me if she faints.'

'Oh Mum! I won't love you or tidy my room any more.' Honor realised he was playing his final trump card, the heart, but she stood firm.

'You never tidy your room anyway, but the love I'll miss. Can you wait till Saturday? You can watch and I'll hide behind the sofa.'

'Promise.' Jack let her go but pointed back at her, as though with a steel-tipped bayonet.

'Promise, scout's honour.' Honor bravely swore.

'Cross your heart, hope to die if you ever say a lie, stick a needle in your eye? Would you swear on your mother's life?'

'I swear.'

'Good old squadge-bottom Mum,' Jack said, softly prodding her bum whilst wrapping his body about her in a hug, before looking up into her face with half-closed eyes and pouting his kissable lips.

Honor winked across at Gem, settled nicely into the sofa, a cup of tea in hand, magazine in lap, and bent down to kiss Jack. How often did Jack swear on her life for playground honour?

'There's a bunch of recipes I've sorted out in the red folder on top of the chest over by the fire if you want to look at them whilst I get dressed. See if there's anything useful there,' Honor said to Gem, before disappearing to her bedroom to get ready for her dinner date.

Had she worn this dress the last time, would he remember, did it matter? She'd wear her mother's old Jean Muir cast-off that she'd given her last year, bought in the seventies. If you wait long enough everything comes back into fashion: Honor's excuse. The problem was, wearing the dress made you feel like you'd been paying a mortgage for at least twenty years, just like her mum.

'Gem, Gem! What am I supposed to wear?'

'Put on the choices and model them for Jack and me. We'll sit here on the sofa and be the judges, won't we,' Gem called back to Honor's horror, in her new role as sofa slug. She was unwilling to hike herself up and about – Honor was only going for a date with Jeremy, she wouldn't have worn anything more special than some old jeans and a jumper.

'Old woman dress,' Jack contributed.

'You're right, it was your granny's.'

'Don't show all your bosoms Mum,' said Jack shielding his eyes from the sheer effrontery of the follow-up number.

'Too tarty?'

'Too Miss Selfridge,' said Gem.

'Not far wrong, it was Top Shop on a bored Sunday afternoon.' And finally, 'The old favourite,' Honor announced, knowing the effect it always had.

'The black one. Wear that Mum, it always looks nice.'

'That's the problem, yes, it always does.'

'Sophisticated yet approachable. A classic,' added Gem, imitating a wine connoisseur.

'Even with the cleavage?' begged Honor.

'Especially. Wonderbras are a brilliant invention.' Gem went back to the recipes.

'Yes but I'm not wearing one. The black it is. Do you think I should holster a Wonder?'

'Go for it girlie. Don't mind me, I'm just waiting for consultation. Something tells me I've been hauled here on false pretences.'

'Oh Gem, I'm sorry, give me five minutes and I'll have a face on. Do you think any of those recipes are any use?'

'Loads, but we could do with a few more starters. I'm just picking out my favourites.'

'Shout them out.'

'Treacle tart, sticky toffee pudding, chocolate mousse tart, plum and almond crumble, tarte citron, white peach soufflé . . .'

'But they're all puddings! What about a few salads and main courses? I think I'd better be in charge of nutritional balance and you can see to the pictures.'

'Is your mum always this dull about food Jack?' Gem said, consulting the thumb sucking, teddy holding, polka-pyjamaed snuggler at her side.

'My mum's the best cook in the world and you'd better believe it,' Jack retorted and jumped off the sofa, running round to the kitchen table. 'Taste this.' He held out a forkful of congealing bacon fat and a crust of soggy french toast dripping with syrup. Gem wanted to say no, but couldn't, not to Jack's enthusiasm.

'Hmmm, best thing I've eaten all week, even cold it's delicious.'

'See, told you, didn't I, Gem. Mum is the best. You must listen more!'

'Who do you sound like, your mum or your teacher, Jack? But you're right, she is. Here's to Honor, the best,' said Gem, clinking cups with Jack's water.

'I must leave the room more often,' Honor interrupted. 'Shifty over and we'll work this out, properly!'

'Quick! Before a man drags you off for his entertainment.'

'No Gem, fifteen minutes before I casually step into the chauffeur-driven limo to be wined and dined for my entertainment; there's all ways of seeing things. Actually I've got to go on the tube.'

'I've always said perspective is everything,' Gem said, holding up her pencil in measurement of Honor.

'Ha, ha, ha. By the way, what happened about the gallery that you saw?'

'Oh nothing much.' She'd been waiting for Honor to ask, hadn't said a thing to anyone, like having a whole box of chocolates in your pocket, the knowledge was almost enough. 'Just a little show in November and a picture in the mixed summer show in August.'

'You're kidding! That's wonderful. Can I call you Gem Bacon for short?'

'Why don't we just call her sausage, I think that's much better,' yawned Jack sleepily.

'Jack!'

'What!' said Jack, chuckling into the sofa cushions.

CHAPTER SIXTEEN

'I have to go now,' Catherine said, climbing out of the bed. She could see the light fading on the other side of the blinds. Looking at it was enough to bring goose pimples to the flesh of her arms, though the rest of her remained warm in the hotel's temperature-controlled atmosphere.

'Hey you can't go. Come back and do something wonderful to me,' Josh said lazily. Unwilling to let her leave he grabbed at her hand, chaining her hard to his side.

'I have to.' She pulled playfully away from him, their relationship firmly fixed in cat and mouse territory.

'But Sarah Jane's still in Hampshire.'

'That's why you don't have to go home, I have other reasons to get back. It feels like I haven't really seen my children for days, or done any work. God knows David's state.'

'Oh gee I'd forgotten, the good little wife has to get home to her happy family.' Josh acted sarcastic before pretty pleading. 'Can't you feed them dinner and sneak back after lights out? David won't notice, lace his dinner,' he suggested whilst kissing her neck and shoulders before pulling her back into bed.

'What would you suggest, doctor, strychnine or methylated spirits?' She returned his kisses with less passion. 'Call me an old-fashioned wife but I've never been one for killing husbands, I always think there's a more amiable way out.'

'Doesn't seem like you believe in fucking them much, either.'

'Why do you say that, you impudent child.' Catherine fixed him with a Mrs Danvers special.

'Scary woman!' She couldn't help her eyes creasing, showing she was joking. 'If you did, you wouldn't have spent the whole day fucking me instead.'

'Touché! And what bliss it was.' Catherine put meaning into that one – well she did mean it, it was a kind of bliss, some of it hard work but nothing she couldn't handle. If she ever ran out of money she certainly had an alternative profession to sell.

The cab driver had sensed that.

She pulled on her stockings and clipped them to her suspenders as easily as doing up buttons. Josh lay watching her, he didn't want her to go, and what he wanted he usually got. His hands resting behind his head he waited for the rest of Catherine's sentence. It never came so he shouted, 'What the hell's that meant to mean?'

'You win,' she answered seductively, as though he really had.

'So you're staying!'

'No, you just win the discussion. We fix up another day for fun, if we both like.' She had to be firm but persuadable, light but essential. She needed him to be begging for more, ringing her at home, dangerously overstepping the mark for the next week.

Her dress was on and her shoes buckled, only a little make-up required and her jacket, to go where her mind was already leading her.

'Tomorrow,' Josh insisted. Catherine's shadow pushed Sarah Jane from his mind. Be a greedy child, she prayed. 'Definitely tomorrow!' He slammed his fist upon the bed. This was what he wanted.

Catherine had got her home run.

CHAPTER SEVENTEEN

Dear David,

I've asked you to come home early so that you can get this message before the children get back from school. Hopefully you will see them before midnight so that you can talk to them and give them these notes, one each. I don't suppose this will surprise you, one of us was bound to do it sooner or later. We couldn't have gone on, could we? Not like we were. In a sense it's just chance that I left first and I think leaving the country completely is easier for us both.

I have gone with Josh to LA and will call you when I reach there and have a number. I know that I will immediately be labelled the harlot, lower than my family's dog, sometimes that's just how it is. Someday I might be able to explain this to you. Believe me, there is a reason for everything.

Thank you David for all you have given me over the years. I am sorry to leave the decision about the children to you. You were right as always, boarding school is probably the best place for them. I was just squeamish to think otherwise. The house was never a real home, there must be one somewhere else for all of us.

Good luck,
Catherine

Dearest Benjamin,

I know you are at a point where you don't like me much, and I know this won't make things any better. I have gone away to Los Angeles for a while to see if I can work things out a bit. I don't know how long I'll be gone but I'll call you very soon. Your father and I haven't been getting on lately (I'm sure you've realised, you're so sensitive and clever . . .

'Don't make me puke!' Ben spat contemptuously.

He couldn't read any more. He ripped the letter into pieces and scrunched them into a tight ball like his fists, which he badly wanted to shove somewhere other than where they remained, thrust into the pocket of his windcheater.

'Fuck you, fuckbloodyshit you, just fuck off . . .' He screamed from his white wrung face and made angrily towards the door, kicking over one of his mother's prized Damien Hirst pieces and cracking the casing. Formaldehyde leaked across the slate-tiled floor, he turned to kick it again. He only had his trainers on and the force of his kick did more damage to his toes than the dead bambi inside, but it's the thought that counts.

His father stood by and watched. David wanted to go and put his arm around his boy, comfort him, pull the strain of fury away, but being physical didn't come naturally. Holding somebody close inevitably meant sex to David. He stood looking as though to speak, as if to say, 'Ben my son, if I could make it any easier I would. Your mother's a bitch but I'm here. She's hurt me, my life's a wreck. My mother couldn't love me either, she left me too.' But for all his expensive education he could only stumble out, 'I understand how you must . . .'

'Fuck you!' Ben screamed back, silent frustrated tears racing from his eyes, faster than he could run slamming out of the room, out of the house.

David watched his son's back disappearing and could do nothing. He was paralysed, his insides fracturing into tiny pieces like a car's windscreen smashed with a hammer.

The light began to fade and he was still standing by the window hours after Ben left. On the periphery of his hearing he listened to a key in the latch, the front door opening and for a minute thought it must be Catherine, back. Then Augusta's voice called out and the spell was broken. He fished numbly in his pocket for the other letter and crossed the room to pour himself a drink, a stiff Scotch to gulp down and another to hold in his hand.

'Hello! I'm home. Mum, Mum.'

There was no answer to her call. Not unusual, they all kept their own hours and Augusta was on her way up to her room to dump her school stuff and hide her fags.

'Augusta, when you've got a minute I'd like a word,' her father called formally to her. She immediately imagined he must have found out from school about her bunking off. Maybe Ben had been grouching about the toothpaste apple pie bed she'd made for him last night, he was such a sneak, maybe he told him about the club . . . A flood of guilty possibilities made their presence felt.

'Okay, I'm just dumping my things. Down in a sec.'

David refilled his glass, he was set on automatic pilot. His daughter's elephantine stamp disappeared and returned in no time.

'What's up Pops?' she said playfully. Best to be jolly in the face of retribution. She jumped into the armchair and looked expectantly at his moribund face, eyes closed, slipping into his drink. He looked strange, she thought. Must be drunk.

'Are you all right, Daddy? What's happened?' The concern showed in her voice as she swivelled off the leather armchair and came towards him, arms open to comfort, roles reversed.

He wasn't prepared for her concern. He jolted suddenly. He felt he was drifting through a dream, a disturbed sleep in public where you start yourself awake, afraid you're missing your stop but can't help yourself drifting back again. Augusta's voice brought him to and he tried to fix a smile but he'd forgotten how to work those muscles. His arm jerked up, the letter in his hand.

'This is for you, it's from Mummy,' his voice slurred.

'Oh goodie, I love letters but where's Mummy? Why's she writing to me?'

'She's had to go away for a while.'

'What do you mean, where? She never said anything this morning.'

'Well, that's why she's written this letter for you, explaining.'

She ripped open the letter hungrily, her young expectant face imagining treats and he watched her, leaning against the wall, as impotent in the face of his child's distress as his own.

'Howya doin' hon,' Josh drawled, happy to have Catherine rigid by his side. They were both sitting upright, in belted luxury, ready for take-off . . . Catherine's jaw was twitching but she arranged a smile to cross her face for her companion, who held her hand.

'Fine. I'm fine, it's just the take-off. I can't stand them,' she lied back to him.

In fact Catherine had never been afraid of flying, it seemed as natural to her as shopping, but she had to cover this terrible feeling that caught her throat and squeezed her sinus, cut into her heart. She had felt sick since waking, frozen inside but churning. It was an oddly immobilising mixture of excitement and fear that she would have to sort out soon. Meanwhile she thought, I have to cover it up. You cannot do these things in life and crumple. You have to be stoic and hardened, brave and bright to survive. She began to chant in her head, I have made this decision and I have to stick to it. I am a winner!

Catherine was a survivor. Look what she'd survived so far. A loveless mother, a step-father's abuse, the hands of her piano teacher pulling into her body as she practised her scales, men, countless men, a husband who raped her, the spite and jealousy of too many wives; herself.

She wasn't scared of leaving the past behind, it was stepping into an unknown future that worried her. Catherine would survive all right, she was determined to, as she was determined to protect Sarah Jane. She would miss the girls, her friendship with Honor, Gem and her sister had been the most true relationships in her life, but at least she wouldn't have to go to the wedding now, put on the show with David and the children, playing happy family in front of her mother. At last she would escape from her mother, and her step-father.

She couldn't let herself think about the letters to Augusta and Ben. They would be better off without her. She had always felt so glad to leave them behind before, why this saddened longing now? It grew hard like a mistakenly swallowed boiled sweet that she couldn't push down.

Catherine looked out of the window, separated from her former world, and gripped on to the arm rest. The plane ascended and her ears clouded over, taking her into another dimension of time and space. She tried to grab at some passing hope to the background roar of the engines.

Sarah Jane returned from Hampshire and switched on the answer-phone in her flat, expecting something from Josh. He had been so strange and distant with her, but she knew he went into these moods, passing clouds that made him surly and unapproachable. Frankly she was glad that this one had descended before the wedding, not during it, or worse, on their honeymoon.

When Josh surfaced from these moods he was always that much more loving and generous with her. Unquestionably she'd put up with his behaviour, there was so much riding on this marriage and the big 'C' word. Commitment. Besides, didn't she love him, wasn't he everything she ever wanted in a husband?

There was only one problem – the voice. Everything else was fine, really it was. The little voice was trying to ruin it all for her, starting up inside her head, raking and unsettling her, sabotaging everything. 'What's to become of Sarah Jane?' the voice would go, and she would answer back strongly, 'She is becoming Mrs Josh Todd.' It was when the voice inside her began asking 'Who am I?' that she could find no answer. Somewhere she had carelessly lost faith with who she was.

Everything had seemed so clear to her as a small child. There was a wide golden path that stretched ahead of her and all she was required to do was walk along it, stay upon it. Her strong long legs could easily walk the distance, the warmth of her sun-blonde hair was a protecting golden crown and her clear blue eyes could see into the future. One day she came across a small road running off her main route, it sparkled and beckoned with the promise of gifts at the end, she read the signpost, 'A Short Cut to Approval'. She was sure as she took it that it would join back up. Instead it led on to a smaller one, and then another, until she was so far astray she was in a maze. Then she could hardly remember the glimmer of the path that she had first set out upon, let alone its promised ease. Now she was about to get into a canoe and, if she managed the rapids, the rewards were endless. She'd be able to have the rainbow and all its wishes; that's how she read it. If Sarah Jane had stuck to that original road she would have had them anyway but she'd forgotten that a long time ago, and now there seemed only the white water to confront as she peered down from where she balanced towards her destination. Happiness.

She thought of the balmy days to come along with her new title, Mrs Josh Todd. She would have a large house with servants, just like her mother, except she would have more. She would have money and accounts in all the smartest stores, she would be pointed at and admired for her beauty and grooming and have fame on a larger scale than her mother had ever achieved. Clever Sarah Jane. And she could give up having to 'make it' for what she was, struggling to have her talents recognised when nobody seemed interested. She could be like her sister, except richer, and spend her time making sure she and the home were beautiful and everything that Josh wanted them to be. That was her new career, the caring, pacifying wife. She wasn't a bad actress, she'd get the role right with practice.

Answer-machines are very handy, you get the full impact of what the other person wants to say, but no right to reply.

The message on Sarah Jane's answerphone wiped everything away. One day she was getting married, all of me and mine is yours, booked rehearsed and ordered. The next day there was a message. A year of planning and dreaming – gone. She'd taken off her jacket, unzipped her boots and was just pouring herself a Bacardi and diet Coke, when she registered Josh's voice and thought, About bloody time too. She missed what he was saying, diverted into worrying what she would wear to make everything right. Nerves, people got wedding nerves. She caught the end and understood it then.

'. . . I'm at the airport now and about to catch the plane with Catherine. I'm sorry about the wedding arrangements being cancelled, but listen, call Bob at the London office, I've spoken to him already. He'll make sure you get a cheque. Okay? I have to go, they've just called the flight. Bye now.' There was a brief pause, she waited for the click of the replaced receiver, she could hear his breath. 'Sarah Jane, you look after yourself.'

For an hour she played that message over and over, the information ran across her brain like a ticker-tape, but how did that help anything? Where was she supposed to take it? Who could she tell? The hideous spectre of her mother's grimace loomed and she picked up the phone and began to dial. Honor's number, sympathetic Honor, sensible Honor, she would know what to do, but all she got was an answerphone. Panic seized her as she tried to find her phone book and Gem's number, she knocked over the glass spilling sticky brown liquid on the crowded, paper-laden table. Transfixed she watched the river's journey to the edge of the glass coffee table, it stilled her to focus quietly on the lemming-like drips, jumping one after another, over the edge on to the absorbent landing of her socked toes.

'The caller is engaged on another call, please wait,' the computer-operated voice repeated. She listened and did as she was told because she wouldn't call Honor at work and she certainly couldn't call her mother. She had to speak to someone who'd know what to do, give her a reason why?

As she waited, Sarah Jane began to feel nicely numb, zombied without even a joint. She sat on the sofa, eerily beautiful, features immaculately emotionless, phone held to her head. She could have easily have been perpetrator or victim, Freddie Kruger fodder or Stepford-Wife Terminator.

At the back of her brain, to the right of her nerve centre, a red light blinked – WARNING.

CHAPTER EIGHTEEN

Gem was lying on the floor, phone to her ear.

'So what happened to you?' she said, waving her legs like flags to an audience. Exercise seemed a good excuse for a chat. She needed to limber up after crouching over the recipe book illustrations for Sarah Jane's wedding present. Working on it served as a masochistic pleasure, she tried to imagine she was digesting it instead of drawing it, that way she didn't have to have lunch. Since the disaster with Josh Todd she hadn't allowed herself any sexual indulgences, so all she had was food, and of course her painting. But it was the food that had put on the half stone in weight.

A fresh canvas and some new brushes and paints to go ahead with tonight, and no interruptions. She intended to paint right through till morning, feeding on the adrenalin that had started pumping through her bloodstream.

'I slept with Jeremy last night and I wish I . . . No I can't pretend that. "*Je ne regrette rien*," as Piaf would say. It's just the sex was so bloody lousy,' said Honor.

'I thought that was his good point, it was just his personality we loathed.'

'I'm starting to think the sex was always awful, but I was just grateful to have him in bed with me,' Honor replied in a bleak whisper. She was sitting in the food cupboard at work amongst the dried and canned goods where her little desk sat, lists of orders still to be done, door closed to the kitchen.

There wasn't the time to be on the phone but she'd done three-quarters of the morning's preparations, got Jack to school and herself in early, fuelled by an ugly guilt hangover.

She needed to confess in order to cleanse. The way she was playing with her necklace like a rosary, anyone would think she was a Catholic.

'You have to show them. Maybe you couldn't be bothered, lazy cow. Don't you know you have to work hard for good sex!' Gem joked to alleviate the drama.

'And bad, it seems,' Honor replied bleakly. 'It was so unconnected. I felt like a stand-in for a plastic blow-up doll. How can
men ejaculate so quickly one moment, then be unable to come for
hours? It's supposed to be fear of commitment but that was all he
talked about. That and me getting better paid.'

'Spunk don't lie, sister,' Gem said abruptly, standing up to do
her leg swings.

'Thank you! I don't know what to do. I should be grateful that
I got a fuck, even if it was courtesy of the Jeremy "in and out" club,
it must be at least six months since the last time.'

'And you're grateful? Excuse me? What's the point in scaling
Everest, Honor, when you're left panting halfway up the mountain
while the other git already got to the top and went home. I wouldn't
even put on my boots for that, let alone my sexy underwear.' Gem
was annoyed until her attention wandered – to how long it would
take for the little piece of fat on the inside of her thighs to disappear
if she kept this up.

'I made him finish it off manually and orally – it sounds like I
made him use an audio-language course for the job doesn't it?'

'Oh my God Honor! When will we ever learn!'

'I'm not unsympathetic to the pressures on the male ego, but
what happens to men? They do it once and roll over after the age of
thirty.'

'Maybe he's not very highly sexed.'

'That's no good to me.'

'Honor, you sex goddess!'

'We're getting to the height of our sexual powers and men's
prowess is on the decline from the age of twenty-two. Gem, what
are those noises?'

'I'm exercising. You've got to start sticking to my adage, get
'em young, treat 'em rough, tell them nothing.'

'I've got nothing to tell anyway, except that old men are
perfectly suited to young women. By the time they die women have
reached their sexual maturity and can go and find themselves some
gorgeous young man to suck their toes into their dotage. When the
men get old they can find themselves some young girl.'

'Etcetera, etcetera. The perfect circle of life for the rich. Have
you thought of politics Honor? I hear the Tories are looking for
leadership.'

'Ha, ha. Jeremy's rich. Still I expect there's plenty more Jeremys in the sea.' She imagined herself pulling the hook out of Jeremy's mouth and throwing his suited body back into the ocean amongst endless doppelgängers.

'Depressing isn't it. The oldest trade in the world. Sex and money.' Gem couldn't imagine herself with a Jeremy type, or in bed with anyone ever again, for that matter.

'What's love got to do with it? got to do with it,' sang Honor tunelessly.

'What indeed! At least one of us have it out of four, not a bad rate, one in four. One in five ends up having mental treatment,' said Gem cheerily.

'Who?'

'Sarah Jane and Josh, love. You didn't think I was going to say Catherine did you? Hey, I've got to go Honor, call waiting's going and it might be offers of work. By the way the cookbook looks brilliant. Speak later.'

Honor got back into the kitchen and rescued a tart from burning, and then herself with a can of Coke. On days like this it was the only thing, synthetic resurrection.

For a change, Gem was on fine form. Some days things can't help going right, that's how it seemed. Gem had decided – men were all boys. Who needed them? Life was so much simpler without them, emptier but simpler. But without them, what would these girls spend their endless telephone conversations griping over? The finer points of the Turner prize or prime minister's question time?

Gem switched over calls and voice.

'Hi, Gem Daley here. What can I do for you?'

'Gem, it's Sarah Jane,' she was barely able to croak.

'Oh hello, how's it all going, bridesmaids' dresses finished?' She couldn't imagine what else it could be about, but a thick silence signified something ominous, and she wondered if she'd been murdered on line. 'Sarah Jane, are you there? Sarah Jane, are you all right?'

'No, not really,' she slurred and then rushed her words, as though on an intravenous drip feeding first mandrex then dex-edrine. 'I don't suppose you could come round, I mean if you're not doing anything. Could you please? I just need to, I mean I'd understand if you . . .' the last bit she stuttered through until the sobs took over and she couldn't finish the conversation. The phone dropped from her hand and fell to the floor, Gem's voice echoing out of it.

'I'll be over as soon as I can get there. Don't worry, I'm coming.' Sensibly organised, Gem was in control.

So many awful things came to Gem's mind as she went over what might be wrong. She calmed herself on the journey with the fact they were at least tears instead of shrieks, but the sobbing was gut-wrenching and all she could think of was death. Who'd died? Not Catherine, she prayed, not Catherine, reluctantly adding Josh to her prayer, as she supposed she morally must.

Whatever had happened between her and Josh she'd had to let go of it. There had been a mix up, her fault, but she'd learnt something: if you pursue a man that you fancy in a crowded room, purely on appearance, ignoring your finer instincts, you do so at your own peril. Better, however difficult at the time, to turn around and walk in the other direction to sanity, rather than love at first sight!

Snakeskin loafers on at the door, beret pulled on top of her head, Gem made sure the answerphone was on and that she had her three Cs, cash, keys and chewing gum (instead of the usual chocolate or condoms). Then she was off, locking up the four Chubb locks on her door. In the hall she undid her bike padlock, careful to tuck her flares unstylishly into her pop socks as safety demanded. With her leather rucksack slung on to her back, she cycled from Camden through a gloriously sunny park, over the Serpentine to Earls Court and Sarah Jane's flat.

She chained up her bike over the notice on the railings outside the flat that stated, 'Any bicycles chained to these railings will be removed,' and rang Sarah Jane's bell. The electronic buzz came and Gem bounded up the wide high corridor stairs to the first floor, and knocked at the open door.

'Sarah Jane are you there? It's me, Gem.' She pushed the door, letting herself into the living room where a mess of human misery lay sobbing. Gem wasn't sure what shocked her most, the state of the flat or the state of Sarah Jane. I hope she never brought Josh Todd back here, no wonder he . . . Stop it, this instant, she admonished herself – that was her mother's voice.

Sarah Jane hadn't stirred at Gem's entrance, she couldn't stop either her noise or her shaking, her back heaved as she seemed to gulp for air. The phone lay where she'd dropped it. The glass also, over on its side, ice-cubes melting their way out to join the Coke over the table and on to the floor. Gem replaced the receiver, retrieved the glass and signed herself up for a day of cleaning, wondering what the hell was going on.

First she went to the kitchen to start the tea on the go. Tea was good for shock, she remembered that from endless episodes of *Z Cars* as a child. The sergeant on duty was always bringing cups of tea (plenty of sugar) to traumatised relatives. Gem wrinkled her noise automatically with displeasure at the burgeoning plant life as she fished around for cups. She involuntarily shrieked as a storm of flour moths flew into her face out of the tea-bag cupboard; the place looked more like a penicillin lab than a kitchen. Kettle on, she went back to say hello to Sarah Jane, to make her presence known.

'Sarah Jane, I'm here, it's Gem. Sweetheart what's up?' She stroked her back, and with a lulling whisper, as though cajoling a child, added, 'Don't worry I'm here now. I'm going to make us some tea and then you can sit up, have a sip and tell me. Just try to breathe slowly, slowly and deeply. Okay? Good.'

Sarah Jane did nothing of the sort so Gem took a deep breath herself, preparing for the onslaught back in the kitchen. She opened the fridge and looked round, bottles, a tub of Flora, some lipstick, a collection of nail polishes and two bulging cartons, one of milk, the other orange juice. She closed the door and hunted in a cupboard for herbal tea that didn't need milk and found some camomile sharing the box with some stale oatcakes and half a bar of nibbled Cadbury's Fruit and Nut. Gem recognised the top of the scrunched wrapper immediately and put it straight back pretending not to have seen the temptation for two minutes, before hungrily biting at the white, moulding, tooth-marked chocolate. Guilty, she binned the rest with a feeling of disgust.

'Sarah Jane, I've brought you some tea.' Gem sat on the sofa close to the bent body and put one arm about her, the other stroked Sarah Jane's thick shiny pampered hair and wished it was hers. 'I've come all the way from Camden risking life and limb, you've got to at least speak to me. It's common decency,' Gem coaxed sympathetically.

At last a tiny voice appeared out of Sarah Jane. 'Oh Gem, it's just I've got this message and I don't understand it. It's on the answer thing. I mean I do, but I just don't want to. What am I supposed to do?' She had heaved her head up from a sodden pillow and dumped herself back down upon Gem, who struggled to press playback on the machine while Sarah Jane stapled her lap, then listened.

There was much about Sarah Jane and Gem that was similar. Their Aryan looks and girlish builds often had strangers confusing the two of them but inside they were quite different. Gem seemed self-sufficient and organised, where Sarah Jane was muddled and dependent. Sarah Jane's exuberance and passion for life, love and energy, far outstripped what most others could muster, but she hated responsibility. She expected nameless others to pick up and care for her, she hadn't the strength for a struggle or the concentration for endurance, not alone. But she did have an energy and imagination for creating happiness. When she entered a party her pores seemed to emit sunshine, as long as the drugs were still going and the drink flowing. Sarah Jane inspired both jealousy and adoration, having seemingly done nothing to earn them. At school others wanted to help her with homework and to be on her team. If she wore sackcloth and ashes everyone else would want to wear them too.

Gem on the other hand thought it was part of life that you should pick yourself up, mend yourself. You had to work hard, prove yourself in life, earn your own money, pay your way. Any man you married had to be an equal, otherwise you would prove incompatible, that's what Gem thought. She wondered how men could settle with women who to her appeared brainless, incompetent and silly, when there were women like Honor and herself around. The problem with men was they never dug beneath the surface, but then neither did she, the wrong colour shoes could have her hurrying in the opposite direction in case she was spotted standing near them. People wanted Gem on their team because she always worked hard and then you could finish early and go for a fag behind the chemistry block. Gem earned her keep.

Gem listened to the voice that had once growled at her, 'I want to fuck you forever,' that had proposed to Sarah Jane, and was now saying something completely different. Telling Sarah Jane her fairytale dream was at an end, where she had gone wrong and what

she shouldn't have done, if she had expected to keep him; justifi-
cations. Taking her clothes off was one, asking where he'd been –
two; nagging for his approval – three; buying him expensive
presents on his credit card – four; talking to other men – five;
getting jealous when he was with other women – six; drinking too
much . . .

It reminded Gem of the seventies reggae song by Prince Buster,
'The Ten Commandments of Man to Woman'. Hearing this, Gem
was almost relieved that Josh had upped and left. 'How dare he
speak to you in that horrible way!' she burst out. Suddenly she felt
terribly protective, it made her wonder if she had a maternal streak
after all.

'How could Catherine do it? Leave her children!' Gem didn't
expect a reply. David, that was easy, slimy sneery hand-under-the-
table David, 'Oh I'm sorry, did I put my hand on your breast by
mistake.' Catherine could've chosen any number of men, richer,
funnier, cleverer than Josh to run off with into the sunset, why ruin
it for Sarah Jane? Why choose your sister's fiancé? Maybe they'd
both met their match.

Now she had to help Sarah Jane, number one priority.

'I'm sorry, Sarah Jane. I don't know what to say. I'm so
shocked. I had no idea!'

'How could they do it. My own sister? Gem, tell me, am I so
awful that Catherine and Josh would do this to me?' Her eyes
begged pathetically for reassurance.

Gem held her face in her hands and said, 'Of course not. You're
beautiful and sweet, you don't deserve it, not in a million years.
Bastards! Catherine, I thought we knew her.'

'What am I going to do now?' pleaded Sarah Jane, tears
descending her cheekbones. 'What's the point, my life's finished
without Josh. I loved him and I thought, I thought I knew he loved
me. I did, I did, I di . . .' She wailed, despair again, and sunk back,
sheltering her head in her arms.

Gem held and soothed her and searched desperately for appropriate condolences. She'd already used half of them. She tried to
think what she would've wanted to hear, perhaps nothing was best
– a human nodding dog to cling to and comfort you, agreeing
absolutely. Gem, for once, a rock in the squall of somebody else's
chaos.

CHAPTER NINETEEN

'Gem how dare you not be in! I've had David on my telephone half
the afternoon and I've got to tell someone!' shouted Honor to the
beep of Gem's answerphone. 'Look it's important, we must talk. I'm
in all night, call, extreme urgency. Oh, it's Honor at six thirty.'

Honor had got home from work after trudging around the new
layout of the supermarket with Jack unable to find anything. She
was relieved to be home until she listened to the short tense
message from David and another from Jeremy.

Sweet Jack could sense it. 'What's up Mum, why the grouch?'
Honor replied with a look. He gave her a wide birth after his nag of
hunger was satiated with a banana and a biscuit, and then settled
himself with a large pad of paper and felt-tip pens to redesign his
favourite superheroes.

Meanwhile Honor unpacked the shopping, made herself a cup
of tea and sought privacy in her bedroom. The bedroom still smelt
of the night before and sex with Jeremy, even though she'd left
the window open through the rain of the day, chancing burglary.
She took a Christmas gift of perfume and sprayed liberally until it
made her cough. Jack had commented on the funny smell that
morning, punching Honor's guilt bag of 'sexless motherdom'.
Unless you are going to be a whore, have a child and you've
taken the madonna life-membership card. Half of her wanted to
tell him the truth – 'Darling Jack, there's something you should
know, your father was here last night and he always did smell
peculiar,' but she could only hear Celia Johnson's *Brief Encounter*
voice, circa 1942.

She shut the window, lay against the pillows of her bed, took a
sip of tea and, feeling a little more relaxed, returned David's call.
Jeremy's she could deal with later.

'Catherine's left me and the children,' David had said bluntly.
She'd only asked how he was and she couldn't think of any
response but, 'What?'

He'd repeated it slowly as if she was terribly stupid, 'With

Josh. She's left me and run off with Josh. Josh Todd, her sister Sarah Jane's fiancé. The wedding won't be happening.'

'No,' Honor replied. 'I don't suppose it will.'

They listened to each other breathe through the phone for a moment, before Honor asked, 'Are you all right David, is there anything I can do?'

'Of course I'm not bloody well all right.' He sounded like a machine gun ricocheting bullets across the line.

There was more silence and sniffs, as he swallowed some Scotch to dissipate the lump growing in his throat. 'It's the children, I've rung you, Honor, because of the children. They don't seem to be taking it very well and I'm, you see I'm not much, I need someone to help them.'

'I see, yes of course. Well I don't know what to suggest quite. Would you like me and Jack to come and stay? I can't think what else I can do?'

'I don't think that's quite necessary but if perhaps you could speak to them. I mean you have a child and things, you know what they are like.'

'David, Jack isn't quite the same age as Ben.'

I couldn't deal with my own adolescence, Honor thought but added, 'But of course I'll talk to them. Do you want me to come over now?'

'No. Just so that you know. I mean they're not in, gone to friends' houses.'

'Do you want to talk, David?' Honor enquired as sympathetically as she could to a man she'd never liked. She wasn't surprised at his abrupt response.

'There's nothing else to say. I've told you everything,' he said briskly.

It felt odd talking so intimately to a man she had known for fourteen years, but had never spoken to properly. 'If you do think of anything, you know where I am, don't hesitate. I'm sorry, really I am.'

'It's not your fault, but thanks anyway.'

Honor swallowed his retort and looped the telephone wire tight to strangle her finger. Her voice remained calm though she was annoyed. 'Try to get some rest, sometimes it gets things clearer. I can come over tomorrow, make you dinner.'

'Yes, that might be nice. I'll tell the children, make sure they're here.'

'Just one thing, David, do you know if anyone has told Sarah Jane?'

'Not a clue, but I don't intend being the bearer of bad news again. I've had quite enough for the time being. Goodnight Honor, see you tomorrow.'

'Okay, about six thirty. Night.'

Bloody hell! Bugger me for a packet of biscuits, I've got to get hold of Gem!

Drunk and desolate, David put the phone down on Honor. The dusk's emptiness filled him, moving through his veins, echoing in the hollowness of his limbs. He picked the phone up straight away and called his office. He'd left work early on Catherine's instructions and something must need his attention. He'd intended to speak to his secretary, a homely girl called Judy whom he'd fucked dispassionately a few times. Maybe the comfort of some obliging flesh was what he needed now. Instead Georgina, a new assistant, a junior lawyer was on the other end, and before he realised what he was doing he'd agreed to meet her in his club for a drink that evening.

Some men in times of crisis go to their families, some to their friends, and some to strangers. David could only bear strangers, who could not judge him for what had happened. He needed somebody who didn't know, who could only see the story through his sorry eyes, to cement his truth and understanding and make him feel better.

Before he left home he had a cold shower, a hot shave and he changed. As he was putting on his tie he thought about Ben and Augusta, something he wasn't used to doing. That was Catherine's job, the children were Catherine's duty, it was agreed. He paid the school fees, but she was their mother, after all! He spent twenty minutes searching for phone numbers and ringing around to locate them and another twenty convincing the parents to let them stay the night as he had to sort things out, 'with my wife leaving and everything . . .' They understood, although he didn't even know them. Augusta's friend's mother even asked him around for dinner, he felt a slight heel for lying that he needed this time on his own.

'Of course, of course,' she'd conceded. He didn't speak to the children, explaining that it was probably best if he didn't. What would he have said?

He went down to the kitchen, made and drank some strong coffee, itching within his skin at the responsibility of fatherhood. He was paid for his decisiveness at work, had become a partner because of his ability, but now, faced with this domestic revolution he didn't know where to start (or even how to work the dishwasher).

As he got into his convertible green Saab, a passing bird's indifference to its newly polished surface splattered over the bonnet. That was the problem with buying a house in a street lined with cherry trees, he'd told Catherine at the time and she had laughed. Selfish bitch! he thought and then remembered her letter – boarding schools. He'd get his secretary on to it tomorrow. At least there'd be a saving on Catherine's shopping bills. He turned the key in his ignition and began to see a glimmer at the end of the tunnel.

Fifty pounds spent in the supermarket yet when Honor looked in the fridge and the cupboards there still didn't seem to be an actual meal for supper.

The Catherine and Josh drama filled her mind. She imagined them on the aeroplane sipping champagne in first class and wondered how they were feeling about Sarah Jane, how long any relationship could last with the strain of that guilt upon it. It didn't really surprise her. They were similar animals. Catherine was too sophisticated for Josh Todd but she obviously had what he wanted, what Sarah Jane lacked. And if Catherine wanted something, she got it. Always had.

'Mum, what's that smell, you're not burning the sausages again?' Jack resignedly shouted over the strains of a *Batman* video.

'I'm doing it on purpose, they taste better burnt,' she lied, then gave way. 'Sorry Jack, I'll do you another.' She pulled the bacon out from under the sausages and stuck a few rashers with the tomatoes into the bread's casing, squadging it down so the juices ran, wrapping it in foil to keep warm, and put a couple more virgin sausages on for Jack. Removing the burnt ones she dipped one into the top of the open Dijon jar, and popped it straight into her mouth.

She thought about her selfishness, not wanting Jeremy to see Jack. She was afraid for her son that Jeremy would appear for a few outings, get bored and disappear; a momentary passion. She wanted to shield Jack from the pain she'd had to go through. She had to believe that Jeremy wouldn't do the same thing again to his son, that Jack would be special to him, whatever happened between her and him.

There was no doubt, Jack wanted a father, someone to call Dad. Other boys had them, why shouldn't he? But did it have to be Jeremy? They didn't talk about it often, but when The Dad Question came up she tried to be as positive as she could, and would tell Jack how clever and handsome his father was. When he asked what he was like she could never bring herself to use the word 'kind' without linking it to 'of'. Jack was too direct. He'd asked, 'But my dad, he's kind too, isn't he?' and she'd replied, 'Mmm.' She supposed he must be at work. What makes a person be a doctor after all? It can't just be for the power of the waiting room.

Things had to be better between Jeremy and Jack than between Ben and David. She couldn't have borne David's lack of involvement with his own little girl, whom he spoilt relentlessly but only with presents. There was a part of her that said, We've managed this long without him, don't let him believe he can nudge in and collect the prize best bits that I've spent all my time and care making good.

Honor had known that when Jack got older she would have to track Jeremy down. Now here he was begging for a favourable introduction and she was offering it to him like a carrot for good behaviour. Jack wasn't any donkey's carrot and Jeremy could never be controlled, not by her. She knew that.

'How do you feel, Jack, about meeting your dad, I mean your real one, sometime?' she had asked in a trying-to-be-casual manner.

'Good,' he said, nodding his head and raising his brows with distinct interest, before putting the straws from his bottle of water into his mouth.

It was as easy as that. Now all she had to do was ring up Jeremy and set a date.

My, how fast life can move when you let it, Honor thought and smiled, putting the tin of sticky toffee pudding into a saucepan of water and turning the cooker on.

Just as they were sitting down to the delights of the Simpsons, the phone rang.

'Tell them to call back, we're busy,' Jack shouted for the caller to hear, as Honor picked up the phone.

'Hello, House of Charm, who's calling?' Honor counteracted.

'Mum please, you're missing the good bits.'

'Honor, it's Gem here. I'm calling from Sarah Jane's, something's happened.'

'I know. I was trying to call you about it, I've heard from David. I was waiting to call Sarah Jane once Jack was in bed.'

'I'm not going to bed, Mum, not tonight.'

'Hold on a minute, I'll take this next door.'

'Mum!' Jack whined at Honor's disappearing back. She signalled back to him 'one minute' with her face and fingers before closing her bedroom door on the TV. 'Gem, are you there?'

'Yup, been here all afternoon. Can we come over? Sarah Jane doesn't want to sleep alone. She's just having a rest, exhausted from all the crying.'

'Sure. What time will you get here?'

'Around seven thirty, okay?'

'Yeah sure. I'll fix up some nourishing soup and make sure the monkey's in bed. I can always sleep in the other bunk if you two want to share my bed.'

'See how it goes, you know me and my homing instinct.'

'Oh go on, it'll be a fun pyjama party, not that I'm trying to belittle the gravity of the situation,' said Honor in a moment of light-heartedness.

'Something's got to lighten the load, otherwise it's going to be a heavy one.'

'We can drink some wine and all get heartily maudlin. So Gem, shock horror?'

'Shocked. That Catherine could have done this to her own sister.'

'That was my thought. Why don't we think, how could Josh have done this to Sarah Jane? We automatically put the blame on Catherine. I suppose neither of us knows Josh well enough to judge from his past behaviour.'

'Hhhmm.'

'What's hmmm supposed to mean? Do you know something about a seedy Josh Todd history that you haven't let on about?'

'Yes, and now's not the time to share it, I'll tell you later.'

'Promise?'

'Promise but I never want Sarah Jane to know,' said Gem, looking across at Sarah Jane sleeping on the sofa. She saw the irony of now being her support, where a few weeks ago she'd have been willing to take Catherine's place. Who then would have been here tending Sarah Jane? Catherine?

'My God, I'm not sure I want to know.'

'Don't ask. See you later.'

Honor went back to her seat, son and pudding.

'Mum, who was that on the phone? You're missing all the really funny bits.'

'Don't I know it. It was Gem.'

'Oh really, what did she have to say?' he asked in an uninterested grown-up tone that she recognised as being her father's, reading the paper over breakfast.

'Oh just her and Sarah Jane are coming over later. You sound like Grandpa.'

'Do I?' He smiled, impressed by himself.

'I suppose I better haul myself up and make soup. Did I get any vegetables?'

'That's all you ever get.'

'At least I got something besides ice pops. Spinach and chickpeas should do it, loads of garlic, olive oil, a whoosh of red wine, but have I got any thyme?'

'Time for what? You're always late.'

'Ha ha it's a herb, get on with *Top of the Pops*. Shout if anything happens.'

'Okay. I'm going to get my guitar and drums and then you can join my band, Mum.'

'Great, we can audition them when they arrive. Sarah Jane was in a band.'

'What were they called?'

'Something too embarrassing to repeat.'

'Oh go on, tell me Mum.'

'The G-Strings, but you're not allowed to tease her.'

'Why's it so embarrassing? Mum, why can't I tease her?'

CHAPTER TWENTY

As Gem put the phone down, she felt slightly chastened by Honor's attitude. She knew that sleeping with Josh wasn't politically correct, but it was no worse than what most American presidents did daily. She'd done her penance and forgiven herself. She wasn't going to show her bloody wound to be doused in bleach by others.

Gem sighed, looking down at Sarah Jane, child-like in sleep with a flawless innocence, pretty in spite of her deeds. Her thick blonde hair curled across peachy skin, her pink lips whispered apart with a sleeping breath. Curled upon the sofa in a foetal position, Gem eased her head back to a pillow without waking the princess. What fairytales we believe as children, set upon our courses as princesses, evil witches, wicked daughters or ugly sisters.

She'd spent all day as agony aunt and therapist, a would-be Cinders skivvying about the flat. Rolling her shirt-sleeves up and finding a dirty tea towel to wrap around her waist, she had tried to get things straight in her head before she began the cleaning. She was not being good out of guilt, nor from pity, but for friendship. She could give Sarah Jane a real gift, one of order. Surely there was some adage about a tidy home leading to a tidy mind. She didn't expect she could do much for the emotions or central nervous system, but that would come in time. Time healed, take just the one day at a time and it got better, even Gem knew that.

Somebody had once expensively furnished the hideous apricot and beige kitchen but finding a bin-liner or plastic bag to sort the rubbish and mould samples into seemed impossible. Pity Gem never took greater interest in science and chemistry, she was sure there'd be a cure for something amongst all the detritus. Perhaps Sarah Jane's hobby could blossom into a new career, providing hospital laboratories with samples, she'd mention it once her friend regained consciousness and a sense of humour.

Gem emptied the sink on to the sideboard and squirted the last of the washing-up liquid into the thundering hot water. Of course, no washing-up gloves, no Jif, one dog-eared J-cloth and a half-flattened dishwashing brush. It would do. She dumped all the cups and glasses into the bowl to soak, the ones she could find. Any hiding and forgotten under beds were probably settled with families by now and she didn't want to break up any happy homes; they were so rare these days. She got back to turn off the taps moments before the waterfall started; it wouldn't have gone amiss, washing the floor, but one thing at a time. She put away old jars of jam, honey and ketchup, then wiped the surface down with the remnants of a mysterious bleach bottle hiding under the sink. The packaging looked like it must have been left over from the last tenant. Finally she set to with the washing up and tried not to look at the skins that floated to the surface where the bubbles were gently popping; the sight made her nose wrinkle up with disgust. Gem liked hygiene with a capital H.

There is something so much more satisfying about restoring order to somebody else's chaos, than to your own. Spend time helping others, curing their ills and perhaps you won't have to look at your own. Isn't the cobbler the worst shod? What was dinner going to be like at Honor's tonight – tin stew? Gem remembered the scrumptious recipes she was transcribing into the unnecessary wedding present. Would it be appropriate to change the bride's name and give it to Catherine instead? Perhaps she should just send it to an agent or publisher as a surprise once she'd finished it and see what happened; just present Honor with a contract. That would be perfect. Half of it was done, there wasn't much point in wasting it all, if it didn't work out it didn't matter, it was fun. To eat or not to eat. That is the question. Whether it be nobler in the mind to suffer the slings and arrows of outrageous fat or hunger . . .

In the living room she picked clothes off chairs, the floor, the table and the disused ironing board and found cupboards, hangers and a laundry basket to redistribute them into. She wished there had been rubber gloves. There was something particularly horrible about another woman's dirty knickers, even if they were your friend's.

As she worked down on her hands and knees with a dustpan and brush, it struck Gem that it could have been her flying off into the sunset with Josh Todd. She imagined herself sipping champagne in first class, looking out of the window at take-off, having sex in the loo with baby-changing facility ... it could so nearly have been her. A squeeze of sadness pinched at her dream until it was blocked out by evidence of his unattractive behaviour which Sarah Jane had been admitting to. Images gleaned from sixties films, *The Party* and *Midnight Cowboy*, mingled in her head, acts of humiliation, the ritual of verbal abuse. She saw scenes from Polanski's *Bitter Moon*, all the lies. Best to think of nothing, she decided as she picked up, tidied, put things back, folded others; her mind an uneasy blank.

As she pushed the clothes to the back of the wardrobe, Gem saw the silver plastic coating that covered the wedding dress. She couldn't help herself, she had to look. She reached in and pulled it out and gently unzipped its cover. It made her gasp, the beautiful pure white dress with its hand-sewn pearls and delicate lace on silk, everything it stood for made her cry. She wept fat wet tears for Sarah Jane's loss and for her own prospects. How long could she keep kidding herself she was a girl, young enough for disco mini-skirts and one-night stands?

She had an awful sinking feeling that what her parents said about her was coming true, that her selfishness and hostility towards people she didn't know (they hadn't ever seen how friendly she got in a club at three in the morning) drove people away.

If she was ever going to find a husband, she would have to change, they'd begin (they were actually referring to her clothes). She was no longer young enough to be choosy if she intended having children. 'You can't go on forever behaving like a teenager,' her mother would say at table in front of her father. Once out of earshot from him, back in the kitchen, she would change the focus to, 'Don't waste your life getting married. Men just use you up and spit you out, that's what your father's done with me.'

'Why?' Gem had always retorted. 'If somebody loves me, and loves me for how I am, they won't want to change me. Will they?'

Won't they? Oh won't they?

No, but if you're not happy you might want to change for yourself, the thought suddenly struck through her self-pitying sobs. It could be her choice, too. She'd not do it for anyone else, but for herself? Perhaps.

As she searched in her pocket for something to blow her nose on she pulled out a wrinkled piece of paper that somebody had given her a few days ago, 'One day workshop seminar, Learning to Love Yourself Once More.'

Hmm, she thought, picking it up, perhaps this would be good for Sarah Jane.

'My God Georgina, has anyone told you how lovely you are? I don't think I've come across such compassion and understanding in a woman. You're really lovely. Quite the opposite to that bitch of a wife,' David said drunkenly to his dining companion, his assistant lawyer. He had told her the saga. She was suitably sympathetic, unbuttoning her shirt to reveal her cleavage.

He was paying the bill at the time with his gold American Express card, and all twenty-six years and five feet eleven inches of her were dazzled by his mature sophistication and ease in his surroundings. She wasn't by that point too sober herself. The champagne and brandy fizzed giddyingly inside her. When he took her tanned hand in his she guided his finger between her lips to gently nibble; after all, his socked toe had been riding up between her stockinged legs like some clawless mole ever since pudding.

David swaggered out of the restaurant more pleased with his lot than for a long time. The lovely, silky, taut fleshed, generous Georgina followed, giggling girlishly behind. Sex with the boss. When they got to his car, he said smoothly, 'Can I give you a lift home, you gorgeous thing?'

'As long as it's yours!' she teased, and suddenly hit by his new freedom, he began to laugh.

Despair can shrink a body and Sarah Jane's jeans seemed too baggy, her jacket looked like it had been borrowed from her dad, and her hair in childish plaits, sticking out from her ears, cemented the image. Only her eyes had grown, large and wounded, a St Bernard dog's piteously pleading for kindness. She walked into Honor's arms like a long-lost mother's, and buried herself into a soft shoulder. Comfortable Honor, honest, solid and strong, patted and rocked Sarah Jane in the way she was used to soothing any sore child.

Jack had had to go to bed disappointed. By eight fifteen the guests still hadn't arrived and there was no bartering to be done. Honor thought it just as well, couldn't see that the emotional turmoil they would bring with them could do a young boy much good. Best he was tucked up warm in bed with Bear, another battered, unrecognisable love-object. Hard to see which was in better shape, Sarah Jane or Bear, but at least Sarah Jane still had both ears and her nose intact. Only the stuffing had been knocked out.

Sarah Jane awakened to a different place, a flat she hadn't seen in months – her own but clean. It seemed part of a dream sequence of events. She did as she was told by Gem, a Mogodonned patient sealed with bromide.

She found her lost security blanket in the form of Honor, and she didn't want to cry any more, just cling. There wasn't a wet eye in the house, the tears had all been used up, a dry shudder and an empty heave were all Sarah Jane could muster. Gem followed in the rear, hearty from ordering Sarah Jane's chaos, fully recovered from her own bout of hysteria, the school prefect organising somebody else into clothes, shoes and a cab.

'I've left my bike in your hall, nobody will mind will they? The miserable cab driver wasn't too pleased about it in the car. Hmm, something smells delicious,' Gem enthused.

Honor shook her head, 'fine', and silently mouthed the word 'soup' over Sarah Jane's bowed head. There were moments to be quiet but Gem didn't notice.

'The thing we've got to tackle tonight is BIG MAMA, how to tell her.'

'Don't worry, we'll think of something, it's not a problem. Let's eat first. Get some food into you, Sarah Jane, and then these three brilliant brains will connive. Come on, sweetheart. All right now?' Honor cajoled, trying to patch over Gem's steamrollering effect.

'Okay,' replied a little voice to Honor's hair.

Honor guided Sarah Jane to a chair, gently easing the jacket from her back, before picking up the ladle and playing mother with the soup, passing the bread and the plate of cheese for her second meal of the night. After the first bowl and couple of glasses of wine, Sarah Jane's restored engine began to purr. It must be the soup, thought Honor, heartened by the medicinal qualities of her own cooking. Gem knew it was the Prozac that they'd searched for before they left the flat. Oh dear, what comes up has to come down. Soon words of anger, injustice, jealousy and outrage began with such energetic vehemence that it frightened Honor.

This can't be the Prozac, thought Gem. It must be something else. Wasn't Prozac supposed to contain not explode the emotions, keep you happy, not manic? She smiled nervously over at Honor, reassurance for both of them.

Sarah Jane's anger wasn't exploding just against Josh and Catherine, but at her mother and step-father too. Soon she was ready to make the phone call. The problem was she didn't want to stop at one, she wanted to tell them all exactly how she felt, rub their faces in her spleen. Her friends tried to calm her down but she was wild in her insistence. The phone rang as Sarah Jane walked towards it. Honor rushed to answer it. 'Hi it's me.' She had known it would be Jeremy, whom she hadn't called back.

'Hello,' she replied.

'Well lover mother?' Honor turned away from the others feeling her face flush, embarrassed at his words. 'I'm coming over in half an hour with a bottle of Chablis, is there something to eat? Can we repeat last night?' She was panicked, dumb with the horror of the idea. 'And this weekend I'm booking some tickets on the Eurostar, first class to Paris. You can bring Jack, we'll be like a family again. Honor are you there, what's wrong?' The confidence of his earlier words drained away in the unresponsive silence.

'Nothing, sorry. Look, Sarah Jane and Gem are over. Now's not a good time.'

'What's wrong, anything you need a doctor for?' he chuckled.

'No, I'll call you tomorrow.' And she put the phone down quickly so he couldn't chirpily respond. She passed it to Sarah Jane to start dialling.

'It's me, Mummy, Sarah Jane. Yes. I'm sorry I didn't call you as soon as I got in but I'm calling now. No, I can't call back in the morning. I have to tell you something – the wedding's off. No Mummy, it's not my fault. No, it's not my nerves, and for once I'm not being ridiculous. It won't be happening. No it can't. There's nothing to patch up. MUMMY WILL YOU JUST LISTEN. I'm sorry to interrupt but . . . there's only one way to say this. No Mummy, he isn't "queer". Josh has run off back to LA with Catherine. Which

Catherine do you bloody well think! Your daughter . . .'

Honor and Gem sat on the sofa by Sarah Jane and studied their nails. You didn't need to hear what her mother was saying, it was predictable. The one surprise was that both her daughters had turned out so sane, relatively speaking. Honor got up and Gem followed to clear the table, start the washing up and whisper. Listening to the conversation was too much like being an emotional voyeur – it made Honor feel sick.

'So, what's happening with Harry? I take it that was Jeremy?' Gem asked, changing the subject and picking up the drying-up cloth decorated with a hundred children's self-portraits, including Jack's. 'Ahh you can't use this to dry up with, this is sacrosanct, Honor. Little Jack.'

'Big galumphing Jack! I know you've had yours framed but I'm surrounded by the paraphernalia of Jack's childhood genius and there isn't anything else. Yup. Harry? What indeed is happening? It's all up to me and I can't decide.'

'Not the Jeremy? But you said he was hopeless in bed!'

'I know, he is, but maybe it's me, a thousand women can't all be wrong! Don't look at me that way Gem. He wants to take Jack and me to Paris, next weekend. And,' she added as justification, 'first class!'

'So what about Harry?' Gem persevered.

'I don't know, it's all a bit scary-serious. He's talking committed relationships. I've not lied, I've told him that Jeremy is about and that I have to think carefully, him being the father of my child and all that. I have this strange belief that somehow it is desirable to be reared by your parents.'

'If they're suitable,' Gem dropped with aplomb. 'You mean you've got to choose.' Gem could feel a note of jealousy creeping into her tone, she didn't like it and Honor felt churlish for presenting the facts in such a negative, self-pitying manner, but she couldn't stop herself.

'Yes, I have to think really hard and make the right decision. Change is scary. I can always use Jack as an excuse, but it's me in the end. I must want to be in a committed relationship otherwise they wouldn't all be queuing up for it.'

Hearing the usually optimistic Honor defeated quite cheered Gem up.

'Once you don't need it, it always arrives gift-wrapped, just like buses. You have to order your choices for the future, write a list.'

'But you can't predict what's going to happen. Look at all this. Just when you thought it was safe . . . dun, dun, dun, dun, *The Twilight Zone*.' Honor nodded her head back in the direction of poor Sarah Jane, still wrestling with her mother over the scandal, the marquee hire, the vicar and her step-father.

'But isn't that part of the joy and excitement of it all, life's adventure, that anything can change?'

'It's all right for you, you haven't got the responsibilities of motherhood. Any decision isn't just about me, it's a question of Jack's childhood, his understanding of life, his morals . . . God, I'm depressing myself! Anyway what are you on, Miss Relentlessly Chirpy, Prozac?'

'No, but I know a girl who is.' Gem signalled with her eyes in the direction of the ranting Heidi on the couch. 'Don't fancy your phonebill much, ho, ho!' She elbowed Honor in the ribs and they both erupted into sshhing, stifled giggles.

CHAPTER TWENTY-ONE

Before the end of the month David was taking whole days off work, the kids with him, touring the countryside for 'fee-paying Borstals' as he jokingly called his research work. Honor had told him about a book, *The Independent Boarders' Handbook*, and advised him to engage the kids in the decision. She suggested he send Ben and Gussy to a mixed modern non-uniform school (so that the change wouldn't be too drastic) where they could have fun with other kids and still be together. David didn't know why he was listening to her, a friend of Catherine's, but anything to get the kids off his back. He couldn't cope with them, they behaved like beasts, they weren't as he imagined his children should be.

Augusta seemed to be taking to the idea with enthusiasm, once she'd got through the first bout of serious tears. David was cheered by her response while Ben flooded the house with a tangible misery that dripped through the floorboards. Although David put it down to age and hormones, he had started to wonder if his own mother wasn't right. She had always told him that he should've sent Ben to a prep school at the age of five. That would have beaten some sense into him.

Ben never had got on with Grandma Stimpson. He loathed his step-grandfather even more, a weak cowardly man hiding behind his moustache and blue blazer, fortified with a whisky smile for his always-right wife, who had to be pacified. Each time they left the privet-hedged confines of the 'tea with Grandma ritual', Ben would think how like his own mother and father they were in public. He wondered whether his grandfather turned on Grandma Stimpson as soon as they closed the door; Ben wouldn't have blamed him, but he doubted it.

Turning on the engine to make their escape down the crackling drive, David would predictably say, 'Now that wasn't so bad, was it?'

Usually Ben and Augusta agreed in bored unison, 'No. When are we getting home?' each time lying better.

After Catherine left, Ben got sick of twisting the truth. One day after the tea ritual he asked, 'When are they going to die? Isn't it about time?'

David wasn't even shocked, tired out as he was by his son's continual rudeness. He snapped back his uncensored thoughts, 'God am I going to be glad to get rid of you to boarding school!'

It kept the kids quiet until they parked outside the house on that Sunday evening. David felt justified; if Ben wasn't willing to play the game of decent civility, he was damned if he would. Inside, there was the welcoming smell of dinner, the fake gas-flame fire blazed in the living room.

'Don't tell me Georgina's here again!' Ben spat in resigned disgust.

'I take it you'd rather cook your own dinner? Or perhaps you'd like to ask your mother to?' his father replied, before going downstairs and shouting back up, 'If you're going to join us, I'd like a little manners and some common decency for once, Benjamin.'

'Common decency is about all you'd understand old man,' muttered Ben too quietly for anyone to hear but himself. 'Common is about your level!'

Nobody mentioned Catherine in the house except David, still tangled in her gall of which Ben's behaviour was a continual reminder. David thought he could make do, but he couldn't even heat tinned soup without spoiling it. He expected his children to grin and live with the consequences. Nobody could change what had happened, they had to bear it. The old au pair was on extra time and extra pay, having been called back after only a week home. The house was kept up, minus the floral decorations, the food shopping done, the cleaner came in an extra day a week and now Georgina was making the family meals; things were coming along nicely. David was drinking too much perhaps, but at least he was beginning to feel a little happier with the prospect of the children going away.

Augusta seemed to have come back a lot better after staying with Honor for a few days, a lot better. He wasn't sure what she'd told her but he'd wished that Ben had gone too. He had refused.

His days spent locked up in his room alone, or with his mates, Ben would forage down to the kitchen for fridge-raids cloaked in hostility, the prince of grievance. He felt it making him harder, intolerant to his younger sister, spiteful to his father, resentful of this girlfriend who in minutes seemed to be settling into his house. Sometimes he even felt like calling reverse charge to his mother just to tell her about it, until he remembered his anger with her too. He had plenty to moan about with his friends, who seemed the only ones to understand. Now he was being taken away from them too. He played with his computer games a lot; a Playstation rigged into his TV gave him a new life of running and zapping karate video enemies to the wall. The more he played the less he had to think about what was going on around him, any school they were due to visit became just another Stalag for inspection. They were all the same, one thing after another melting together, one meal following the last. Filling in time, for what? Life was a pointless charade, a rigged game.

'Ben!' Augusta stood knocking on the other side of Ben's self-constructed bolt. 'Ben it's dinner-time. Daddy says you don't have to come down but don't expect any food unless you do. It's your favourite, fried chicken and cornbread. Come on Ben, shall I wait for you?' Augusta whispered to the door in an act of friendship, the nearest she came to being able to say she loved him. She couldn't chance it any more. The last time she had, he'd spat at her in condemnation before adding, 'You don't even know the meaning of the word!'

Not that anyone seemed to in their family.

'Don't bother. I'm coming.'

She waited anyway, sitting on the top of the stairs, hands flattened beneath her bum, knees brought up to her resting chin. She thought about how Honor had told her not to mind how Ben behaved towards her, to them all. That he was the oldest and the most hurt and when people said nasty things they were only ever saying them about themselves. That when you were happy and loved, you could afford to be loving to the rest of the world, and that nasty cruel cranky people were the ones to feel sorry for because they can't show kindness. They don't know what it is, and when they're shown it, they can only be suspicious.

Of course it was shit, the only people she and Catrina felt sorry for were the ones who hadn't got a clue about how they looked, like Honor, but still Gus used for her own purpose the chant of, 'What you say, is what you are!' to annoy Ben and get the last word.

Other plots hatched in her mind, something Honor had said about looking at the positive aspects, concentrating on what you've got, which she translated to 'what you can get'. Augusta was practising on her father until she could get away to boarding school and then America for the summer, maybe forever. She rang her Mum every day and Catherine promised her golden cornucopian dreams that Augusta intended to collect. She wanted them for Ben too, but he said he never wanted to see Catherine ever again. Fool.

The door to his room clicked open and he vaguely raised his eyebrows under his slouch, in acknowledgement of his sister, as he kicked her aside to go first. 'You know Ben, if we go along with them, play their game, we can really milk this one,' Augusta said to the back of his hunched form. 'We can get anything we like . . . we just have to think of it. Catrina says that you get four holidays a year, presents from the boyfriends and girlfriends. Listen, I bet Josh Todd knows all the *Baywatch* babes . . .'

'Oh shut up, Augusta, stop talking crap! Don't you ever get sick of the sound of your own voice?'

'No, don't you get sick of moaning? Oh Ben,' she stopped him in the corridor with her hand pulling on his elbow. 'Can't we try to be friends a little, stop arguing, just us two. At least we can be together against them,' she sneered, jerking her head in the direction of the kitchen. 'I told Georgina to cook fried chicken and cornbread, that it was our favourite food and if she wanted to be friends with our family . . . you should see the amount of cookbooks she bought trying to find the recipes. She's been practising for days trying to get it right, you can tell, there's masses.'

They both burst into smirks of laughter at the preposterous image of Georgina trying to ingratiate herself, of anyone trying to please them. 'And I told her the only pudding Dad really likes is Baked Alaska with meringue and ice-cream, but to keep it secret because he loves surprises.'

'But Augusta, he hates surprises, and meringues.'

'I know! Pretty funny huh? Sit back and watch.'

Both of them went into the kitchen laughing. Ben was impressed with his sister.

'What have we to congratulate for this change of humour? I can't keep up with your mood swings. Sit down, is it a private joke or can we all join in?' their father asked quizzically before growing slightly nervous at the tone of their laughter. They reminded him of Catherine. He was always having to tell her she laughed too loud, too easily.

'No, it's private,' Augusta replied, slipping a sly-eyed look at her brother, across the table.

'I think it's lovely you get on so well. I always wished I'd had an elder brother, so I could get to date all his friends,' said Georgina, thinking she was in the swing.

'Do you think any of my friends would fancy Gussy?' Ben answered in disgust. 'Get real!'

'But it works both ways, you get to date all the friends that she brings home.' Georgina was determined to keep cheery though a sense warned her it was going to be a difficult dinner. She had set herself these sights and intended to fulfil them; she'd have this address as hers, already a dress hung in the wardrobe. It was going well with David, if she could just get along with the children . . .

'Hardly the point since we're going to be locked away in a boarding school next week. Eh Dad, you'll soon have got rid of us, and then you can have our home for just you and your girlfriends.'

'That's quite enough, Ben. Can we maintain some sort of civilised behaviour, hm?'

There was silence as dinner was placed on the table and the vegetables passed around that bewildered David with their authenticity. 'Splendid effort,' he said.

Encouraged by David, Georgina bravely tried to engage in conversation, break up the raging silence. Every topic she raised fell flat; she gave up and listened to the tick-tock of the kitchen clock and the sounds of food being devoured. It was only once Ben had finished off three pieces of chicken, four cornbreads, half the sweet potatoes and slurped his apple juice down that he turned to his father. He felt nourished, ready for confrontation, and anyway he had to get out the words that kept going round his head, the over-rehearsed questions. He didn't care about the answers.

'It didn't take you long Dad, did it, to find a replacement for Mum, or did you have her there waiting on the sidelines?'

'Ben, don't be so rude. Georgina's just cooked us a, urghhmm, lovely meal, she is a friend of mine and I'm sure she doesn't want to listen to this childish conversation.'

Georgina had found it hard enough to get through dinner and

had stuck to her wine. She would've preferred the silence to the conversation that was now underway, the whole topic made her prickle with unease, twitch in her skin. She got up from the table to put the pudding into the oven, she hoped this sweet tip of Augusta's would appease David.

'Oh I forgot, we can't talk about anything that's embarrassing like getting rid of nasty children or mothers, or dumping anything else, for that matter. Do you remember, Gussy, our favourite nanny Mia that Daddy and Mummy got rid of? You were four and I was six, they thought she was stealing money and then Daddy found out it was the gardener, silly Daddy. But nobody told Mia and we weren't allowed ever to speak to her again. Do you remember how we were sent up to our room and watched her out the window, crying down the street. We weren't even allowed to say goodbye.

'Strange, all those years with her and one day she was gone, just like Mum. Now that's what I call being civilised!' and he burped as an appropriate punctuation. 'Oh pardon me!'

'I don't want to discuss this. I refuse to talk to you when you're like this Ben. How dare you be so insolent as to talk to me in this way? I won't have it! GO TO YOUR ROOM – NOW!'

'Daddy is that true about Mia, that she never did it? Dad, is it true? We were never allowed to speak to her, you said she was a common thief and she was the one nanny we loved. I loved Mia and she loved us and you sent her away for nothing?' Augusta was in tears of recrimination. 'Ben is it true?' she pleaded.

Ben didn't bother turning around, he was busy pulling a Coke from the fridge and an apple to go with the bar of chocolate he had upstairs. He wasn't staying around in this pigswill.

Georgina had turned her back, started clearing the plates, she couldn't touch her food. She closed her ears and tried to think of something nice, a dress she'd seen in a sale that she'd go back for tomorrow. She went to the oven and peered in at the perfect browned castle peaks of meringue. At least this would cheer him up, she thought.

'Surprise David,' she said, placing Augusta's double-whammy on the table. 'It's your favourite.'

But even the Baked Alaska didn't seem funny any more.

CHAPTER TWENTY-TWO

Three months had gone by since Sarah Jane and Gemma had seen each other, the chalky remains of summer still dusting mid-September as they drove to Norfolk together, car packed to bursting with hat boxes and presents. Wrapped dry cleaning lay elegantly across the back seat like some footless waif on a *chaise-longue*. Central London passed into the distance as they eased on to the motorway, music blaring to their party-mood excitement. Disco, disco, singing along to the words. The fun of escaping together in weekday naughtiness, office blocks full of working people trailed behind.

For Gem and Sarah Jane the weekend started as they travelled to the wedding, giving themselves plenty of time to enjoy the full spectacle. That's what weddings should be about. Not bungling about late with mismatched socks, bored through the ceremony and stuck in the corner of the room with Aunt Cynthia discussing hybrids. A good wedding, and you don't mind if you haven't had a snog at the back of the marquee, let alone got the full business in the bushes with the best man, who turns out to be engaged and won't speak to you over breakfast the following morning. Too often, wedding fantasies are ruined like white shag-pile by red wine, followed by fearful resentments: 'I didn't catch the bride's bouquet, and I should've been the next one up the aisle...' Recriminations and regrets all the way home.

'What are these tapes you've got? It's like going through a retro market, *Sounds of the Seventies*, *ABBA's Greatest Hits*, The Mamas & the Papas, Burt Bacharach, Al Green, didn't he go strangely religious? Haven't you got anything decent like the Swingle Singers.'

'Oh, you're such a gay young thing these days. It must be all that magazine coverage. Claiming you're twenty-five, I saw in one paper! Have you no shame at thirty? I'm afraid you won't find any Goldie in my car, I've thrown the house out into the jungle, man.

Put on the Reverend Green, we can be saved together.'

Sarah Jane slotted the cassette in and turned up the volume, pretended to map-read before giving up to stare out at the sun-patched suburban landscape.

'Hmm not bad. It's just I'm a bit wary of old stuff, after the treatment centre and all that letting go of the past. I don't want to let it back in via The Carpenters. "Why do birds suddenly . . ." ' she crooned, bursting into song.

'Sarah Jane you've got to stop taking things personally, they're only songs.'

'You're asking me to break habits of a lifetime?' she accused mockingly.

'I had to, why shouldn't you? It's not enough that you have to pay these therapists with your life savings, they then expect you to work at it, even after you stop seeing them.' Gem had spent the last two months going once a week and a hundred pounds an hour to Jimmy Salve, fashionable psychotherapist. She knew what she was talking about.

'I keep finding people staring strangely at me in supermarkets as I chant, "Keep it conscious." Pity you can't just buy it like a tin of Bird's custard.'

'Oh no, then everybody would have it!'

'Do you think going to see Jimmy will tip me over the balance and I'll never come back?' Sarah Jane had booked a session, after her period of recuperation in an idyllic country treatment centre where she had 'deep pore cleansing inside and out' as she so neatly put it. Her parents had been sent a large bill which they had sent straight to Josh's agent.

'What like me? When are you starting?'

'I've already started. Jimmy is brilliant, thank you for telling me about him, it's like being back at school getting homework. I've got to write letters to my sister, mother and step-father this week, saying just how I feel about them – the truth! Then I read them out. Scary, but at least I don't have to post them. Anyway that's next week's work, this weekend I'm just going to enjoy myself. This is such fun being with you. We can swap the latest.'

'I know, Jimmy's brilliant, all the fathers and mothers we never had. Talking about relatives, have you heard from Catherine?'

'I told you about that last letter didn't I? All about how she ran off with Mr Fabulous to save me from having to humiliate myself for the rest of my life.'

'Yes, over the phone, maybe she meant it.'

'I'm sure she was trying to do the right thing, but it was hardly in the "best possible taste", I mean she could've talked to me about it first. Asked me perhaps, but no, Catherine has to be the Fat Controller. The big sister, always sorting out everybody else's lives. Look at hers! Not that I'm judging, let go and forgive, in Jimmy-speak.'

Gem didn't want to stir the waters so she let the silence wash over them, and Sarah Jane get back to the map-reading in her where-the-hell-are-we-now style, map upside down. Gem felt two-faced guilt descend, wished she hadn't asked about Catherine, she'd had a letter from her that morning.

Catherine and Gem had been writing to each other ever since she'd eloped with Josh. Sometimes Gem felt like a spy ringing up Sarah Jane to see how she was, the kids, and David, to keep Catherine supplied with inside info. Gem did it to placate the crying, drunken, self-pitying phone calls that woke her up direct from LA at four in the morning. Poor sad Catherine who they all thought had everything, was now teetering on the brink. Living the glamorous high-wire life. Keep the money, the house, the filmstar world – if you can, sweetie. Sarah Jane would have already fallen, Gem didn't doubt that; Catherine was an old hand, she could keep the plates spinning, mask firmly in place. It was just a question of time, how long could she survive living as someone she despised?

In the latest instalment in Gem's leather bag, casually slung behind her driving seat, Catherine had written, 'If I left what would become of me?' For Catherine seemed to have run out of options: no going on and no going back, back to what?

David meanwhile had adjusted quickly to being looked after and cared for by Georgina firmly installed in the shortness of weeks as Catherine's pliable replacement. She was already changing Catherine's designer interiors. Each day a new set of floral Austrian curtains appeared, while the Philippe Starck furniture was hidden, pending the arrival of Colefax and Fowler replacements. Tastes differ between women, but David didn't notice.

Georgina was starting to plan the new nursery in her head after a month. Of course it would mean moving Augusta's room and getting the attic converted, unless Augusta shared with Ben . . . Still they were hardly ever there, their empty rooms were a waste of space now that they were at boarding school most of the time. When she went back to work after two weeks, where would she put the nanny? She fast-forwarded her ambitions till they were almost real.

Ben had been home waiting out a suspension for drinking, drunkenness and violent behaviour, having desecrated the school walls with aggressive graffiti. He hadn't been expelled yet, because of his extenuating circumstances. The school was willing to over-look the drugs, as long as he was able to reflect upon his deeds and his father paid next year's fees in advance. It was nearly the end of the summer term anyway.

Ben didn't give a fuck. He hated everything and everyone, he wanted to go home, but his home wasn't home any more. He couldn't see anything as his own, and was afraid to tell anyone about his fears and losses. For all his normal exterior, he felt unable to comprehend the outside world, while inside he had fits of rage that shook so spasmodically he felt he was being throttled. At other times he was an unanchored blob floating in a void, lost in space – the space where his brain and heart should be. When he read *Fortean Times* he wondered if he'd been abducted and brought to an alien planet in an adjacent sphere. Ben spent most days getting stoned with his old mates, listening to music so loud it flooded him. Nothing mattered much in this state. In the mornings he awoke bright with anger that made him want to rip down walls, or so lethargic he couldn't wank himself out of bed till the afternoon. Once up, he'd put on yesterday's clothes that had also been the day before yesterday's clothes, and slunk silently on kitchen raids that filled him with carbohydrates and sugar until the next day. His father would barely talk to him, Georgina couldn't bear to look at him, neither wanted to smell him. They tried to pretend things were fine, ignoring the stinking adolescent noise that shadowed their domestic bliss.

Late at night Georgina would wake to the angry shouts of David on another transatlantic call to sort out what he called 'the Ben problem'.

'Bitch from hell! He's your bloody child. For God's sake you're his fucking mother, you do something about it you selfish cow . . . If you're not bloody careful you'll find I've put him on the first plane over to you, then think what you'd do . . . Right fine, August they'll both be with you. I look forward to it, shall I break the good news?'

Augusta had warned Ben of the school pupils' motto, 'Do it but don't get done'. Do brothers ever listen? She'd raised her eyebrows to her friends in disbelief at her own kin's stupidity, getting caught spray-can in hand writing an illiterate, inelegant 'This skool is shit', a joint that she'd sold him stuck in his mouth. Very clever, NOT!

The school they were both at was considered to be progressive, its approach being to encourage the students' self-expression, but as they had explained to Ben, if only he'd vented his spleen on canvas in the art studio they could have hung it on the wall and used it as a springboard for discussion. If only he'd been able to come up with good enough explanations for his negative thoughts, he could've stayed on for the rest of the term.

He couldn't communicate, barely grunting, yes or no. If they'd looked inside his head they would've heard his running commentary, 'But were they bothered! Fuck no!' Ben repeated to himself. Nobody cared so why should he!

Augusta herself was running a rather successful drugs boutique. They were mostly the soft things that you could find from rummaging around your parents' drawers and cupboards, lumps of dope and bags of grass, some coke she'd found in her mummy's make-up drawer, but she was a bright girl, good at chemistry, and was busy learning about the medicine cabinet's yielding possibilities, along with the help of a drugs rehab leaflet from the town library.

In her tuck box lay a Sainsbury's bag of assorted goodies gleaned from visits to Granny and friends of parents, repackaged into old sweet wrappers and Smartie tubes. Her best cover from the teachers was her age and her popularity, amongst the other students she was never short of invitations. Augusta was enjoying boarding school, and she told her daddy so. She didn't tell her parents how rich she was getting, her resources were secret. She would count it late at night locked in the loo and sleep well, secured by her flourishing independence, filling an empty hole. Augusta was going to be a successful businesswoman, when she was older, on a global scale, though she wasn't sure whether she'd stick with her main commodity – less for moral reasons than business ones.

In letters to her mother she wrote, 'It's a pity really that Ben can't enjoy himself, but I don't think he could enjoy anything, he's such an old egg he's even getting acne. Yuck! Do send him some special zit cream please, for our sakes. Love Gus. PS, loved the DKNY jacket, is there a matching skirt or dress? Have you seen the new Moschino shoe range? I'm an American size seven.' Gus was Augusta's new identity, her reinvention as fully fledged sophisticate.

Sarah Jane put a new tape in, rap remixes of seventies disco, a new version of '*Voulez-vous Couchez Avec Moi*' came on: Lady Marmelade.

'God, do you remember this one back at school?' Gem said, remembering it from the disco the night she had got off with Josh.

Sarah Jane laughed, 'This is brand new, you are time-warped Gem.'

'Yeah, yeah. God this brings back memories. Do you remember all those unspoken rules that seemed so deadly serious when we were teenagers, what you could and couldn't do, what they would and wouldn't respect you for. How girls who were on the pill claimed it was as a period stabiliser, that they weren't possibly using it to have sex with their boyfriends.'

'Ahh those were the days when you didn't have to know how to put a condom on a boy sexily, or worry about it splitting, you just got on the pill when you were fourteen and started practising. Do you think it's just luck that my AIDS test came back clear, or does God intend me for some special mission on this earth?'

'I think we're both incredibly lucky. Special agent Sarah Jane – the Woman from Aunty, you know like the Man from Uncle!'

'The Woman from Aunty? Sounds like I'm a tea lady at the BBC.'

'Aunty, how are Augusta and Ben managing in their boarding school, all those drugs and sex on tap?'

'Not at their age, not my little niece and nephew! All I can report is that neither one is pregnant so that's a success. Mind, they do say that they do it younger these days, they're certainly developing younger. I went to see them after rehab so I could make my amends to them and their father. Augusta's out of teen bras and she's not even teenage. I think they must be putting hormones in the water. God knows what the holidays will have done to them, with Catherine and Josh in LA?'

'Do you think it's morally reprehensible to send under eight-eens there? Poor things. We all have our journeys.'

'Isn't it nice not to have to lie about what you want any more as long as you can cope with your own feelings,' Sarah Jane said, off on a tangent.

'Ahh the wonderful freedom. I am not responsible for anyone else's feelings?'

'I'm practising that at the moment. You don't mind if I try out on you – slag bucket?'

'Sweet tenderness, I must think of some term of endearment for you – douche bag fit?' Gem replied jokingly.

'Thank God it's not me getting married tomorrow. I know I've gone back over it enough to bore my own hind legs off, but I have to remind myself what my sister saved me from. Josh used to come out with some of the sweetest sayings, kinda give you goose pimples as he slapped you around the head with them. I don't know why I put up with him – it's not as though he was so fabulous in bed, not with me anyway, maybe he was using it up on everyone else. I suppose the money and glamour helped, helped getting the drugs. Was he good with you? You did go to bed with him didn't you? I mean everyone else did. Chance to screw the famous movie slag.'

What had Sarah Jane been saying about not having to lie any more? Gem kicked herself, this was one of her best friends directly asking her a question she didn't want to answer truthfully, whom she cared about hurting. She knew she wasn't meant to take on anyone else's pain, but Sarah Jane had enough to cope with trying to recover. Did she need to know this? Did she know already, was she joking or just being flip?

'Where are we supposed to be going? Isn't it this turn off? Sarah Jane, quick look, or we'll end up in Scotland for two weeks! Is it this one or the next one, quick?'

'Just a minute, I'm looking, can't you slow down?'

'We're on a motorway.'

'Does the sign say Norwich? Just stick with anything that

points to Norwich.' One calamity transposed so easily by another. Gem knew where she was going, realistically swerving off at the last minute. Sarah Jane reached for the water bottle and glugged some down, before remembering to offer it to Gem.

'No thanks.'

'Honor told me you were going off to India by yourself, is it true?'

'Yup, I'm finally hitting the hippie trail aged thirty-three.'

'It's not so old.'

'Thanks, that's reassuring!'

'No I think you're really brave. I don't think I could go by myself.'

'Well don't, come with me. We can do a road movie together, you don't need Hollywood, when there's Bollywood. I'm going before Christmas for the winter. All we need is the title.'

'I've got it, I can see it now in big lights across Leicester Square, *Blondes in Bombay* or *The Blonde Bombay Connection*.' Sarah Jane was enjoying this. Now she wasn't going to be a moviestar's wife, her old energy was restored. She wanted that fame more than she ever had, and not on anyone else's coat-tails.

'Are you sure you're not thinking of the cinema in Greek Street with the adult bookshop downstairs? Why not just go for *Busty Blonde* and *Dirty in Delhi*?'

'Oh, I didn't tell you I've been offered something at the Donmar, proper serious acting as well as that TV thing. Move over Josh Todd, there's a new babe in town!'

'That's brilliant. I didn't know. It's going so well, what's the TV series?'

'It's a detective avenger crime girl. We start shooting week after next. Nineties Jason King, without the 'tash.'

'I'd refuse to grow one too. Yuck! Bristly face hair brings me up in a rash.'

'No, but they're quite useful if you don't let them near your face.'

'Have you been sitting on somebody's face recently Sarah Jane? We've been driving all this time and you didn't even say! Tell me he's not another actor?'

'No he's not. He's just an editor who came to interview me from a magazine.'

'So you wanted to make sure you got the whole double-spread star profile?'

'Gem I didn't, but as it turns out . . . Anyway he made the first move after this waiter spilt a drink on me and he got his napkined hand on my lap.'

'I bet he did! So you obviously didn't slap it back as unprofessional conduct.'

'Well I did, but you know how it is once the physical barrier's been broken.'

'One thing led to another?' Gem asked. She nodded. 'Where? Not the loos?'

'No! It was daytime,' she said, affronted. 'We went back to my now tidy flat.'

'Good. Where he did amazing things with his goatee?' Gem laughed in an exasperated fashion at the predictability of Sarah Jane's behaviour.

'Exactly. He's quite gorgeous but really intelligent and funny, and I think he quite likes me too. The only trouble is I'm going to have to start reading.'

'Why change a Sarah Jane?'

'I feel like a cultural face-lift. Does that make sense? Will you come to the theatre with me Gem, before you disappear?'

'Sure, but poetry readings or foreign films, get Honor for those.'

'So, what about your dating material?'

'Who me! Nothing since the dawn of time. I've become the professional celibate I pretended to be when I was shagging like a dog on heat, anything I didn't know with a nice butt who I couldn't have feelings for. Now I've become this super-mature woman, the next wedding's mine. I'll go in for some fancy Hindu ceremony in India and end up as the bride of Shiva, I expect.'

'Like the bride of Frankenstein? I think you'd get on with Jamie. If we bump into you selling Hari Krishna incense on Soho Square, I shan't introduce you.'

'I don't mean to be coarse but I expect my dual personalities, as you say, are too flat for a man used to your stature.'

'I'm not saying I don't trust you, it's just men I have the problem with and trust being the basis of love, it's all pretty sad. But Jimmy has faith in me.'

'We all do,' said Gem staring guiltily on the road ahead, thinking, I am not worthy of the title of friend, not even with a small f.

'But what about the one you brought to that fateful dinner, the last time we were all together? I mean us four with Catherine. Pity the old tart, I mean the divine loving human being, can't be with us tomorrow for the wedding. I expect she'll be there in spirit, she always manages to get invited to everything. I wonder what I'd do, if she turned up?'

'What about David?'

But Sarah Jane's answer was disrupted by a distant sign signalling relief. 'Yippee, a service station. I'm dying to pee. We can have murderous thoughts over cow-dung pie with year-old veg and sweeties.'

Gem started off towards the relaxation of highway catering that beamed its oasis vision ahead of them in solid greying concrete, cheered by primary-coloured promotional banners. Entertainment, fodder and petrol, all of life's needs in a car-park.

CHAPTER TWENTY-THREE

'What on earth is your sister doing for so long? She must have been in the loo for close on twenty minutes. We're never going to get there. Georgina, sweetie, you couldn't just go and check?'

'Of course darling, she's probably gone to look at magazines or tapes and doesn't realise we're in the car,' said Georgina, trying to smooth his rage.

'It would bloody serve her right if we left her stranded.' He wasn't going to be soothed. He fumed to the silent passenger, his son, who hulked up the back of the car with his voluminous cotton clothing and over-long limbs. Pressed against the window, Ben's cheek was flattened white by the glass, whilst he gazed to a distance that his father couldn't guess at. In his head he was snowboarding.

David looked at Ben through the rear-view window. The incongruous messy form in the neat expensive car, mismatched items like this father and son, how was one with the other? Nobody wanted to be on this journey, but they all were. There had only been a few conversations so far, and those were between Georgina and David about work, and one awkward discussing of wedding outfits involving them all.

Wedding talk was irritating David. Georgina had already hinted at her desire to be married in the months that had gone by since Catherine had left. The summer seemed too ridiculously long to David. Though there was no sense of time passing, things had changed and Augusta and Ben would next week be back at school, thank God. He wished that Georgina would go easy, he didn't need to replace a lost nagging machine.

David was taking Georgina's efforts for granted, expected dinner at eight thirty, the house, Ben and Augusta to be organised and tidy. He had forgotten what it was like to be without a wife, she had stepped so easily in to fill the emptiness Catherine's departure had left. Georgina saw Augusta as easier than Ben, in that you could at least talk to her. David wasn't sure which was better, the shrieking machine-gun fire of his daughter's voice or the iron aggression of his son's weighty silence.

When Augusta was born, David always thought of her as his. It was a long time ago. As a baby she'd always looked like him, people commented on it, and as she grew older he felt it a mark of betrayal that she should have taken on Catherine's persona. Since her mother had left, every time he looked at her Catherine stared back, chiding him. The fact that she was female and becoming a teenager, which was one of those times that mothers were there for, to deal with, was another pull at his noose.

He couldn't forgive Catherine for her timing, he just hoped that she had filled Augusta in with all the details of puberty when they were with her in LA last week. She'd certainly returned with a new wardrobe. Too old and sexual for her age, he noticed men staring at her in the cafeteria and didn't like it. David hoped she had something for the wedding, she'd said she had. He would get Georgina to veto it, to help. Georgina could talk to her about the other things too, it wasn't that he was squeamish about accidents and blood, but menstruation was not his field. And why the hell should it be, he didn't intend dealing with it. Didn't schools deal with all that stuff, facts of life, they bloody well ought to for the amount of money he was paying them.

'Now where are Georgina and Augusta!' He strained his view impatiently towards the ladies' loo where they had disappeared. He didn't want to be late for their hotel booking.

They were off to the wedding.

Even Ben wanted to be at Honor's wedding. That was why he was putting up with the journey, though he didn't think it was healthy to be in such close proximity to his father. Honor had shown him the one bit of sympathy and sense he had had from any adult, she seemed to understand what others condemned, shouting at him for his 'selfish behaviour'. Honor was half decent – respect! Jack was cool.

Ben hung out at her place some evenings or weekends and she fed him, didn't ask questions or try to make him talk. She was draggy about drugs, wouldn't let him smoke spliffs but otherwise it was cool and he sort of understood that she didn't want drugs around Jack, Jack was a kid. He baby-sat Jack for free. She wasn't his mother, she cared. How Honor and Catherine could've been friends when they were so different, Ben couldn't figure out.

Ben would even put on clean clothes for Honor's wedding, more than he'd done for Catherine the whole time he and his sister had been in LA. David had been surprised at Ben's enthusiasm to go, he'd half-hoped that both Augusta and Ben would refuse petulantly, especially since they had only got off the plane days before. He and Georgina could have gone alone, had a dirty weekend together in a country hotel, instead it had turned into a family-style outing. More stressful than the trip he'd envisaged.

David had thought they would return full of hideous behaviour and foul-mouthed resentment, but they both surprised him by being less difficult than expected. Though Ben didn't really speak any more, not to his father, at least he seemed less strung out, not so confrontational. David had to admit that it must have been a good trip. They were definitely going for a return visit at Christmas, he had decided. This time queen bitch could bear the expense.

Ben put his hand into his pocket to feel for his security touchstone. A large lump of 'black' that he had taken from Josh Todd's 'goodie jar' before they boarded the plane home. It was safe in his jacket, cling-film wrapped. He'd hidden it in the baseball glove Josh had given him that had belonged to somebody famous, as though it meant anything to him, but it was a good place to hide the dope in. It had been such a large piece that he'd cut it in two, kept one with him now that he could stroke and roll between his fingers, his piece of magic, the other bit still sat in the bribery glove, back in his room. Each morning he'd wake for a large spliff that seemed to mellow the voices continually waging in his head, turn down the volume control on the world. He never knew whether somebody was talking to him or not, usually a smile was all that was required with a slight nod of the head. He had a real carrot of a joint this morning to get him through the journey and it had made him feel slightly nauseous to begin with. He tried to slope the feelings that made him panicky, thoughts that it might wear off before they got to the hotel, he shut his eyes to allay the anxiety. He could slice a bit off with his nail and eat it, but it always made his head zoom and he didn't want to get so out of it. His father might sense something; however sad his dad appeared, he should be careful.

Augusta was standing in the ladies in her tiny knickers and pink glittery shoes that looked like they were out of *The Wizard of Oz*, with heels fit for the streets of the Bois de Boulogne. She had little white socks on, out of which stretched her long thin legs. A tight T-shirt covered her arms but stopped before her belly button and got nowhere near her flower-covered bottom. In one hand she held her trousers, the other upon the hand-drier button.

'Augusta! What on earth are you up to? We've been waiting in the car for ages and where are your trousers? You're almost naked.' Georgina shouted at her in her haughty high-pitched voice that switched so easily from coquette with David to head prefect with his children.

Augusta swung around, the bunches of her hair neatly scrunched on either side of her head hanging into her face like a pair of cocker spaniel ears.

'Oh hi Georgina, I'm trying to hurry. I'm drying my trousers, I just leaked all over them. Really boring! Can you see my knickers are still wet? Everyone started to get weird about me drying my knickers under this thing. I mean it's not as though there are any men in here.'

'I'll get you some sanitary towels? I didn't know you'd started menstruating.'

'No I hadn't. This is my first time, it's quite exciting becoming a woman on the motorway. Could you go and get me some Tampax?'

'But Augusta do you know how to use them, wouldn't you prefer some towels?'

'I'm not sitting with a cushion between my legs all the way to Norfolk. I've already got a Tampax up there, a woman gave me one and I've watched loads of the girls in my dorm put them up and I've practised. Let's face it, it's hardly one of the great mysteries of life. It's just that I'm going to need some for later, I expect. I don't suppose Dad would be happy with blood on his cream seats.'

'No. Of course, if you're sure Augusta. How are your trousers?'

'Almost done. Buy a box of Quality Street too. We can celebrate.'

Georgina left, slightly dazed by Augusta's uninhibited style, to join the newsagent's hordes amongst the sticky kiddie sweets and top-shelf magazines to locate the 'feminine hygiene' shelf. She looked and chose a pack of regular, even though Augusta would probably go for super plus in her bid for womanhood.

She stood in the queue and remembered her own screams of horror when she'd discovered blood streaming unnaturally between her legs. Her mother had had to come running up the length of their Basildon garden, and had insisted she go to bed for the afternoon and lie quietly, nursing a hot water bottle with the blinds down and a mauve candlewick bedspread over her. Her periods had always been a painful embarrassment, as her mother had told her they would be. A woman's cross.

'Has Georgina spilt the good news Dad, Ben?' Augusta finally appeared with trousers on, bounding back into the car, joining the rest of them with more energy than a kangaroo. Her eyes gleamed an excited mischief above a cat's smile. 'Has Georgina spilt the good news yet? No?' she asked again, grabbing the box of chocolates to tear greedily at the lid and pulling out all her purple and green wrapped favourites before offering them around.

The car waited, its conscious occupants embarrassed. Ben wasn't aware of Augusta saying anything but he liked her smile and the taste of the chocolate toffee that circled his tongue. Georgina had already whispered what had caused the delay to David and he had cleared his throat, 'Quite,' closing the matter. But Augusta wasn't going to be closed.

'From now on I can get pregnant whenever I like!' she beamed proudly and when no response other than horrified amazement greeted her announcement she petulantly demanded, 'Well, aren't you going to congratulate me?'

CHAPTER TWENTY-FOUR

Hitting the service station, Gem and Sarah Jane dashed for the loos. During the journey, they had glugged their way through a litre of water each, clearing out their systems for the expected wedding onslaught. It was going to be that kind of celebration and they wanted bodies pure for sullying. This wedding was important for both of them.

Gem was close to confessing her indiscretion with Josh, she felt warm with Sarah Jane as they laughed to the loos and borrowed each other's lipstick. She felt she had to tell before she left for India. With her exhibition, the wedding and a million other excuses, she hadn't been able to face it yet; it would probably be the night before she left. She was glad that Sarah Jane had already found a near-replacement, hitting the serial monogamy trail again in search of unconditional adoration. But this time it might be different.

Sarah Jane's problem was she always waited to be picked, like some succulent fruit off a roadside branch that no man could bear to pass without tasting. Whilst the whole thing was beginning, she would hold her breath in anticipation, calculating from the amount of phonecalls he made to her in any one day how promising the situation might be. Each week she would withhold her decision, hiding herself inside until it might be safe to show a toe . . . For many men, giving her body was enough, they thought they had her, but the drugs always kept her separate. She needed that. You can do things on drugs you'd never dream of sober (you can do things sober you'd never dream of stoned). Sarah Jane never made the choice herself, never really picked what she wanted in men. Not in the way some voracious women hunt a target, sight the beast, aim and go in for the whole thing ring-shopping at Tiffany's. This one sounded no different but maybe things would change. Maybe.

Gem hoped so, for her sake, as much as she wished for it herself. If Sarah Jane could get it right, there had to be a chance for her.

Some friends you can have a good time with, you may know the same people, be comfortable in your similar pursuits, laugh at the same jokes but though they might pat you on the back, wish you the best as you spiral upwards in success, most will groan inside with ill-concealed jealousy. They will want to hold you down, beside them, thinking, Why her not me, why should she get the baby, the job, the man, the praise – I'd be so much better at it. It's hard not to want to be the fish that got away.

Luckily, we are not all dedicated to each other's destruction, but if you cannot rise at the same pace, how can you want someone else to succeed? If you could only work out their trick (it is only a trick!) you'd be up there too. Or would you?

Gem and Sarah Jane did not spend their lives in each other's pockets, might not, after the wedding, speak to or see one another for a year but it didn't matter, because they wanted the other to succeed. Beneath the jibes and silly jokes that masked their care, there was concern and love.

The serviceway café offered them a resistible menu but they both felt they had to have something just to fill the hole. Dinner that evening at the main house where they were staying with Honor and some of her family, was a long way off. Post-dinner was girls only, a small hen night for Honor.

Sarah Jane looked grimly at her plate of sadly oiled chips that could never have been potatoes in a previous life, and the sponge bread that sat curling away from its eggy contents in a make-believe sandwich.

'I don't know how you can eat that, do you want some orange?' Gem offered some of the fruit that she was busy peeling. She was still self-conscious about her eating habits, though fewer old chocolate-bar wrappers littered her car in self-disgust.

She was trying not to vomit any longer and was looking better for it, her hair was thicker, her skin less sallow and the hollow grey/purple bags beneath her eyes had disappeared. Unfortunately, no matter what Clarins promised there seemed to be no way to get rid of the wrinkles, and the only solution to her prematurely yellowing enamel-less teeth was capping the lot; she was saving up for that. With a good make-up job nobody noticed but her mother, who chastised her for not brushing her teeth before discussing some new fresh fruit jelly recipe. But that was her mother who had known her for over thirty years and was still discussing 'interesting things to do with jelly' with her.

Times when Gem had tried to explain her feelings always ended in rows, it sounded like she was blaming her mother for the life she had (or rather for the one she didn't), for the way she felt towards men, towards herself. Now she tried, on Jimmy her therapist's advice, to love them and leave them, not to seek their parental approval, just to love them. Some days it was bloody hard.

When she'd gone into therapy Gem hadn't announced it. 'Oh Mummy, by the way I'm talking about you every week and discussing the way you brought me up so badly.' Sometimes she itched to tell, but that was her illness and a modicum of sense prevailed to keep the peace. They had done the best they could with the limited knowledge they'd had, that's what Jimmy told her.

Her new behaviour didn't pass without comment.

'What's happened to you, Gemma? You don't care about us any more,' Anna Daley said to her daughter, having been unable to draw her into an argument about the council clearing up the rubbish in their street.

'Of course I care about you and Daddy but not Richmond's refuse debates.'

Gem had thought for a moment about showing her mother her and Honor's cookbook, but she couldn't bear the thought of criticism before it was on sale. Her perfectionist mother, too scared to achieve lest she fall and fail, always had plenty of advice for the rest of the world. From editor or colleague fine, but Mother, no. She wouldn't take the verbal abuse, or feigned interest from Father now she was working with her anger and punch bag. She was learning to insulate her marrow from the barbed parental comments, and to fill her own love tank.

The book was looking brilliant, sharp and bright. It had been snapped up by a publisher immediately for the Christmas market. Though Honor didn't appreciate it, she worked in a well-regarded small Soho restaurant that fed the publishers, editors and media who worked there. The look of it was the thing, the way the recipes had been laid out amongst a collage of painting and cut-outs, Matisse with food. Gem had kept it and its success hidden from Honor and now she was giving the contract to be signed, and a bound colour-photocopy proof, to Honor as her wedding present. It was to be called *Human Stuffing (and other things to do with food)*. Gem would give her the book and contract that night, so she could take it back to London signed. Meanwhile Honor would be honeymooning.

'You know the whole idea of the book came about because of you, Sarah Jane.'

'Did it, why?'

'Because we couldn't think of a wedding present for the girl who we thought had everything. We did try, we looked all through an Argos catalogue.'

'Thanks!'

'Then we remembered your cooking.'

'What cooking?'

'Exactly! A book of easy recipes for fulsome delicious food, to sustain you through the Hollywood horrors, like the best cardigan.'

'Ahh I'm so touched, thank you. How wrong could you have been.' And she leant across the Formica turquoise-and-beige striped wall-matching table and gave Gem's arm a squeeze and her cheek a kiss.

The man on the near-side table stared in interest.

Gem reciprocated but didn't tell Sarah Jane that she wanted the book dedicated to her, without which it wouldn't have existed. She would ask Honor first.

The cafeteria was filling up with those who wanted tea. Old women hobbled by with aluminium tea services whooshing their contents on to the wood-veneered plastic trays and over the cellophane-covered shortbread biscuits, children becoming ob-stacle courses in their way. Each time the door swung open, youths appeared with the noise of Terminators, searching for parents, thirsty for coins and Coke. A couple married and unspeaking for twenty years settled on the next-door table to Gem and Sarah Jane, the gaudy pretence of a Devon cream tea before them. They began to eat silently, each pouring their own tea, milk and sugar into their own cups and stirring with long white plastic toothpicks. Both looking as sad as a wet seaside, advertising marriage as a life sentence.

Gem made horrified looks to Sarah Jane, hidden behind a propped hand, and silently mouthed to leave.

'Time to go before we're put off marriage for life. Ready steady Gem?'

The couple both turned and stared as Sarah Jane and Gem got up and left, their eyes following them to the door before returning to the lipstick-pink jam glossing their plates.

'Spooky. Dead relationships or what? Arhh!' Sarah Jane ghoulishly relished having narrowly escaped.

'There are people living these lives,' Gem answered matter-of-factly. 'And this is with the sun shining, imagine if it was raining and grey!'

'Tell me about it! I think that was Josh and me, a year after the wedding, except we would've looked worse, Gary Oldman in Coppola's *Dracula*. What a relief, I'm never going to have to have a meal with him again.'

'Why?'

'You know, he ate like a dog, he shagged like one too. Did you notice his eating? It's the little things that all add up,' she mused. Gem let it pass with an uneasy smile, hoping the comments were coincidences. Then Sarah Jane screamed out, 'Let's go raid magazines and sweets!' and the subject was dropped.

'Quick put your dark glasses back on, I can see you staring off a cover and I don't want to be mobbed.' Gem had spotted several Sarah Janes staring at her, naked but for flimsy underwear, from a magazine for the thinking man.

'Ha ha ha. You're right, I thought that was next month.'

'Don't worry you've got no clothes on, nobody will recognise you.'

'Here, will you buy these for me and I'll get the chocolate. What? I can't go and pay for five copies of me naked.'

'I don't suppose they'll think I'm strange? Shall we get a few intellectually stimulating discussion articles you can read to me for the rest of the trip?'

'No. Let's get some new tapes, Rod Stewart's greatest hits. You'd like that wouldn't you? "Wake up Maggie I think I got something". Any Motown?'

'Arethra – "Respect". That's what we need.'

'Oh let's just get these and get out of here, I'm never going to find the *Artist's Newsletter* here. One day I will find and apply for that prime teaching post in North Alaska.'

'Here,' Sarah Jane gave her an armful of tapes and a fifty-quid note, 'and here's some water and money.'

'Do we need all of these?'

'They're presents for the car. Learn to accept them gracefully on her behalf.'

'Thank you Gem, on behalf of my little Trixibelle. Eek, what's this?' Gem waved a tape out in front of Sarah Jane's nose as though it was somebody else's used condom. 'You old rock chick, the Rolling Stones, honestly?'

'Would you have preferred Tom Jones?'

'Yes, yes, yes! Welsh sex on a stick.'

'Wouldn't an ice-lolly do?'

CHAPTER TWENTY-FIVE

'So this is the pile we've all been waiting for,' Sarah Jane gasped as they drove through an imposing set of wrought-iron gates, woven into a peacock crest.

'Do you think it's big enough?' Gem said, sighting the distant mansion.

'I can't believe it! It's bigger than our home. I mean Mummy's.'

'Sarah Jane, your roots are showing. I was going to say it's a lot bigger than your one-bedroom flat. I think it's bigger than my block.'

Gem and Sarah Jane had at last got to their destination. The early-evening sun caught part of the house, an edge of lawn and a row of cedar trees that cast their shadows like ink-black friezes upon the green. It looked like a National Trust picture postcard, and it seemed unbelievable that it could be any mortal's home. A cinema location for a wedding.

'Gem, you're acting as though you've never been to a country house before, a proper one. You're not going to embarrass us are you?' Sarah Jane retorted snappishly, joking to Gem who sat gawking open-mouthed at the design of the set. She jumped back from dreaming of her own inclusion in the scene and put the car into gear to cruise down the driveway.

'Undoubtedly, with my loutish Cockney ways and coarse West-London manner. I shall shock everyone with my artistic boho behaviour, my 'tash will grow Dali twirls and Ian Board and Buñuel will meet in my foul mouth.'

'I knew I couldn't rely on you to behave like the one Hugh didn't marry, Kristen Scott-what's-her-name in *Four Weddings and a Funeral*. I should have paid to have you kennelled. I won't have to keep running after you with a pooper scooper will I?'

'Good job you brought one. Something extra for the breakfast hot plates, ma'am?'

'Disgusting. Who is she? I've never seen her before in my life.

Gem, did you know that Honor came from a family of such distinguished breeding?'

'What do you mean? Did I know her folks were loaded?' said Gem with a Cockney accent as credible as Dick Van Dyke's in *Mary Poppins*.

'Yes.'

'But it's not theirs, is it? It's her grandmother's. She only married into it two years ago in an old people's home. Met this old bloke, fell wildly in love, went back to his place for coffee and never went back. Dirty stop outs.'

'What a wonderful story Gem. A real tale of hope, that's what I like to hear. I love real life fairytales. If I never find true love in my prime, I can book myself in to the old people's home and retire to this life the week after.'

'I don't think there's a guarantee, otherwise nursing jobs would be at a premium, but let's be positive. Honor's step-grandfather might have a brother.'

'I think I'd prefer a grandson.'

'We'll have to do some investigating tomorrow at the wedding. Maybe I can get the son and you could be my daughter-in-law?' Gem thought it might be possible.

'I don't know if I can cope with any more exotica in my family, our relations are complicated enough. Did I tell you I just got a new brother?'

'No! Your mother didn't take the wonder drug, did she?'

'My mother have more? I don't think so. She couldn't properly appreciate us and therefore has a warped view of the joys of children, and the rest of humanity. To be absolutely truthful, it's worth not getting married just to skip the wedding preparations.'

'I'm proud of you. I think Jimmy's making you remember your self-confidence.'

'Now I've just got to "unconditionally love" her and my step-father. Harder. Where was I? Oh yes, it's my dad. He did a marry-your-secretary course, ended up with the son he always wanted and never stayed around long enough in the past to find out he'd got. He must have loads somewhere.'

'Have you met the baby?'

'I haven't even met his secretary.'

'You mean the baby's got a secretary already, isn't that rather young?'

'No, silly! I mean his new wife. Catherine and I weren't even invited to the wedding. But of course I love them both.'

'Of course. Hey! I get a feeling I'm going to like it here.'

They'd got to the end of the long crunching driveway and in front of them was the main doorway and a selection of cars that didn't seem to post-date the mid-seventies. There was a yellow Carmen Ghia, a turquoise Austin Healey, a mink-brown Bentley and a divine-pink Cadillac. The only car that seemed to shriek in its surroundings was a Volvo estate circa 1997.

'Now let me see, guess the parents' car?' said Sarah Jane as Gem began to park.

'Not necessarily. Don't you remember how wacky Honor's dad could be? It might be the bridegroom's family.'

'Wedding decorum, the bridegroom's side can't stay in the bride's family home, they might see the wedding dress! If this is Granny's collection, I can't wait to meet them.'

'Let's get our stuff in and ring the knocker.'

Sarah Jane rang and thumped, whilst Gem hauled the bags over and felt ashamed of being duped into buying a practical modern Golf. That was the old her, listening while her parents fuelled her insecurities about breaking down on motorways and being raped by psychopaths and schizophrenics on the loose. After this wedding and with the book advance she was going to buy an MG, something that expressed her personality and verve. Slick, cool, confident . . . And she'd go on a mechanics course, then if she did break down she'd mend it herself. There was no need to be patronised by smarmy, macho garage men prodding you with their enormous bills. 'No answer?'

'Nope, but this door's open. Do you think we should just go in?' Sarah Jane asked hesitantly, a little in awe of the hugeness of the mahogany carved door.

'Of course, don't be silly. Give it a push.'

They walked into the marble and polished wood hallway. The floor was mosaic with Neptune rising out of the waves, a round rosewood table shading his face – larger than Gem's whole kitchen. On top of the table, an oriental blue-and-white bowl positioned in the centre burst with anemones and sweet peas. Everything in the hall seemed to be wreathed and garlanded, with the contents of a couple of gardens and the deep cold silence of centuries. Ivy wound its way down the banisters as though it was growing through the stairs, and the lilies that stood tall and beckoning on either side of a double door gave off their heady perfume.

'I thought lilies were for funerals? You don't think . . .?'

'No I don't. Come on, let's leave our bags here. Something tells me we should go through the . . .' Gem stopped bossing and paused as though choosing from an overwhelming choice of play-school variations '. . . big doors.'

'You know I always expect the worst where weddings are concerned these days,' said Sarah Jane, justifying her lily thoughts whilst following Gem into a world of technicolour. Sometimes you hear that word 'ablaze' and you think, oh yeah? But this living room seemed to come from the centre of the spectrum, thrumming with stripes and spots that clashed and jumped and yelled at your pupils, shot joy into your heart and made you laugh out loud.

No good for hangovers, or the morose with a sickly disposition. It was ridiculous, it was fun. Made by somebody who had lived through the thirties, forties, fifties, sixties and saw colour as the gateway of modernity. It was Matisse and Delauney, Hodgkin and Hockney, Beaton and Bauhaus, Heron, Frost and Hitchen and their work jumped out of the walls and up from the rugs.

'Now that's what I call interior decoration!' exclaimed Gem. 'Let me die and live in this heaven.'

'Wild crazeee! Hey look, that's the marquee. And isn't that Honor over there with Jack and those people playing croquet?'

'Isn't this the most fabulous place? Even if nobody else turns up we're just going to have a brilliant time, I know it. What are you waiting for, let's go say "hello".' Gem turned to Sarah Jane, who was already off and running over the croquet pitch.

Gem trotted off in the direction of Honor, the civilised pretensions of late-summer croquet momentarily disrupted by Sarah Jane's flying form. Teacups remained balanced upon stone lion heads in the genteel landscape where you half-expected to trip over a bath chair. To the right stood a Victorian conservatory, its goldfish, spouting cupid fountain and tropical greenery left unexplored. Straight ahead stood the blue tent teeming with silver moons and stars for the next evening's dinner reception; tables folded in the corner leant against towers of stacked gold and red velvet hire chairs. Behind the tent and in front of the Chinese summer-house was an old funfair merry-go-round.

Tomorrow the place would be filled with bustling, dedicated people, putting all of it into order. Tonight was the anticipation of tomorrow and its excitement. Getting ready to watch the spectacle of joy.

'And are these the treasured bridesmaids, Honor?' said Winifred, Honor's grandmother, looking like a Katharine Hepburn stand-in, from under a large floppy straw hat embroidered with wide stitched sunflowers.

The family had an early supper and disappeared into the various wings of the house, 'to preserve their energies for the big day'. Honor's brothers disappeared, rather reluctantly on seeing Gem and Sarah Jane, to the local pub to meet up with the bridegroom. 'To get him drunk and convince him to get on an overnight train with a strip-a-gram and no clothes,' they explained as Honor dismissed them with a laugh. The dinner was cooked and cleared by staff, Jack was tucked into bed with a hot-chocolate treat to rot his teeth and sweeten his temperament for the next day's activities. There was nothing for Honor to do but relax. Everybody told her so, it must be true.

Jack was beginning to have last-minute nerves. His granny sat on his bed holding his hand, she didn't want to call Honor in case it was catching. She stroked his head and whispered soft words that would lull and dissipate his fears. He sat up as suddenly as he'd first flopped into bed, and said, 'I don't want a step-father, I want my real dad. How would you like it!'

She laughed and said, 'But I do like it. Great-grandpa Fred is my step-father. I couldn't imagine a nicer one except for your Harry.'

'What if he gets wicked and beats me?'

'Then you can come and live with me and Grandpa. That's a promise and I shall beat him black and blue with the kitchen broom.'

'But what if Mummy loves him more than me, what am I supposed to do then?'

'She won't ever love him more than you, it's not possible, you're her baby, her boy. You come first and that lasts forever. Nothing can be more. I should know, your mummy was my baby once.'

'But it didn't work like that in Cinderella.'

'No. But that is a story, more to do with finding the magic that lies within us to save ourselves from the things that pull us down and make us grey.'

'What do you mean, Granny? I don't understand. Sometimes you say things that I don't know about.'

'You understand about the light side and dark side of us. About the sunny times that make us laugh and have fun?' She looked at her grandson's serious expression, his vital little face absorbing her words. 'Sometimes it seems as though a cloud passes over us and we want to make everybody feel as cross and sad as we feel at the world when we're unhappy. When it seems like everything makes you angry and you want to cry every time something goes wrong?'

'Like when I can't find my yo-yo and nobody cares, nobody thinks it matters, but it does to me.'

'And then you get cross and the crosser you get the sadder you become.'

'How do you know, Granny?'

'Because it works like that for grown-ups too. Sometimes you spend your whole life trying to get back to how you thought you felt as a child, sunny and warm all the time, though it might have only been a moment. Some people never find it, though they buy every grown-up toy thinking it will give it back to them, because they can't remember, they're lost.'

'Like when I got lost yesterday by the river and I couldn't find my way home?'

'Exactly.'

'But you remember what it's like, why can't they?'

'We all have to learn our own magic, how to get rid of the dark, cross, sad part inside of us, like Cinderella, and then we can enjoy everything, have the things we love, get rid of nasty feelings like being jealous and know we are loved always for ourselves, and not what we do or have.

'You see, Jack, when you love with all your heart it's for ever and it doesn't change, though you may not want to live with them, or other friends arrive. You don't love your special Bear any less when you get a new teddy, do you?'

'No, but I don't talk to him as much because I've got other toys to play with.'

'But he's still the special one.'

'Oh yes, Bear's the special one. He's going to be with me for ever.'

'And that's how you are to your mummy and she is to me. She's my special girl, my only one though I love her brothers and they're special too they won't ever stop me loving your mum. Do you see now?'

He nodded a sleepy yes, closed his eyes and turned to his side. She had talked him quiet and comforted him in his exhaustion.

'Granny?'

'Yes sweetheart?'

'Did you always talk so much when you were little?'

'Yes sweetheart.'

He 'hmmed' in understanding, his suspicions verified, before slumping his muscles into the bedclothes. She watched him, not moving from her perch on the side of his bed, stroking his silky hair down upon his warm, soft face until his body's last involuntary spasm; the sign that he was entering his dreamtime.

How like Honor he was. Poor little chap, she would have an excuse to spoil him whilst Honor was away on the honeymoon, she would teach him how to play tennis, fly kites and use a mallet on the croquet lawn properly, she thought happily.

She brushed his sleepy hot head with her lips before lowering the lights and leaving the door ajar for him, for Mummy's bed visits, or night pees.

The three girls were alone in the warmth of the living room and the chill of the champagne. Honor was adamant, 'Not too much! I don't want a hangover for the first time I get married!'

'Why? Are you saving it for the second? Who is going to be the lucky second?'

'May we all enjoy each other's weddings as much as this one!' Gem added.

'May we all enjoy each other's brothers, as this one,' giggled Sarah Jane.

'I'm sorry Sarah Jane. How much have you drunk? Which one

did you have your eye on? Don't tell me, I think you've taken a fancy to Simon.'

'Aren't you going to open your pressy?' Gem interrupted and pressed the purple-and-green beribboned present into Honor's lap.

'All right, all right.' As she started to pull at the ribbons delightedly, she looked at her friends' excited shining faces. 'It's not a fancy toaster, is it? Let me guess, a set of matching dining coasters?'

'Closer than the toaster.'

Honor had reached the contents and looked slightly bemused. 'Is this a hint? Do I need a cookery book? I mean it's lovely and truly I don't have any.'

'Look at who it's by. It's only a copy of the proofs but you get a sense . . .'

'It's the book! Gem you did it, you finished it. I never thought, I mean you just didn't mention, I thought it had been forgotten. What did you do with it?'

'The contract's inside. I sent it off to my agent who got a publisher for it straight away. All you have to do is sign on the dotted line.'

Honor was overwhelmed, the surprise was so complete, she gave Gem a hug, like she'd give Jack for being brilliant.

'You do like it, don't you Honor?'

'What can I say? It's wonderful!' she said, turning the pages of its spiral binding. 'Gem you're so clever, it all looks so beautiful and my name's all over it. I can't believe it. It's the best present I've ever had,' she managed to blub out through the tears of what she supposed must be joy.

'They want you to do an introduction, it'll be the last thing in along with our dedications. I thought we might dedicate it to Sarah Jane, after all we wouldn't have done it without her. When you read the other side, you can see on the contract how much we're to be paid, fifty–fifty if that's all right.'

'Of course. Of course I'm shocked by it all, I haven't done anything, only copied out some of my old recipes. I can't demand payment, you've done all the work.'

'But it wouldn't exist without your recipes.'

'Or without Sarah Jane.'

'Are you sure you don't want me to do the introduction? Just a thought,' said Sarah Jane, helping herself to another glass.

'Hey, better than that, we could lay you out upon a table naked and put all the food across your body like a human platter for the launch party. Like Meret Oppenheim did for the Surrealists.'

'Not for every meal? I don't mind being photographed or drawn for prosperity covered in food. Sounds quite sexy, but I'm not going to have a load of journalists picking finger food off me for a couple of hours.'

'Not even ones with goatee beards called Jamie?' Gem teased and Sarah Jane giggled and blushed while Honor cross-examined her, before agreeing, for 'Art's sake', to reveal her extrovert body if need be for publicity purposes.

'Why not, I'm almost naked on the front of this magazine this month.'

'Which one?' said Honor. Sarah Jane fished out a copy with a flourish.

'Wow, don't you look fantastic, like a mermaid.'

'Thanks! How many young execs are wanking over it tonight, what d'you reckon?'

'A nation of them.'

'Another bottle's needed, more champagne anyone? And toasts.' Gem popped the cork on another. Honor stood and offered, 'To the book and to all of our successes, both naked and clothed.'

Their glasses clinked and their eyes met in agreement. They settled back languorously on the floor where they were sitting in front of a fading fire, emotionally fraught but happy.

'Honor you never told me you had so much talent in the family. I thought from the way you talked about them that they were all spotty adolescent youths.' Sarah Jane turned the tables upon Honor. She was already thinking of tomorrow. So was Honor, though she was trying not to. She didn't mind it being so sudden, but the anticipation was almost killing her.

'I still see them like that because they're all younger than me.'

'How could you tell I liked Simon?'

'Something in the way you stuck your tongue in his mouth at the first opportunity and the way you went wide-eyed when he told you the pink Cad was his. At least my brothers will keep you away from the bridegroom. Isn't that traditional that the bridegroom goes off with the bridesmaid on the wedding day?'

'I think your morals are stuck, as though either of us would touch . . .'

'Your sullied goods!' Sarah Jane and Gem chorused and laughed.

'Thank you, girls, for your kind words of support. My favourite girls in all the world. More champagne I think.'

'What happened to the one glass?'

'It magic-ed itself into just the one bottle. Anyway, I never drink too much, just the right amount and everything is perfect.'

'I'll second that, here's to the right amount,' toasted Sarah Jane.

'The right thing,' added Gem.

'The real thing,' said Sarah Jane and her voice held a wobble of emotion. They knelt there together, the three girls, Sarah Jane, Gem and Honor, the night before Honor's wedding. Not so long ago they had all thought that the next wedding would be Sarah Jane's and it hit them all at the same moment. Honor put down her glass and put her arms about Sarah Jane and Gem followed. All holding each other, they didn't know whether to laugh or cry.

'Is this supposed to be some American bonding buddy movie?' Sarah Jane sniffed through her tears into laughter. 'Come on guys, group hug,' she mocked, in an American accent.

'No, a Coke commercial, "It's the real thing, what the world wants today, Coca-Cola," ' and they fell back giggling on to the thick weave of a Jean Cocteau rug of a fish-eyed woman, praying and weeping as her Icarus tried to fly into the sun.

'Those children are the fucking limit!' David shouted as Georgina lay singing an Elton John song in a tub of suds in the marble gold-tapped bathroom and thought, 'So what's new?' She was weighing in her mind the cost of David as a husband, as a father to a yet unconceived child. Of course he wouldn't talk about their children like that because they would be well brought up. She'd make sure they had a Norland Nanny. David as a cantankerous boring drunk of a husband in their Chelsea home, seemed to be the price. Surely she could find a husband with a house in the Boltons for the same price, but what if she didn't? There was no reason why there couldn't be a husband number two. He must have friends.

'What's the matter darling?' she trilled back.

'The matter, as you so neatly put it, darling, is the fucking kids have gone and had room service delivered when I'd made it quite clear that we were dining downstairs at eight thirty.'

He stood in the doorway fuming, a large Scotch in hand.

'Never mind, we can do the same. Get an early night, order some champagne and smoked salmon,' she pouted sexily, eyes fluttering.

'Where do you women get the idea that men are just made of money? Champagne indeed!' he said, turning to re-fill his glass from the mini-bar only to be disappointed. 'I'm sure the house wine's perfectly good!'

'Let it be my treat,' said Georgina, unwilling to let go of her idea of an evening of sex. He raised his eyebrows in amazement, then he understood.

'And if it's sex you're thinking about, I don't feel like it, if that's okay. I'm tired, all right? Order what you like, I'm going down to the bar.'

Catherine was drunk too, on champagne. Lost in Josh's villa in the Hollywood Hills, she had U2 blaring on full volume, the CD on repeat. Josh was away filming, she could do what she liked, why shouldn't she? He said she could, he said, 'I want you to treat this as your home,' so she did. She'd had just enough champagne to send the wedding telegram through to Honor, she had thought about ringing direct but wasn't brave enough, drunk enough.

Catherine needed a little drink these days to do most things, and you know how sometimes that one bottle can't quite hit the spot, so she'd opened the second. Three glasses out of the second bottle of vintage Dom Perignon and she was slumped in a drunken heap on the sofa, again. She found it hard to be alone, missed the noise of the children squawking, hated going to bed by herself. It was rare these days for her to get to bed without waking in the living room first, mouth gluey and dry with alcohol, corners stuck with lipstick and spittle, cigarette-stinking *prêt-à-porter* creased with dried sweat, the mindless babble of TV. She had fallen asleep with the effort of putting her cigarette out, her hand lay in the ashtray, the butt still grasped in her fingers. The glass next to her was on its side, smeared with her glossy lip colour. The music filled an emptiness, Bono's voice boomed, 'If God Will Send His Angels,' echoing from one side of the modernist palace to the other, but nobody listened.

CHAPTER TWENTY-SIX

'Thank God, the wedding's not until this afternoon,' Sarah Jane spluttered, her head surfacing through the hot water to lie Ophelia-like, floating in the deep claw-footed Victorian bath. She was talking to the air as much as Gem, who was concentrating on carefully brushing her teeth in their surrounding bleeding gums.

'Wha'd'ya thay?' Gem shouted back through a mouthful of cosmetic whitening toothpaste and the roar of the sink taps that washed the foaming blood away.

'Not so loud! I said, good job the wedding isn't this morning. The thought of another glass of champagne makes me want to heave.'

Gem turned the taps down to a stream. 'Can gi gask you a perfonal quefchum?'

'If you can with that toothbrush in your mouth.'

Gem spat and rinsed, rinsed and spat, before asking, 'Why was I woken by a male voice and much giggling this morning, or was I dreaming?'

'I'm sorry, did we wake you? I told Simon to be quiet.'

'You dirty old cow!' Gem said with admiration. 'Are you trying to beat some land-speed record on cradle snatching?'

'He's only a couple of years younger than me. Don't judge me by your thirty-something status! He's cute though, isn't he?'

'So you've sorted your lift home tomorrow, the Pink Cadillac is his?'

'You're not mad are you?'

'Hereditary possibilities . . . Of course I'm not, who am I to judge. He's a record producer, isn't he? Strange you hadn't met before, you kinda look alike.'

'I know, but we're making up for it fast. Best thing is he's a human being, just like me. Except without the breasts or fanny.'

'That makes you believe he's human? I don't know where you get your ideas from!'

Sarah Jane smiled, misty-eyed. 'He's so sweet.' She sighed. 'He says he wants to make me a star. I had to break it to him gently that

I already was one and that I can't actually sing, but he said since the Spice Girls that didn't matter, and that I could be on *Top of the Pops* in a year. Cool huh!'

'Simon says, "Simon says put your hands on your head." Gem says, "Kiss and tell, was he any good in bed?" '

'Gem, he was sublime. But, in President Clinton's words, we didn't have sex.'

'You mean you didn't penetrate the baby-making hole on the first date? You can save it for behind the marquee during the speeches.'

'You're just jealous!'

'I know. Does he have a friend? Hey what about Great-grandpa Fred's brother?'

'I'm not married! I haven't escaped the manacles for nothing. I want sex to be fun!'

'God! How I want that too. To stop feeling sick with guilt or resentment each time I've done the evil deed.' Gem suddenly turned grave, she knelt down by the side of the bath and stared earnestly at Sarah Jane; it was now or never. 'I think I've got to tell you something . . .'

Sarah Jane began to laugh thinking this was part of a joke, her wires today weren't connected for sombreness.

'Don't laugh, this is serious. I understand if you never want to see or speak to me again. I . . .'

'I know. I know what you're going to say.'

'What?'

'That you had sex with Josh. He told me, suggested we try a friendly threesome. I wouldn't, he got cross and hit me, like they do.' Sarah Jane spoke as plainly as a children's presenter.

'You knew all along? I'm so sorry. I didn't know it was him. I swear I never . . .'

'It's not your fault. Actually it is but don't beat yourself up about it.'

'He said his name was Billy. I picked him up in a club, like I used to do all the time,' she said in vacant justification.

'He called himself Billy, how perfect – Billy Liar. Poor thing. He was just desperate for everyone to love him. He only thought they would if he shagged them, he never even enjoyed sex, but couldn't say no. He faked the best orgasms of any man I've known. Poor Catherine, lucky me!'

Gem listened amazed, watching Sarah Jane lovingly scrub her elegantly pointed toes. 'I might even have that Simon behind the marquee tonight, just for fun.' She looked at Gem and it seemed like they'd swapped roles. 'C'mon Gem, lighten up.' She scooped a handful of bubbles from the bath and deposited them dripping on Gem's face, turning on the shower to rinse her hair.

'Thanks,' said Gem glumly and got up to wipe her face and pull some clothes on in her adjoining room, door left ajar.

Still drunk, Sarah Jane babbled on, 'We're going to have a great time today, I can feel it. The past's gone and I've forgotten it, so you must too, all right?' She popped her head up, squeezed shampoo on and massaged it vigorously.

'I know. Thanks,' Gem accepted with resignation. 'It takes a little time readjusting my spine, not having those guilt boulder-shoulders. I was beginning to feel like a cast member of Dallas. Can I borrow your lipstick, it worked wonders for you last night?'

'Sure, but I think it might have been the inhibition-releaser of that bottle of brandy we steamrollered into when Simon came back from the pub.'

'I'll stick to the lipstick. Just give me five and I'll be smiling wider than the Grand Canyon. I can't tell you what a relief it is, I could garotte myself!'

'I know, but who'd get to clean up? Imagine my relief that this isn't my wedding!'

'That's rich from you, Miss Hygiene! Do you think she's making a dreadful mistake?'

'No, but it's easy to misjudge, especially when someone looks like that. They told me in the treatment centre that if I was instantly attracted to somebody to stop, turn around and walk, FAST. But Honor didn't shag him straight away.'

'It was me who told you that. If only I'd used that technique with "Billy".'

'Oops, done it again with Simon, never mind,' Sarah Jane said as casually as though she'd spilt a glass of water. 'Still,' she continued through the shower, rinsing her hair, 'when you're fucked you're going to attract something similar, but when you're reborn, like me, the mirror image is fine,' she congratulated herself. 'Besides, Honor's fine. She's always been so sane.'

Gem came back into the bathroom to put on her make-up.

'Beauty prejudice,' she announced. 'I mean if you're good looking, you've got to be gay or a bastard. There must be exceptions, I hope.'

'Of course there are, what about me!' exclaimed Sarah Jane, springing naked and dripping from the bath, nymph-like in her total physical perfection. 'Hey, we'd better hurry down to breakfast, pass me the towel hon. I'm just bunging my jeans on.'

'Shout when you're dressed, we can slide down the banisters together.'

'Are you that desperate to have something between your legs?'

'You said it.'

'What are you girls up to this morning?' Honor's grandmother inquired.

They were all sitting around a large table, feasting on an old-fashioned English breakfast. Smoked crispy bacon, eggs – scrambled, boiled, poached or fried, steaming yellow kedgeree, solid home-made herb sausages, tomatoes grilled and speckled with thyme, fried mushrooms, kidneys sautéed and smeared with Meaux mustard. Loaves of bread made into toast to go with the thick bitter marmalade, purple damson jam or sweet clover honey: the house's produce.

'We thought we'd drag Honor off for a quick walk before she gets swallowed up by the beautician factory at twelve.'

'What? Expect me to walk on my wedding day! Okay. Jack, fancy a walk with the football down to the sea after breakfast?' asked Honor playing footsie with her son beneath the table.

'Sounds a very sensible idea. Expend a bit of energy and get out of the way of all these lovely young people turning our house into the Chelsea Flower Show,' Honor's granny said, as though amused by the whole spectacle surrounding her.

'The sea. I'd completely forgotten about the sea. Let's go for your last single-woman swim Honor,' insisted Sarah Jane as though it was a last rite.

'Yeah, let's go swimming Mum, where are my goggles and did you pack my armbands and can you carry my surf board, Mum, Mum, let's go, now, please?' Jack insisted, tugging with the urgency of a jailed man discovering an open door.

'Okay, okay, let's wait until everyone's finished breakfast, but I don't have to go in. My swimsuit's packed.'

'Spoilsport.'

'You can go in, in your big knickers,' said Jack, and they all laughed.

'With my belly and bum? I suppose it would frighten the sharks away. Isn't it going to be freezing? It's not exactly the middle of summer.'

'It'll be lovely. I went with your granny yesterday, Jack. It's had the whole summer to warm up,' Winifred said, turning conspiratorially to her great-grandson. Even with her daughter as Jack's grandmother and herself a great-grandmother, she still felt more than ever like a young girl. 'Goodness knows why you need costumes, it's perfectly private down there. Fred and I never use them, do we darling?'

'What's that Wini? What you saying?' Fred's twinkling eyes appeared from behind his newspaper, his mouth copying the upward curve of his dandy moustache – a happy rotund man. 'Are you being mischievous old girl? It's those polka dots you're wearing, always brings out the mischief in you,' he teased.

'Oh, do you think I should stop wearing this dress? Don't you like it Fred?' She winked at the girls as she spoke, women's games.

'Goodness no. I mean yes, I think you should have all your wardrobe changed to polka dots if it makes you happy.' And he dropped his paper to clasp her hand amongst the dishes on the yellow-and-pink dotted tablecloth. Together Wini and Fred emanated love like a laser, glowing and spreading through the room.

The three girls walked the ball-kicking Jack across the field and down the beach.

'Doesn't it make you go all googly and syrupy inside when you see two people so happy?' Sarah Jane was talking about Honor's grandmother and Fred.

'That's you and Harry. You'll be like that,' said Gem.

'Old you mean. I hope so.' The sun shone through the sea breeze, warm on to their faces, breeding hope. 'When it comes to the crunch it's so difficult. What if I've picked the wrong one out of all the men in the world?' Sarah Jane and Gem looked worried. 'Joke? Last minute commitment-terror. He's gorgeous. I love him.'

'I wish you weren't going away, Honor,' said Gem, hugging Honor's arm to her side. 'I'm going to miss you. Do you have to?

Couldn't you just put a spiral staircase up through your ceiling into Harry's flat and live happily ever after? Why do you have to go the whole way and make us all sick with envy that not only have you got the perfect man, you go and live the idyll too! The problem with you, Honor, is . . . you don't know when to stop having a good time. Most mortals settle for less.' Gem knew what she was talking about.

'I know, I know, the gods' mantle can be a heavy burden to bear,' Honor replied laughing. 'It is a shame with the book and everything. Seems like bad timing but it can't be helped. I'll be able to put all this new research into our next,' she added optimistically. 'Gem, can I just say, thank you so much for the book. It's the best surprise I've ever had, honestly, it's wonderful. I can't wait to show everyone.' She smiled back at Gem, giving her a squeeze of appreciation as they walked along the sand, watching Sarah Jane running with Jack kicking the ball backwards and forwards in the distance. The sun glinted off the wet sand as the sea slowly lapped back out with the tide. A seagull flew over squawking a noisy salute before dive-bombing his dinner between the waves. A red sailing boat hovered on the horizon just to make the Norfolk seascape perfect. A soft warm wind blew the dune grass like a row of swaying hoopla dancers and two white clouds floating in the blue sky collided and became one.

'Honor did you see those clouds up there, there was two and now there's only one, they merged perfectly. It's an omen, Big Chief Gem-Gem say, this will be a happy wedding day. You have my blessings.' Gem began illustrating her predictions with Red Indian sand dancing, patting her hand across her mouth as though to whoop up a war or start a fire.

'Thank you, you daft brush! Come back here, I haven't finished talking to you.'

With Honor's stout command she trotted back to her side.

'Gem you know you have my new house in Spain as your eternal family home. See it not as if you're losing a friend but gaining a holiday house. It's all a matter of perception.'

'Dear Honor! Don't I know it, my glass is positively overflowing. For God's sake I'm happy,' she screamed into the wind that whisked her words away. 'I also know that if you and Sarah Jane can find a man, I'm damned sure I'm not going to be left behind, if a man is indeed the icing on the cake.'

Sarah Jane suddenly ran up shoving her towel and a request at Honor. 'Hey, hold my stuff. Look at this Jack,' spinning off into a cartwheel that left them all laughing as she collapsed into the sand, incapable of fulfilling her boast.

'SHOW-OFF!' they shouted back and Jack jumped upon her shoulders with all the enthusiasm of a conquering gladiator.

'HELP, HELP. Honor, get your rascally son offa me, I'm suffocating.'

'Sorry, show-off godmothers have to be taught a lesson, especially those that go around seducing my younger brother.'

'But I didn't do anything, and how do you know?'

'I saw Uncle Simon coming out of your room this morning. I bet you were snoggin' him,' said Jack.

'Jack!' said Gem and Honor in unison.

'Sarah Jane snogged Simon. Mum look she's going all pink. You were right, you said she'd be embarrassed. Did you sex him? I asked Uncle Simon and he said you didn't. Did you lend him your toothpaste, he said he was just borrowing your toothpaste, was he?'

'Nice line in euphemisms your brother's got,' Gem commented, elbowing Honor.

'So did he borrow your toothpaste, Sarah Jane?' said Honor, peering through her mass of curls like a sleuth at Sarah Jane, and raising her eyebrows to the sky.

'Mum if you're not careful the wind will change and you'll stay like that. That's what Grandpa says.'

'What's going on here? I think it's time for tickling, young man; you know too much too young. What has your mother been teaching you?' Gem came to the rescue, helping Sarah Jane in her defence.

'It's not Mummy. It's Granny I swear, stop, stop. Help. Mum help!'

'You deserve each other. Last one in the sea's a sissy. I'm dropping your stuff here. You better get your water wings fast before they blow away.' Honor refused to take sides.

'Wait for me Mum. Get off, Sarah Jane, otherwise I'm telling Simon of you.'

'Otherwise I'm telling Jamie,' added Gem laughing.

'I give up, you bullies! But I can't be captured by your

earth-bound reasoning. I belong to the universe . . .' Sarah Jane's voice trailed away into the sea as she stripped and ran, naked and bounding, a Venus returning to the waves, screaming to the wind, body splashed by freezing brine.

The four returned like wet puppies from the beach glowing with exhilaration, covered in smarting salt-dusted goose pimples. Honor could feel her breasts lift as soon as the first freezing wave had hit them, her muscles, shocked into working, still hadn't warmed enough to slope back down again. Sarah Jane's hangover had been drowned by the sea and Gem's hair looked in need of serious attention.

The house they had left the hour before had been transformed again into a hallful of neat strangers with Honor's mother, Martha, ordering them all into position. The swimmers looked like things the cat had dragged in and left on the doorstep to live or die. An efficacious woman with a catering tag and prim pinched smile accosted them with a curt, 'Can I help you?'

'Not unless you get us a cup of tea, we're freezing. Mum,' Honor called over the woman's shoulder, 'we went for a swim.'

'Look Granny at Mum's boobies all sticking out,' laughed Jack, childishly pointing at Honor's freezing bombes.

'So they are, Jack,' said Martha immediately, ruffling Jack's thick mat of sea curls and laughing with him. 'There you are, Honor. You are naughty, why didn't you tell me you were off? The hairdresser's going mad up there with nobody to play with. Go put her out of her misery and I'll bring up a tray with some sandwiches and something to drink. I had to send your brothers into town to get the sound equipment because the DJ rang to say he'd had his stolen at a service station, poor thing. Apart from that I think everything's going according to plan.'

'We told Granny and Fred,' said Honor. 'I thought she might have . . .'

'Ah well! Dad's fussing the vicar over at the church just sorting the last things, he can't believe it's all going to go to plan. He's basing himself on Spencer Tracy in *Father of the Bride*, don't tell him I told you. I think he and the vicar must be testing each other on their lines. There should be enough hot water for showers.'

'Poor Dad, I'll try and look like Liz Taylor at twenty-two but I don't hold out much hope, Mum. Don't worry they can have cold showers,' she said in Sarah Jane's direction. 'I'll have the hot perfumed tub whilst they paint my toenails,' Honor teased, girlish with excitement, as they ran upstairs.

'Jack, once you're dressed come down and help me, will you?'

'Okay Granny. I think she wants me to teach her how to use my Gameboy,' he said in a cheerfully resigned tone to Gem. 'She's hopeless at it, can't even reach level two. Even Great-grandpa Fred's better than that!' Gem kept quiet, frightened she might be tested by her six-year-old godson.

'Oh Honor, you look beautiful!' chorused Gem and Sarah Jane.

'Bugger off you two.' She poked her tongue at them.

Honor's face was covered in a green and brown freckled face mask. She looked like a Godzilla beast with her hair twisted up and knotted around strange multi-coloured antlers which seemed to protrude from her scalp. She was lying on her towelling wrap on a make-shift table having her flesh heaved, wobbled and manipulated whilst some put-upon assistant had the impossible task of painting her toenails as they hung beneath the table.

The command was ignored. Sarah Jane whipped out a Polaroid camera, and snapped the scene into posterity.

'I'm not saying I'll use it for blackmail . . .'

'Don't tell me you just want me to lie to my own brother and say he couldn't hope to meet a nicer girl!'

'If you call that a lie, then I'm afraid you must.'

'Please, not on my wedding day, not in the eyes of God, anything but . . .!'

'Yes, I'm afraid so. Anyway, you're supposed to be quaking with nerves and shuddering on this momentous occasion. Stop being so jolly. Otherwise I shall start crying and singing, "It should have been me . . ." '

'Ahh I'm sorry, but you try looking like a mint choc chip ice-cream and retaining some dignity. Mum's been forcing champagne down me, something about calming me down, now I can do anything.'

'Oh my God.'

'Ain't no stoppin' me now I'm on the loose . . .' she sang tunelessly to some old disco beat. Honor was having fun, it was her wedding day and she wasn't going to waste the opportunity.

'I think we better have some and catch up.' Gem reached out too late, her friend had grabbed the bottle and was lifting it to her lips. 'Sarah Jane!'

'I was joking.' She put the dripping bottle back down in the ice bucket. 'I'm waiting till the reception. We've still got our duties.'

'Right, out of here, you two. Go do something constructive like chat up my brothers and bring me some peppermint tea. Mum's already told me I'm not allowed coffee, coffee breath, whatever that might be. Has my brother Thomas arrived yet?'

'There's another? Quick where's my lipstick. Sorry I don't want to kiss your face but all the best, Honor, good luck and remember, we're with you all the way. Just do something about the make-up!'

'Don't worry, we will,' said Karen, the put-upon beautician.

'Thanks. See you later. You are going to put on your brides-maid dresses, aren't you?'

'Yes. We'll see you in an hour. That'll give you time to have that talk with your father before we go off to the church. The one about men and women.'

'Oh go away, you two.'

'Knock, knock. Room for one more with a tray of toasties? I can't get this damned door otherwise the whole lot will go over.'

'Just a mo, Mum, I'm in the bath. Karen, can you get the door?'

Honor had finished with the kneading beauty treatments and now lay soaking her skin in lemon verbena perfumed oil bathwater. She was determined to smell like a glorious whorehouse walking up the aisle. So much of her time she smelt of food, hands like fishy fingers, garlic ingrained nails, hair mixed with the soup of the day, while her skin absorbed anything that got fried in the kitchen. If only for one day she would smell of flowers from the crown of her head to her pink chubby toes. Poor Karen was opening the windows, suffocated by the perfumes after massaging her with every invigorating essential oil going. Opening the door she saw her chance to escape for ten minutes.

'I'm just down in the kitchen having a cup of tea for a tick. All right?' she shouted back already out the door.

'Fine.'

'I'll be up after to see to your face and hair.'

'Not much to be done with my hair but make-up, I want loads, bring the garden trowel.'

'What's that all about? You don't need much make-up. Don't be silly darling. You're beautiful without it. Where are the girls, don't they want something to eat?'

'I'm just getting out of the bath, you couldn't go and knock on their doors could you, next door to Jack's. Is he here with you?'

'No he's downstairs helping in the kitchen and having a sandwich. Don't worry about him, he's fine. Your dad said he'd have a game of croquet with him later. You just relax, I'll get the girls.'

'Come in,' Honor answered to a new knock at the door and there stood her granny Wini.

'I thought you could do with some crystallised violets to suck on. So your breath smells as beautiful as this room. Reminds me of Penhaligan's. Are you sure you've got enough perfume on, dear-heart?' She patted Honor gently on the back, looking around the chaotic room before giving her a gift in a little old, beautifully embroidered bag covered in tiny flowered stitching.

'This is for you but you must give it back to me later; that way you will have covered all the superstitions. It's tiny enough to tie on to your suspenders if you want to be saucy and who doesn't on their wedding day. Old, blue and borrowed, everything else is new, isn't it?'

'Well, Granny, I had thought about wearing my old school knickers but I've given in and splashed out. Actually I didn't, Harry gave me my underwear as a present.'

'Ahh, that's a shame, it won't be a surprise for him.'

'I'll have to think up something else. I couldn't stop him, he did insist. Predictably Taurean and generous, like me.'

The rest of the women arrived and sat around. Gem and Sarah Jane, starving after the swim, showers and make-up routine, dived into the sandwiches, mindless of smudging nail varnish and lipstick that would have to be redone.

'Gosh these are delicious, what's in them? It's so unfair that there should be so many good cooks in one family. You should start marrying outside your profession, you're as bad as doctors, or lawyers,' said Gem, eating heartily for once, before continuing, 'it never happens with artists. We're too jealous to share our creative-genius moods with anyone else in a family. Otherwise they might discover we've just miserable gits behaving badly like anyone else.'

'God forbid that you, Gem, could ever be like anyone else!' said Honor through a mouthful of melting cheese and Parma ham.

'Here I am baring my tortured soul to you over a, hmmm.'

'Thank goodness the food's finally shut her up!'

'Mrs Summers, I couldn't have one of those teas?' asked Sarah Jane politely.

'Of course, but can you please call me Martha? I hate all the awful formality about weddings, don't you?'

'I don't suppose we'll have that problem at this one, Mum. Thanks for being so brilliant. I know you won't believe me but I couldn't have been here without you. My favourite women in all the world in one room. Thank you God,' Honor said, putting her arms up to the ceiling, punch drunk with another wave of joy.

'Ahh darling Honor, it's only what you deserve. But it is true you couldn't have been here without me, or Dad.'

'Or me! Don't forget me!' Martha's mother Winifred chirped up and stood. 'I wish you all the best my sweetie. I've got to find Fred, otherwise he'll never be ready. You know men, never find anything, just like children. I expect I'll see you all later.'

'Thank you, Granny, for letting us do all of this here. Invading your house.'

'It's an absolute pleasure, Fred loves all the commotion. Makes him feel like he's in the army again, commanding the troops. Goodness knows how we ever won the war with him on our side. Can you imagine anything more frightful!'

The door snapped tightly behind her as she tottered off down the corridor. Independent, energetic and as vibrant with life at eighty as her granddaughter on the eve of her wedding.

'That's how I want to be when I'm her age. Honor, you are lucky to have such an inspirational family.'

'I want to be like that now!' said Sarah Jane. 'She's got such life force.'

'It runs in the family. Please raise your glasses to the glorious Summers clan,' Gem rejoiced, holding her tea in mock toast to the centre of the room. 'May it always be.'

'May it always be what?' asked Sarah Jane, a bit slow.

'Always be summer, silly!' said Honor.

'I don't know if I've got the energy for you three. I might have to go put my feet up for twenty minutes. Call me if I'm not back here and dressed by one?'

'Don't worry Martha, we'll send Jack in. The most effective alarm clock.'

'Yes, I'll be quite used to it after two weeks of you away, I expect.' Karen reappeared at the door ready to start again. 'Ahh, Karen, have you everything you need, good. I'll see you all later then. Oh and if anyone feels like they've got a spare half hour, I'm sure Simon could do with some help putting the marigolds over the tent walls. Sarah Jane, perhaps you . . . Only if you have the time,' Martha added with a secret, knowing smile.

CHAPTER TWENTY-SEVEN

Gem and Sarah Jane stood side by side in their exploding, tightly laced corset dresses like golden crowned eighteenth-century exiles, extras run off the set of *The Three Musketeers*, hair in ringlets, cheeks rouged and bow-painted lips. It wouldn't have been totally surprising for Oliver Reed to stagger into view grabbing one of the wenches in a louche Lord Rochester manner.

Instead, they held on to Honor's white satin and gold lace train, mere courtiers behind their queen, and followed her up the church aisle as though practising for their own turn, some day.

Honor held on to her father, as warm and as close as she ever could remember being. She felt as much pride to be standing next to him and his solidity, as he felt in having this beautiful woman glowing upon his arm.

He had teased her in the car on the way over, as they slid about on the glossy leather seats of his father-in-law Fred's chauffeured Bentley, about how pleased he was that she was at last to be placed on a pedestal, as her name suggested.

'Ha ha, Honor-ed indeed, did I have to change that much to get there? As long as I get my "loved and obeyed". I'm glad you didn't tell me that sooner, that you couldn't have honour without marriage!' Honor felt cross. She didn't find it funny that marriage brought conventional acceptance from a man as weak as she perceived her father to be.

'We did wonder after Jack, but you've done it in your own time and I'm proud of you. You and Jack, you've been so brave for so long it's about time you allowed someone to help you in life. To be your lover, friend and support, like your mother is to me.'

'But Dad, what about all the other women?'

There was a pause, she couldn't have gone back, made a joke, blustered over. It was something she had to know and if she didn't ask it now she never would. 'The mistresses that we all knew about and we were never able to mention.' Honor felt suddenly brave and protected in her dress, on this her day.

More, she felt close enough to her dad now to ask.

Hippolyte Summers was taken aback. After all his years in diplomacy, well cosseted by his wife's care and consideration, he didn't expect this to be a subject he would ever have to discuss, especially not on his only daughter's wedding day. He and Martha had long ago buried it as the relics of a dinosaur age and knew there would be no *Jurassic Park* rebirth. 'You know, they were only women,' he blustered, embarrassed by Honor's anxious expression. He knew she was only trying to come to terms with her past, her future. Honor wasn't trying to castrate her father, not in the back of the Bentley on the way to her wedding. After all, she needed him to walk her down the aisle.

Only women. Like me or Sarah Jane or Gem . . . she thought, feeling an old bile of resentment rise within her. But she had to let it go, it was only a thought.

'I succumbed to women when weakened by stress and away from home for too long. I'm not going to say that they were all nothing, but none of them could ever measure up to your mother, and I would never have ever left her for any one of them. What you don't understand is your mother is so much stronger than me, more compassionate and forgiving than anyone else I've known. The way we laugh together has healed my stupidity. She's my strength and my light, and my reward for anything good I might have done in my life.

'Friends that can make each other truly laugh outlast everything, and if you make your husband your best friend and your closest confidant, that's the most important thing.'

'Daddy, I do love you. I just wish . . . wish I'd spent more time listening to you, getting to know you, instead of hating you for how you behaved. Why did we spend all those years being polite and ignoring each other?'

'Because, my darling, beautiful daughter, sometimes it takes this long to get close again, but you know I've always loved you from the moment you were born and I held you in my arms and you weed all over my best tweed jacket.'

'Which one? Not the one with the yellow stain down the arm?' Honor sniffed through the tears which were rolling down the hills of her cheeks, ruining Karen's perfectly applied make-up.

'That's the one.'

'No wonder you never wanted to get rid of it,' she said laughing and crying all at the same time.

And they drove on for the rest of the journey, Honor's head resting upon her father's shoulder, comfortable at last, enough to be blowing her nose on his handkerchief; she'd finally got close enough to walk away.

With every eye in the church upon her, the mass of beaming faces merged, Honor felt like she was floating, floating down a river of love. For once the destination didn't matter any more, the journey was such bliss. At first she couldn't stop her face-wrenching smile bursting into giggles, especially with the cliché'd organ music playing, 'Here comes the bride, big fat and wide, slipped on a banana skin and had a bumpy ride.' Jack had been singing that to her all week. She heard Jack behind her smartly hiss, 'Stop it Mum! You're not s'posed to laugh in church. This is serious!'

The embarrassment passed as she eased into enjoying the attention and ignored her protesting stomach. Then she was by Harry's side, and though she wasn't sure if it had taken a lifetime or a second to get there, she knew it was the right place to be.

Sarah Jane started to cry as Gem and Jack sat together holding hands, sniggering childishly once dismissed from their duties.

The small full church fell silent for a moment before the first baby's cry, followed by the scuttle of a father's feet, exiting with baby, and the creak of the mediaeval door shutting out their noise.

Then the vicar's voice took over with the marriage ceremony. Hymns that hadn't been sung since school followed prayers eternally locked in churches, and then Honor's mother began to sing.

Honor had pleaded with her to sing 'Ave Maria' and she did to a stunned audience who whispered, '. . . Never knew Martha could sing so beautifully.' 'Didn't you know she used to be a professional, sang at Glyndebourne before she married . . .' The church boys' choir sang eunuch-inspired Purcell, a dream of English music that would make the most hardened European patriotic, and the most cynical dewy eyed.

Paper tissues were being shared in a most unhygienic manner, not only between Gem and Sarah Jane. What can you catch from tears?

How to be brave enough to make so many promises in the eyes of God, thought Gem, they must intend to keep them. But to promise anything, as long as you both shall live, with life expectancy increasing into forever?

Gussy sat reluctantly wearing Georgina's slip under her translucent organza dress, but she'd slipped the jacket off defying both her father and the church's chill. Now she cried as Honor and Harry made their vows, cynicism fudged to despair, mascara smudged about her eyes with angry tears. How can this ever last? she thought rebelliously (Gussy's school project for the holidays was the suffragettes). Love's a fairytale fallacy to hook girls to the kitchen sink of men's desires. What man has ever made a woman more than pregnant! Look at my father, and that sad little money-grabbing desperate Georgina. At my mother . . .!

It was one of those weepy weddings. Some cried for their lost innocence, some for the impossibility of their own pledges, some for those who could never make them, some for those who never had. Honor's mother Martha cried with elation and, she hoped, for the happiness that awaited her daughter, now adult, but a girl for so long.

Honor and Harry joined as one, floating back down the aisle, attached like untouchable Siamese twins. People they had known all their lives were behaving reverentially to them as though they had gained a different status amongst their own.

Outside the confetti rained everywhere as they streamed out of the church into the sunlight and the photographing rituals began, somewhere between the tombstones and the begonia borders.

Families meeting families. Friends bumping into friends, unrecognisable in their big hats, wedding-day glamour, polite best behaviour and pearlised lipstick. Reserved in their usual greetings, not the time or place to mention last week's legover ('You didn't tell me you were going to bring your wife? Is this the one you haven't slept with for a year? Who's she pregnant by then?'). Those conversations had to be saved for later, over or under the brandy course. For now polite 'hello, nice to see you, what a lovely dress your wife's wearing' would suffice. 'Thanks, I got it from Mums To Be, have we met before?'

Then they were off in their cars, bridesmaids in the pink Cadillac shockingly parked on the village's grass verge as Simon jumped out to get a packet of condoms from the corner store. It was too big to be parked anywhere else.

Harry, Honor and Jack were cosy in the Bentley. Jack, talking through the corrugated tube intercom system to the chauffeur, commanded, 'Home, James, and don't spare the horses,' and giggled. 'Did you recognise the posh voice? It's me, Jack,' he said, pressing his face to the chauffeur's window, unable to keep up any pretence requiring seriousness.

The chauffeur smiled back and said, 'Home it is then, sir, as you command.' And Jack was thrilled with the game before jumping between his mum and Harry and beaming up at them. 'Stop the smooching you two! You're not allowed to in front of the children. It's true, you can be arrested, that's why children can't go and see 15 films, because of all the sex. Isn't it!'

'Do you want a great big lipsticky kiss then?' said Honor, teasing him.

'Of course he does not, Honor, what man would, eh Jack?'

She lifted up her veil and came towards them both with a serious vampire's intent upon her face, half-smile and full appetite, and burrowed down upon them so they were both covered with the mark of Honor – Chanel Rouge Star.

When they got out at the other end, it wasn't necessarily the entrance that Honor had intended to make to her own wedding reception, giggling and dishevelled, hair in her eyes, make-up all smudged and her husband and son looking much the same. Everybody laughed at their appearance, took the photos for proof before any of them had a chance to dash upstairs and wipe the smear campaign off their faces in the quiet retreat of Honor's room.

Jack finished wiping himself first, slapdash clean and off downstairs to find distant relations and friends his size. To indulge in small people's war and games, food and feuds, battles and sieges still to be organised in the garden; he also wanted to go on the merry-go-round.

Honor felt a twinge of embarrassment at being alone for the first time with her new husband. She didn't know what to say, then she realised she didn't have to say anything, with Harry she could just be.

Downstairs Dionne Warwick sang out from the speakers and up through the floorboards, 'I Say a Little Prayer for You'.

Normally that song always made Honor's heart jump, but her heart had jumped so much in the past few days it was permanently floating in the sky of her throat. She looked towards Harry and smiled, her husband, my that felt strange. He looked back at her from the mirror where he was standing wiping the last smear from his cheek. The care and love and warmth that she felt for Jack she now knew she felt for someone else, but in quite a different way that was strangely almost the same. She couldn't untangle the jumble of feelings but she knew they were all good ones, and that's what mattered.

Just as she finished replenishing her mouth with lipstick Harry came and wrapped his arms about her in a big bear hug. 'I love you, little thing,' he said.

'Me too,' she said back.

'What took you so long?' her mother fussed towards her as they came down the stairs. It made Honor blush as though they'd been having illicit sex instead of enjoying their marital rights.

'We had a lipstick fight on the way back in the car. Your daughter attacked Jack and me. Martha, she is a dangerous woman,' Harry kidded with his new mother-in-law. She wasn't so different from his own mother who had died shortly after his father last year. Martha made a good surrogate mother.

'Now you're down, how about some champagne or Bucks Fizz or Kir Royale? Relax and enjoy yourselves, it's your party after all and it would be such a waste if you didn't. Everybody seems to be getting on wonderfully. What lovely bright friends you both have.'

Harry squeezed Honor's hand and they strode into the pre-supper party. The room seemed to have divided into the Scots contingent and the English. The brave and bilingual made forays into the other's camps. Where to start with so many friends and family, who to speak to first and everyone saying the same thing, one basketful of praise after another, everyone so kind. Honor found herself becoming intoxicated by the whole scene, she couldn't drink anything but water. After one sip of Bucks Fizz faces began to blur, voices moved in and out, she had to get outside before she fainted.

There she found Jack playing war and smearing his trousers with mud and grass, the suit jacket already discarded on a nearby tree stump.

'Jack,' she called out to him.

'Hi Mum.' He returned a wave and was back up a tree with the speed of a monkey. Sarah Jane and Simon, her little brother, were on the merry-go-round. She wasn't quite sure about all that. Sarah Jane would break his heart, she knew that, but maybe it had to happen at some point, he had broken enough himself.

'Well done!' said Gem, appearing suddenly with a big hug. 'You did it!'

'I know, amazing, huh, and not a Jeremy in sight.'

'How did Jeremy take it?' asked Gem.

'Oh, about as badly as you could imagine.'

'Good,' said Gem. 'There is a God. Divine retribution.'

'I didn't tell Jack who his dad is. I don't know if I've done wrong but what with the wedding . . .'

'But you are going to tell him?' Sarah Jane asked anxiously.

'Yes of course. But he's still only just six, another year or two. When he wants to know, connect up the face and name. It would be unfair otherwise. I couldn't say, Jack this is your dad and now I'm getting married to someone else and we're going to live in another country, where your dad used to live before he came to search for you back in London. Nice one. Hard enough leaving his friends, starting a new life, let alone having to deal with a newly discovered father.

'We decided, I mean Jeremy and I, to tell him he was his godfather and would always send him special presents. Do you think I was wrong?'

'If it felt the right thing to do, we can only do what's best by our own reckoning. Hey, think of it this way, later on you can just remove the god part and be left with plain ordinary father. Handy. Not that he's ever been more than perfunctory in either role.'

'We all have to do that at some point. I mean make parents into ordinary people, remove their god-like status, better at ten than twenty-five,' Honor said philosophically.

Looking around at all her friends there seemed to be only one person missing. Catherine. Poor old Catherine. What a mess we can make for ourselves when we're intent upon it, she thought, on the other hand what a mess we can make when we're not even looking. Then she saw David coming towards her, Augusta and Ben dragging behind. A young woman was with him as well, who must be Georgina. She'd heard about her from Augusta in less than glowing terms. 'That's Georgina,' Gem whispered and nudged before drifting off.

Maybe Catherine did the right thing after all, she thought looking at David, before feeling a flood of compassion for him and the family that surrounded him. This time next year, she thought, that girl he's walking next to will be pregnant, and maybe he'll give himself the chance to start again. Or maybe not.

'Well done Honor. Congratulations! You've done it at last, given Jack a dad, eh?' said David, awkwardly holding his hand out to shake hers. Which made even Georgina look at him askance.

'Ignore the arsehole,' whispered Gussy shockingly whilst hugging Honor. 'He's been an egg all weekend! You should have heard what he said to Aunty Sarah Jane,' and then loudly, 'you look so beautiful.'

Ben followed with another hug and mumbled, 'Yeah you look great.'

Honor felt strangely detached. She could almost have been at somebody else's wedding, in a third eye's dream state, watching herself within the scene. She needed five minutes to gather herself, get used to the condition. She excused herself from them all just as the supper gong sounded and eager guests, knowing the feast they would get, thronged inside.

There was an oak tree at the corner of the path that Honor went to instead. Putting her arms about its wide girth, she was comforted by its solidity.

'Dear God,' she said, 'I so hoped this day would come but never totally believed and now you've brought it to me, I don't quite know what to do with it. Please give me the strength to be part of it all and just enjoy it. Thank you for everything you've given me, my family, my friends, Jack and now Harry. I know I'm truly blessed with your care.'

Peace replaced the horrid turmoil inside her, and she walked away easy as though having touched the Blarney Stone, or bathed in the waters of the Ganges. When Honor walked calmly into the marquee everyone was seated. Her father stood up and cried, 'Here she is. Honor, we were going to send a search party out for you.' Harry beckoned with his smile to her, she knew he hadn't been worried.

'No need, Dad, I'm home and dry. Aren't I allowed to be late for my own dinner? I thought it was a bride's prerogative to be late for something and arriving late at the church with my father, as everyone knows, was impossible. Hippo's never late for anything. A girl's got to get some attention around here somehow.'

Everyone laughed and the sea of chatter began along with the feast. She sat down, cosseted between her father and husband.

Around the room sat Honor's eighty favourite people, and even a couple she didn't like so much but who came inextricably linked to ones she adored, she even felt warmth towards them.

If you can't feel warmly towards the world on your wedding day, when can you? Cold, crisp Aunt Penelope in sweet ice-pink. Awkward cousin Jonathan who had bound her to a bed as a child and made her kiss a toad to see if the fairytale would come true and left her there for the afternoon in disappointment. Fat hooray Humphrey from the restaurant. Of course David, not her favourite person. The aptly named Sissy, girlfriend to her old friend James and lastly Chas, Harry's snotty partner. Such was her compassion she could love them all, but it didn't mean she had to talk to them, not on her wedding day.

She delightedly noticed Gem's confusion at being seated between Gregorio, whom Honor liked, and Harry's handsome sculptor brother, Arthur. She wished she'd had the camera to take the pictures. With so much to look at, how was she supposed to eat. She wanted to slow the clocks down or hold a video camera on top of her head; she didn't want to waste time eating.

'Darling Honor, are you not going to eat any of this delicious smoked salmon and caviar? You must have something.' The gravadlax and roe sat untouched and gleaming upon her plate like a plastic Chinese restaurant window display in Leicester Square.

'All right, just for you, my dear husband,' and she nuzzled to his neck, 'you may feed me.' And they took turns feeding each other as if for some sickly commercial for life insurance and everybody 'ahhed' with the sentimentality of it all. Honor hardly spoke to her father, except to reassure him that she was fine every once in a while, when he would turn to squeeze her arm. They'd said everything they needed to say in the car. Instead they shared jokes amongst groups of people that gathered about their table, like politicians waiting to sign their autobiographies in Harrods, deflecting serious questions.

The wine changed, the pheasant in Calvados was served, steaming garlic, roasted potatoes, parsnips sandwiched in cream, tomatoes and gruyère steamed their delicious aromas straight to open nostrils.

All at once it was late, the giant paper marigolds were hidden in the tent's shadows, candles were lit upon the tables and the gold and silver stars alighted, sparkling upon the ceiling as though the earth's blanket was closing down upon them all. Lanterns were lit that hung from above, plates were cleared, salads dispensed with. Before the cake could arrive Hippo, Honor's father, had begun the speeches.

People make jokes about speeches, about boring people to death with little-known facts that should remain so, about embarrassing incidents of youth and childhood. But when you are a bride there is nothing more wonderful and less embarrassing than to listen to your father rabbiting on for hours about you, his beloved daughter, for it might be the only time he ever does. Proclaiming his pride and joy, drunkenly enthusing over any minor molehill you may have clambered to the top of, and discounting those you have been felled by, for none of your disasters count on your wedding day.

When you're in love, what can be more mesmerising than to listen to the faltering anecdotes about your husband from his brother or anybody who cares to mention him, for everything about him is fascinating. As with a new baby, all your interest is focused upon the miraculous invention of life that lies in your arms, for there is no world beyond it. It is the beginning, middle and end. That's how it was with Honor. Speeches are for those ringing with love in their ears so that the words become almost irrelevant. When it was finally Harry's turn to speak, the rest of the room could have disappeared in that moment and Honor wouldn't have cared a fig. It didn't matter that what he said wasn't wondrously witty or sweepingly sentimental, it seemed so to her and that was all it was really meant to do.

Nobody was overheard saying, 'What a wag! Harry's speech was the funniest thing I've heard in a long time.' But they could be overheard saying, 'I've never seen a man look with such adoring love upon anyone as he looks at Honor.'

And that was true. Just like her granny's, Harry and Honor's love was the kind that ignited the room with its generosity. It wasn't a love to set the world on fire but one that would keep the embers glowing and your hands and toes warm without socks or gloves through Arctic conditions. It wasn't the raging, out-of-control flames of greedy, devouring sex.

Sarah Jane and Simon had disappeared outside the tent to practise a different kind of love, the roaring kind, as urgent as a fire alarm.

Inside the telegrams were being read. Bellows of appreciative, alcohol-fuelled laughter greeted a couple of witty 'incapable of being there' friends. Honor read and laughed as she stumbled through the lines. The third telegram started out much the same as the others. 'To the two dearest H's, Honor and Harry. Have a wonderful day, wish I could be there. Missed you at mine. Josh and I married yesterday in Las Vegas. Send my love to my sister. All mine always to you. CATHERINE.' It wasn't true, just something Catherine had made up, drunk and alone with a phone. People who didn't know cheered, another wedding, another town. Honor sat back in shock but it was nothing to how Ben, Augusta and David felt. The divorce with David hadn't come through yet.

Augusta quickly made the most of the situation and began to boast to the teenager sitting next to her who her new step-father was. Ben sloped off with Harry's teenage cousin for the promise of drugged oblivion. David meanwhile carefully poured three glasses of wine and downed them in quick succession to calm his anger and humiliation. The brandy hadn't arrived on the table yet, Georgina was relieved to see, and with David's solitary gulping she took the chance to start talking to another man across the table. She didn't like David drunk, nobody did, and she was discovering she didn't much like him in social situations, when he became brutally aggressive in holding his end up. Alone together was the only time it felt as though it could work and like last night, not always then. Georgina was balancing things in her mind and was seriously wondering whether she should invest any more of her time and energy in this man and his ungrateful, brattish kids. Some men were wealthy and had never been married, she thought as she found out a little more about Chas, Harry's snobbish partner.

Sarah Jane didn't notice a thing to do with the telegram or Las Vegas, such was the perfect thrust of passion that she found seated upon Simon's lap, back up upon one of the horses on the merry-go-round. A shriek from Aunt Penny heading the wrong way to the loo left her disgruntled and unseated for mere moments, but they rose again to join the moon above their heads.

Honor had told her mother Martha about the whole Sarah Jane and Catherine incident, the hen night (censored version), Josh and the dinner where she presumed it had all begun. That night. The evening when she first introduced Harry to the gang and he hadn't tried to sleep with her to her immense disappointment.

This is why we have mothers, so they can rally us through the hard times. 'That's enough telegrams for now darling. The cake can't wait any longer. Everybody,' Martha clinked a glass impatiently with a fork to get everyone's attention and to stop them all drifting off. 'Harry has made this wonderful French wedding cake himself! Without Honor knowing, he was downstairs sweating away at this beautiful labour of love all day. So can everyone have their glasses ready to toast. Everyone got champagne?' The cake appeared carried by two of the overworked waitresses. Of course it couldn't be any old Boucheron. Profiteroles filled with caramel cream and covered in glass shard toffee that glinted like a glacier, balancing upon each other like a deck of cards. The whole thing was in the shape of a heart that bloomed into a rose with the help of a few dozen strawberries. An arrow of dark chocolate-dipped profiteroles pierced the centre and on either end were some crude marzipan effigies of Honor and Harry.

Everybody's attention was drawn to the spectacular cake, except Sarah Jane and Simon still busy gathering dew, experience and post-coital lines of coke. So much for Sarah Jane's anti-drug resolutions.

'Wow this is crazy stuff,' said Ben to his new friend Jimmy, back from their quick toke, looking at their mirage of a cake.

'I'm not sure but I think that's how it is. Cool huh! Roses out of hearts.'

Honor leapt on to Harry, all smiles, hugs and kisses, 'Oh Harry, you are brilliant. I love you so, It's great. I didn't realise you'd been slaving over a hot stove all the time while I was languishing upstairs, you poor sweetheart. Where's the photographer? We can't cut the cake until it's been photographed.'

Gem appeared, Polaroid in hand. 'Say Thursday,' she said to them.

'Why Thursday?'

'Because it produces just the right amount of pout, I find. Great. Now you can just smile if you like. Can someone pour some champagne in their glasses?'

The official photographer stood behind Gem, relegated to second-class status, taking snaps across her shoulders. Arthur, Harry's brother and best man, held her glass to her right, Gregorio doing her bidding.

Once the champagne was in all their glasses and the knife placed firmly in Honor and Harry's hand, Martha and Hippo the proud parents raised the toast.

'We give you, the bride and the groom.'

'The bride and groom,' the room echoed back, the cameras flashed and cheered as the knife descended through the cake and the juice of the strawberries from its centre bled out on to the plate. The heart struck to its core.

'I would like to raise a toast to our hosts on this most marvellous day, Honor's grandparents, Frederick and Winifred.'

'Frederick and Winifred, may we all be as happy and as in love.'

Somewhere in the back of the tent a tired and lonely voice reciprocated, 'Hear, hear,' before slumping, head upon the table. 'Take me home,' he slurred into a napkin, but Georgina wasn't listening, nobody was. David was gone, just as the party was really beginning.

The cake cut, the dancing began and the tables moved back. The DJ from London, primed, put on the first disc requested.

'And this one's for the bride and groom.' A trumpet started to blow and Herb Alpert and his Tijuana Brass smooched into 'This Guy's in Love'.

Honor could hardly dance for laughing, collapsing upon Harry's shoulders. He held on to her silly form, struggling to hold back his own laughter, whilst kissing her face and trying to lead her in a waltz. Honor couldn't stop herself, riddled with hilarity, wasn't this how it was all supposed to be? The complete Cinderella. This was how every good story was supposed to end – ridiculously and marvellously, happily ever after . . .

★ ★ ★

A wedding is not the end of a story, Martha and Hippo, Catherine and David, Wini and Fred could tell you that. Honor and Harry were just at the beginning. They had only met four months before, perhaps a longer engagement than most war brides. Most things they didn't know about each other, if they had they might never have married. In four more months Harry, Honor and Jack would be living in Spain, working a restaurant together, learning a new language, new customs, a new life. Jealousies, taking sides. What happens then, away from the familiar comfort of family and friends? The madness of first love makes the hysteria of a wedding possible, all the reasons, needs and dreams are played out in one day. No matter the modern fashions, girl gangs or the political incorrectness of wanting white-laced, pink-loved and sugar-trimmed weddings, as long as Sarah Janes, Gemmas, Catherines or Honors find fairytales in library books it will ignite a wish that must be a hereditary gene. The dream of the wedding, the marriage, the happy ever after . . . that never was a fail-safe, white-wash solution.